All Shall Be Well

All Shall Be Well

An Irish Inheritance

A Novel
by

Lillian Lewis

iUniverse, Inc.
Bloomington

All Shall Be Well
An Irish Inheritance

Use of the poem "Death of an Irishwoman" by kind permission of the estate of Michael Hartnett, The Gallery Press, Loughcrew, Oldcastle, County Meath, Ireland. From *Collected Poems* (2001).

Use of the poem "Pity the Islanders, Lucht An Oileain" by kind permission of the author, David Quin.

iUniverse books may be ordered through booksellers or by contacting:

iUniverse
1663 Liberty Drive
Bloomington, IN 47403
www.iuniverse.com
1-800-Authors (1-800-288-4677)

ISBN: 978-1-4759-2025-3 (sc)
ISBN: 978-1-4759-2026-0 (hc)
ISBN: 978-1-4759-2027-7 (e)

Library of Congress Control Number: 2012907568

Printed in the United States of America

iUniverse rev. date: 06/13/2012

For
Natalia, Liam, and Ariel, and of course,
Katherine, Rachel, Gabrielle, and Jennifer.
Remembering where you came from.

And on one occasion He said to me, '*All shall be well*,' and on another occasion He said to me, '*All manner of thing shall be well*.'

One meaning of this was, He takes heed not only of the great and noble but the small, the humble, and the simple … He does not forget them. Another understanding is this: many deeds which to our eyes are so evilly done and do such harm that it seems impossible any good will come as a result of them. But we should understand that our present reason is blind and stupid, and we are incapable of recognizing God's Wisdom. You will discover for yourself His intention

> *All shall be well*
> *I make all things well*

And He wants us to know this so we shall be at peace … and rejoice in Him.

From the Long Text *of* Showings, *Chapter 32*
by Julian of Norwich, May 13, 1373

Girl with a Pearl Earring
(circa 1665) Johannes Vermeer
Mauritshuis, The Hague

Acknowledgments

To Claudia Parish for cover illustration, book design, maps and more; to Stephen Shimek, my husband, for listening for four years and for chapter drawings; and to Mark Hein, friend and colleague, for shaping text and cranking up the author. Much gratitude to all.

Death of an Irishwoman
by Michael Hartnett

Ignorant, in the sense
She ate monotonous food
And thought the world was flat,
And pagan, in the sense
She knew the things that moved
At night were neither dogs nor cats
But pucas and darkfaced men,
She nevertheless had fierce pride.
But sentenced in the end
To eat thin diminishing porridge
In a stone-cold kitchen
She clenched her brittle hands
Around a world
She could not understand.
I loved her from the day she died.
She was a summer dance at the crossroads.
She was a card game where a nose was broken.
She was a song that nobody sings.
She was a house ransacked by soldiers.
She was a language seldom spoken.
She was a child's purse full of useless things.

From Collected Poems, *2001*
The Gallery Press,
County Meath, Ireland

1

Showings

If Morgan had known just how this Irish wake was going to turn out, she probably never would have come thirty-five hundred miles, economy class, on the last of her vacation money. Then again, the Irish immigrants could not choose their fate either. Could they have known the long loneliness they would endure in separation from the motherland? Perhaps if they had, they never would have embarked on that journey either.

It was a full flight. O'Hare to Shannon usually was, especially as summer approached. Everyone moved quickly, for a Friday night, to store things as the captain announced imminent departure. Morgan's mother used to crash the duty free in Chicago, stuffing her cloth Marshall Field's shopping bag with cigarettes, Frango mints, nylon stockings, and Beefeaters gin. It was always like Christmas when Rose came to County Mayo. Morgan felt like telling her mother that Marshall Field's was sold to some outfit in Minnesota. Everything was changing. For a split second, Morgan forgot there was no one to bring those cigarettes to.

Morgan Kenny was on her way to Ireland to bury an old-maid aunt, a great-aunt on her mother's side, whom she hadn't seen since she was twenty-five years old. Great-Aunt Mary was the last of Morgan's Irish relatives. *The last of the Kenny clan,* she thought. With Morgan's mother and grandmother gone, old Mary was the end of her link to the old world and the old times. That Irish connection had given her mother and her grandmother Lily a particular Irish-American identity. They were Chicago Irish, Catholic, and Democrat from Mayo. Within those parameters, they belonged.

That was the odd thing: For all the family's "Irish talk," Morgan was not the Irish flag-waving type. She identified herself more as a former Benedictine—even as a sometime Catholic—than as Irish-American, which posed a question: What was compelling her to make this trip to bury an old auntie she barely knew? Sure, she'd kept up a few Hallmark communications each year, more of a duty she felt than an act of affection. "You have to perform the rituals," her grandmother would say. Maybe she had to do that. Do what Rilke said about real mourning. *Maybe I should have "ashed my hair" when my mother died, "rent my shirt" when my grandmother died.* And perhaps by not doing it, she still carried them all.

A May drizzle beaded the plane window.

"'Tis a soft day, 'tis," Morgan could hear her grandmother say. "Beltane it is. May Day." *Rituals.* "We had our rituals," the old woman would say. "Of course, we had the Maypole and dances, too. My father, God bless his soul, would take our cows to summer pasture, and me and my sisters would string flowers on them and ourselves. Simple pleasures, lassie. We went through the town with the cattle, and the whole pub watched us, and Shanley's bakery—and often came along."

"Back then"—it was always "back then"—"the Irish had a saying for everything," Grandma Lily contended. Morgan's father would counter with "Irish malarkey thinking," as the Kennys sang and wept their interminable melancholy for the "Other Side." "Happy on neither," he maintained.

But on this trip, Morgan seemed to be carrying all those from the "Other Side" with her. All those who had told her magic-filled "Irish malarkey" stories and had raged the rages with the spirits—they all were dead. All the intense ones, the peppery about-to-explode aunts who laughed and swore softly and danced on Christmas morning with cigarettes blazing and cups filled with elderberry wine—all were gone. The old-time people who used to sit in her auntie's kitchen with a glass of amber liquid on Easter morning and told your fortune with a wink or pressed a "fin" into your palm and said, "Quick, spend it, before the devil knows you've got it." Aunt Mary was the last of that *Dancing at Lughnasa* breed. Yeats may have written of Lady Gregory and Maude Gonne, a highbrow bunch, the Irish literati; but Morgan's Mayo peasant stock were no less "beautiful lofty people never to be seen again." Morgan's thick, single braid had become undone, and her wheat-colored hair fell over her eyes. *No, I don't suppose I will ever see their likes again.*

The plane was taking altitude now, and the passenger next to her smiled in the silence and took a swig from his flask, sighing into the plane's lift. At thirty-five thousand feet, that brief moment before dark, the setting sun spread the entire sky gold vermilion.

Golden images lifted into Morgan's imagination as well. Pages from the family scrapbook, you could say. Aunt Mary and Aunt Aran standing in front of their thatched roof cottage with Grandma Lily, a tiny cross window on either side of the green door.

The "veil" must be thin now because of Aunt Mary's passing—or maybe because of Beltane? Morgan thought of the Celtic calendar. "Sure, it's easier to see and hear those who've gone before at these special times," her grandmother told a neighbor.

"When the veil is thin, one can cross to the 'Other Side.' The transportation's absolutely free!" Morgan had heard Grandmother Lily say this so many times. Morgan's mother, Rose, enjoyed the Irish malarkey, too. When Morgan was a child, she believed as a child. She knew the "veil" was thin on Christmas, Easter, weddings, First Communions, and other times of drink. Many spirits live in the bottle and yearn to be set free, she knew. And Morgan herself became acquainted with Queen Mab, like all the others in her family. It was a curse, and a sign of Irish prodigality.

The rattle of the beverage cart dragged Morgan back to this side. She had respect for the Irish curse. She had to decide each time and each place.

"Coffee, please."

At times, she seemed satisfied enough with her father's dismissal of the Irish as a race of "charming superstitionists."

"Don't let those 'bead rattlers' fool you—they're pagans, heath dwellers. Just look at your aunt Mary." Rose would chuckle agreement with her husband. It was true. Aunt Mary never went to church—but then again, she was not comfortable in Castlebar's department stores, either. You could say the same for banks, offices, or anywhere with secretaries and their clipboard questionnaires.

"She's simply a hermit exhilarated by God's creation," her mother would say. (In the United States, that read "a little queer.") Aunt Mary was a wild woman, living "on the back forty," still living in the ancient spirit of the god of the grove. But her praise for divine abundance was more in the line of wonder at a hank of onions or a clutch of eggs or a dripping chunk of honeycomb, than at the Holy Trinity. Still, she never questioned her God's judgment about her life of precariousness. And when she swore, she invoked the Holy Family.

Grandma Lily defended Aunt Mary's oddness from those who questioned her Catholicity by saying she did not need the rebuke of the Church to live a moral life. Nor did she need a Lenten rule for self-denial or fasting. She certainly didn't need that virtue, since she had already cultivated essentiality just by being Irish in those times before the Celtic Tiger.

In spite of Papa's warnings, the Kennys were all casual believers in the "Irish malarkey" supernatural—whether it was the intervention of lost-and-found saints or the Holy Ghost's urgings or just the *veritas* that comes in pints. But there were simple everyday malarkey things, too, like Ma's keeping a tattered Irish pound note in her handkerchiefs "so I'll never go broke." Or Grandma Lily always scooping up the bubbles in her tea and quickly drinking them, for they were signs of money—"Coin comin' for ye, if only ye can catch it!" They all caught that malarkey bug.

How ironic: Something very "malarkey" was happening to Morgan right now, in this plane.

As the plane settled into its cruising altitude and magazines and computers came out, Morgan felt a closed-chest sadness about her aunt's passing. It was the feeling of something unanswered or undone. *What is it that I am meant to remember?* Morgan mused. *What would be the question for Mary? That's what this feeling is all about.*

"Death is never the end of the story." She heard that quite distinctly.

Is that you, Mary? I'm not sure; I believe you are trying to contact me.

The old house came into view.

The thatched roof on the Kenny cottage came flying off—blown away, as it were, by a big wind. It was small, small as a dollhouse. The whole thing lifted like Dorothy's house did in Kansas. Morgan was high above it—but there was no dollhouse furniture in it.

Plane turbulence. The overhead light flickered on. Morgan closed her eyes. Instantly, she saw Aunt Mary—not as the pathetic old woman she had last visited, but young, as she appeared in the photo Grandma Lily kept at her bedside. Papa said the photo reminded him of Vermeer's *Girl with a Pearl Earring*. "Aunt Mary never seems to age," he would say. And indeed he, young enough to be her son, died a decade before her. She wore the innocent *puella* countenance all her life, even when she was eighty—she was the servant girl, obedient and secretive. Enormous blue-gray eyes, work bandanna 'round her hair, a model for Vermeer.

The eyes in the snapshot were speaking to Morgan now.

"All shall be well, and all manner of thing shall be well." Morgan strained to recognize those words, but forgot them the instant the eyes winked at her. The eyes sang, "When Irish eyes are smiling, sure they steal your heart away."

Morgan forced her eyes open, but her mind's eye kept the *Girl with a Pearl Earring* before her.

"Mary, Mary, I'm so sorry I didn't get to know you," Morgan whispered to the image. "No one seemed to know you. We all took you for granted."

Finally, the tears from years of ancestor-hunger, stored up in her heart, overflowed. Truly weeping, Morgan continued on in a prayerlike mode, "Hail Mary, Aunt Mary, you were probably full of grace. I'm sure the Lord is with thee."

Morgan surprised herself. She had not expected this much emotion—or sanctimony. It wasn't guilt, but a desire to know her aunt—and it brought her more loss. She felt that those Vermeer eyes wanted to tell her something more. Wanted her to know.

"What do you want me to know, Mary?"

At that moment, the right wing of the plane lowered. The passengers' gasps coincided with the voice of the captain warning to buckle up, for more turbulence was coming. Always a white-knuckle flier, Morgan stared with her eyes tightly shut into the eyes of the "Girl" who had just died. Mary spoke softly to Morgan again, who seemed to reassure her of something. "All shall be well"—but there was something more.

Entering a liminal space seems to be easier for the Irish, Morgan thought. *Maybe they're just spacier than most.*

The plane began correcting its position. Everyone was silent. A little child began a wailing cry. Everyone inhaled, again. The eyes were smiling. *"When Irish eyes are smiling, sure the world seems bright and gay ..."* Was this wobbly sensation Aer Lingus at thirty-five thousand feet, or was it all these old family feelings and people flooding back for a purpose?

The whole plane sighed as the captain announced that Shannon was in sight. Approach imminent.

"Hey, you don't have to believe in the 'Irish malarkey' thing for it to happen to you, *musha*," her mother used to say. *God, how I miss her, nagging and all.* Morgan's mother, Rose, was born in Chicago, but she told the stories the exact way they were given to her by her mother, Lily, Mayo brogue and all. Morgan didn't have that gift. No gift of gab was hers.

Morgan felt like telling her mother she had seen her dead Aunt Mary—really seen her. There was some humor in this, because Rose was dead, too. But perhaps Rose was the only one to have believed in the family *genius.* All of which was quite normal in the ancient Celtic world—though rather eccentric in this one. Still, no one had identified Morgan's special gift.

Rose had not cultivated her own gift with Morgan, the gift of moving between the worlds like a shaman. She may never have considered Morgan a candidate because from the time she was a wee child, Morgan wanted to become a nun. She entered the convent at eighteen, immediately after high school. That seemed to be the end of expectations as far as her parents were concerned. But whether Morgan Kenny had the gift of "sight" or not, she'd continued to see her Aunt Mary for several days thereafter. It would remain to be seen if the gift maintained.

Everyone said Grandma Lily had the gift of gab, and there was no question she had her carpetbag of tales as full as the tailor's. She handed them down to Rose, who "inherited" but never handed them down to Morgan. Timing changed things. Morgan entered the nunnery; and without grandchildren, Rose lost the impetus to hand on the stories. So with her, most of them were buried.

Morgan loved to hear the homemade tales and burnished family gossip, but what she did receive she got from her grandmother. She did not disappoint Lily, and Lily did not disappoint her. Though her grandmother's memories were golden, the realities of her childhood in Castlebar, County Mayo, had been harsh. Grandma Lily's mother and stepmother were born in famine times, the 1840s. She and her sisters were little more than ragamuffins, living on a cattle farm and consuming tons of turnips, drinking seaweed tea, "without a penny to cross themselves." Soul memory softens the bellyache and swollen feet.

Morgan had been a frequent visitor to Ireland with her mother until Rose died, five years ago. The Ireland Morgan knew was a romantic version she had absorbed from her grandmother's memories: Irish poems recited on feast days, step-dancing classes, the old fifties movie *The Quiet Man* with John Wayne and Maureen O'Hara, and the old forties film with Victor McLaughlin, *The Informer.*

Perhaps Morgan had escaped this world, and the obvious mistake of the convent, by making a country three thousand miles away her avocation and home. She even did her graduate paper on the ninth-century Kerry madwoman from Slieve Mish, on the Dingle Peninsula. She'd been drawn to the subject because of Aunt Mary's oddness. Aunt Mary could have been called "the wild woman of Mayo." She was every bit as dotty, disheveled, and disorganized as Morgan's fantasy of a wild hermit, but she also was a wonderful mix of brogue, malarkey, and hospitality.

Aunt Mary was the youngest of the three Kenny sisters.

Morgan's grandmother, Lily, was the oldest. Lily's mother had been wife number one. Little was known of her, because the father allowed little mourning before the second wife was taken.

This time, Anthony Kenny married a girl so poor she looked to the marriage as a hedge against being sent to the poorhouse. Some said she was a white witch or that she sang magic chants. Americans would just have called her "intuitive" or "a psychic." She was the mother of Aunt Aran and Aunt Mary. She also died young, exhausted by pregnancies and early-life hunger.

Little Mary knew adversity from childhood on. She was a motherless child. In truth, she was an orphan with a gentle soul. She never went to school beyond those first years with a neighbor woman, Mrs. Naughton. She never married. Always the servant. A simple, uneventful life, most would say. Morgan's heart went out to her.

But maybe it wasn't so uneventful? Morgan's inner voice threw her an interesting exception: *What about the visionary Julian of Norwich? Chaucer remarked that she'd never made a journey, even to Canterbury. She never left her cell, but she "saw the whole of creation in a hazelnut." Could that have been possible with Aunt Mary, who'd never left Mayo?* Morgan hoped so.

The question remained: What was it that brought Morgan all this way for an aunt she hardly knew?

Sure, there are some things to settle in Castlebar. Little is left. The house and land. I almost forgot the Lady's Well.

How was it that Aunt Mary was lodged in a corner of her soul? Maybe there was something more for her to know of her aunt—and herself. No matter. Something, internally, was helping Morgan to take steps into uncharted territory. Something was changing. Obviously, there was the dying—but something else was emerging, too.

As she edged toward her fortieth year, she knew a new leg of her journey had silently begun. The life maps she had relied on for years were out-of-date. Maybe Mary's death was the occasion to search for new ones. It was time.

Attendants were getting ready for landing. Morgan's stomach struggled against the wobbly downdraft.

Unconsciously, she did the "nunnie thing," filling a small space of time with Hail Marys or a list of Praises. Something new was forming in her mind. The passionate language of Julian was with her in the moment and began flowing through her: *"Beloved One, thank you for calling me into Life, for holding me in your Love. For knitting me out of yourself. Let me find your Will. Amen."*

* * *

The Girls "Back Then"

Lily was Morgan's grandmother and Rose's mother. She was the oldest of the Kenny sisters of Castlebar. She was florid, expansive, a dancer in her day. She was a teller of the Irish faerie, "a spiritual race of people arriving before Patrick." She also told of the utter poverty of her family, and indeed of all Ireland. She had a sense of humor, saying the Kennys were godlike, since they could make something from nothing! Stone soup, no doubt.

The most astounding historical fact to Morgan was that they never had "the electric" when Grandma was growing up. She told her grandchildren, "We didn't miss a thing. We had one another, the treasury of story and prayer, and of course, the feasts."

In a fantasy of running away from the farm and a life of drudgery, she came to the States as a kitchen servant for a rich Irish family in New York, the Lymans. A "Molly," as they used to call them, the young Irish girls who escaped the Great Hunger by somehow getting ship passage and becoming scullery maids. "The downstairs people." It could have ended badly—but Lily met her true love, a handsome young man from Ireland, Eugene, who was a sailor on the Great Lakes. He invested in America and left her a pretty penny.

Aran was the thinker, the planner, the scrapper and thatcher. Everyone said she was hardy and handy. But she was more than that. She was the mother to Mary when their mother died. She had great loyalty to their mother's memory, as well. She'd been her right hand when she became an invalid, and their mother passed to her the gift of "sight," blessings, and curses. Aran was the one who kept the family afloat with her entrepreneurial invention of the pastry business (read *poochine*) when her father's cattle languished. She was still in grade school when Lily left for New York. In middle age, she married Emmet Neary, the "boy" next door, to save their field. Not an insignificant gesture. She was the second leg in the stool.

Mary was the last of many Kenny children (only three had survived). She was born around the Great War. No one would dispute she was the prettiest of the three—some even said beautiful. Long-legged and blonde, she was "Nature's child," neighbors would say. It was truly amazing that she never married. She had a lilting Irish soprano much desired in choirs and gatherings. She stayed in the family home her whole life.

"It was the eyes," said Morgan's father, Francis, who knew Mary from the time she was a young woman. "There had to be something behind those mysterious blue-gray eyes." Morgan's mother took a more prosaic approach, saying there was little mystery either in her life or in County Mayo. But then again, Rose could have sprinkled a few more good words about everyone.

So that was it. That was all Morgan could dredge up. She'd never heard anything much about old Anthony Kenny, her great-grandfather, except that he had buried two wives and left his remaining three daughters the fifteen-acre farm, a house, a barn, and a holy well.

But Morgan's inheritance was yet to be seen.

BELFAST

Mayo

NEWPORT
WESTPORT
CASTLEBAR

Omey
Island
CLADDAGHDUFF
CLIFDEN
Galway

GALWAY

DUBLIN

Clare

SHANNON

Limerick

DINGLE

Blasket
Islands
Kerry

Cork

Ireland

2
Shannon to Mayo

At Shannon Airport, half the passengers were readying packs of cigarettes to light up and collecting their duty-free spirits. Morgan got through customs. She saw her name floating over the crowd. A young boy in gray trousers with a stripe carried the sign MORGAN KENNY—TELEGRAM.

"I, I am Kenny. Morgan Kenny," she told him confidentially. He handed her the yellow envelope. AUNT MARY BURIED YESTERDAY. NURSE SHANAHAN FROM GRAILSIDE HOME CALLED. GOOD LUCK, NANCY. P.S. NURSES STILL STRIKING.

Something is wrong here. I'm the remaining relative—don't they have to consult me?

At the same time, an R. Hackney Service driver stood holding a sign: GALWAY – CONNEMARA – MAYO. Within a few minutes, four tired travelers were dragging luggage across the parking lot.

The Irish spring still held a chill clenched in the low-slung clouds, promising a slow, rainy day. Yes, a "soft day." But for this sunny moment, Morgan felt a pang of hope. *Odd for a funeral,* she thought. She wasn't sure about what she hoped, but it was part of that "new beginnings" feeling.

The perfectly pressed, perfectly packed, quart-sized gentleman in his late sixties stood beside a perfectly preserved blue station wagon (possibly a mail wagon from the sixties) with all its doors open.

He lined them up like schoolchildren, repeating their names: "Mrs. Timmons, Miss Kenny, Mr. Matthews from Glasgow, and me are goin' the full route to Castlebar. You sir, Mishter Grady, go to Letterfrack."

Morgan caught the younger-looking man, with shoulder-length reddish-blond hair, reddish stubble, and jet-blue eyes, sizing her up. She had no hope that Ireland would offer her a memorable adventure; the man with the red hair, it seemed, never thought life was worth living without one. She looked at his outsize dusty boots and mused at the old adage. "The size of a man's feet give the measure of "that" private part, so they say."

The quiet man, whose casual stature was not unlike that of *The Quiet Man*, seemed a good starting place for possibilities.

"What do you think is a decent payment to Castlebar?" she asked him.

Grady gave "the Yank" a smile. "He can easily get 75 punt from each of us. That's about 400 quid. Not too shabby. Let me try to negotiate a group rate."

Morgan liked his spontaneous authority and easy manner. She liked the look he gave her, too. It may have seemed corny, but he fit her traditional ideas of Ireland, and he seemed to fit the big man, John Wayne archetype in *The Quiet Man*, too.

He reported that "Reggie" ("short for Remigius, and you can add to that Aloysius," as they later found out) needed a total of 300 quid. In just that short exchange, she felt taken care of. She was "letting down" now.

Reggie would make three stops: Galway to pick up books from Kenny's Bookstore for delivery, Letterfrack to drop off Grady, and Castlebar for the rest. He slipped in a few extra stops for the bookstore.

"How far is Castlebar from Shannon?" Morgan looked at Grady with more than a little guile. Although she'd made this trip a dozen times in her life, she had no sense of direction in Ireland. How far was Mary's farm in Mayo from the airport?

"As the crow flies? 140 kilometers, a hundred miles, but the real miles? Maybe double."

She was so very tired. Her mind was flooded with details—*But if Aunt Mary is already buried, who buried her? Aren't I the official relative for all of this? And another question … how can I handle a wake without a body?*—and this new information had interfered with her true feeling.

Well, this looks a lot more interesting than the bus.

As she stepped up into the royal blue paneled station wagon, she couldn't help but think of John Ford's *Stagecoach. That was a John Wayne film, too. This ensemble is a fair comparison with that one, including the driver. Reggie's the stage driver—with a tweedy porkpie cap, a big smile, and bad teeth. Everything else fits the film.*

Introductions went around. Mr. Matthews with a British accent, a soft Scottish burr underneath, gave a crisp banklike impression in a three-piece suit, tie, brown felt hat, and newer faux-leather attaché case. Not quite smiling, he lunged for the passenger seat. With a tip of his hat to the assembled, he flattened his London *Times* and removed himself from the crowd.

The second passenger was a chatty, stout woman in a very wrinkled business suit with a green plaid jacket and enormous purse. Her name was Mrs. Timmons. She seemed to know Reggie.

"Are you stayin' at Timmons' Teatime in Castlebar, Reggie?" she asked.

"If you say, your Ladyship." Reggie called all the women "Ladyship," and the men either "Guv" or "Mishter." Reggie and "Lady" Timmons fell into conversation.

The Quiet Man, Grady, was the third passenger. A rumpled, professorial type with a meerschaum stuck between his teeth, fortyish with thick shocks of gray in his strawberry-blond hair, wanting a haircut. His ultimate link to John Wayne was the cowboy-style boots. He was big enough to carry them well. She had to admit his felt hat was a little more from *Raiders of the Lost Ark* than John Wayne's tweed.

Without a word, the Quiet Man stacked everyone's luggage on the rack, several of his own cardboard tubes, and a collapsed walking stick, and then crawled in next to Morgan.

The final passenger was "the Yank from Chicago," Morgan Kenny, a late thirty-something dishwater blonde—athletically proportioned, with good bones, as they say, and sensible walking shoes.

The "stagecoach" was full. Morgan was in the middle, wedged between Mrs. Timmons and Grady.

"Good mornin', folks. My name is Ignatius Remigius Aloysius, but please call me Reggie."

He was sizing up the coastal map in his head.

"So-o-o-o, three of you are goin' to Castlebar. And you, Mishter Grady, are goin' to Letterfrack. Brilliant! That's exactly where 'Kenny's Bundle of Books' is goin'. Let us be on our way to Galway City, where I have connections for the very best Irish fry-up. Black pudding experts of Galway!

"Figger the path we'll take. I have a wee errand in Galway, at Miss Kenny's—the bookstore Kenny, that is. She's got this 'Bundle of Books' program, and I am one of her deliverymen whenever I get up this way." Morgan caught Reggie's professional voice—Reggie the Tour Guide, who undoubtedly knew everything about everybody.

"When we're up to the Twelve Bens, I make a few deliveries for her. Okay, then a wee detour at Letterfrak, Mishter Grady, but we are in good company with fine weather, are we not?" Grady smiled, realizing Reggie was smoothing over the extra mileage in order to slip in an extra passenger.

Reggie took out a wrinkled map and pointed to Galway, loosely drawing a loopy line to Castlebar by way of Connemara.

"We'll be takin' the road out of Galway City toward Outregard, and then the Connemara road should be lovely this time of year, should it not? We'll make a right at Recess (emergency stop only), striking due north through the Twelve Bens, Ireland's humpback mountains, on to N59. A quick stop at Letterfrack to let out our boy, Mishter Grady. Can we lunch there at Lady Margery's?" He smiled at Grady.

Grady never ate at Lady Margery's, it being too dainty for his liking. He frequented an old pub run by a fallen-away Franciscan, who made "monster sandwiches" for hungry walkers and boasted of homemade monastery beer.

"Now then, that's a spot where we could have a beverage stronger than tea, if you fancy." Carrying on without a hitch: "Then straight on to Castlebar along Killary Harbour, the only fjord in the whole of Ireland, with glimpses of the romantic Abbey of Kylemore. And then the famed village of *The Field* (by God, Richard Harris was brilliant!)—Leenane. And Westport; by then, we might need another wee stop.

"Is everyone settled now? We're off!" That was the voice of an experienced "track man." He pressed his foot to the floor and Morgan expected noise and coughing black emissions, but the vintage wagon took off with a purr.

"How is it that you're comin' this way, Missus?" Reggie turned his head.

"A death in the family. My great-aunt from Castlebar died."

The stout lady turned slightly to catch Morgan's eyes.

"I'm from Castlebar. What's that your name is?"

"Kenny. Morgan Kenny."

"What's that your Auntie's name?"

"Mary," Morgan turned to her. "Mary Kenny."

Mrs. Timmons thought for a moment. "No, I don't know her. I thought I knew everyone in Castlebar.... Yes, I remember now, there were some Kennys that lived up on the hill, but they've been long gone. *Seandun*, folks used to call it, 'Top o' the Hill.' It's got a perfect view of Crough Patrick, that hill. That's an old, old estate, dear … abandoned for years."

"*Seandun*—yes, that's the name of my aunt's farm! But she's been in a nursing home for a number of years. Grailside."

Mrs. Timmons "surveyed" the town in her mind. "There is no Grailside Home in Castlebar. Definitely not."

It was Grady's turn to put in his two cents.

"There's a Grailside Home in Connemara, though, out by Renvyle House—at the very tip of the peninsula. Great Atlantic view! Right on the sea," he said. "Mystic."

"Are you sure about that?" Mrs. Timmons countered.

"Yes, people are always seein' banshee out that way." Grady raised his eyebrows. He was enjoying it. He put his calloused hand over Morgan's and squeezed it, to give her the tip-off that he was about to do some teasing of Mrs. Timmons. It was a spontaneous gesture of intimacy that was new to her.

"No, I don't mean banshee. I mean, are you sure there's an old people's home way out there? I didn't think there was anything out there except that old gentry hotel."

"I am very sure—but maybe you are right, and it is Claddaghduff, Missus. I've gone out that way, to Omey Island, several times a year for a decade. It's a gold mine of Neolithic artifacts. It's also an infant burial ground. We're still digging there."

Mrs. Timmons seemed to take exception to this last statement, giving Grady a glare. "Prehistoric babies?"

"No, infants only since the Christian epoch. But right up into the present time."

"Babies ... not buried in the church grounds?" Mrs. Timmons reddened.

"That's right. A terrible injustice, if you ask me. The priests denied unbaptized babies access to 'holy' ground. So the mothers came to the peninsula to bury them. A *killeen*." He turned to the Yank. "It means 'little church.' It's a well-known spot. The few people who live on Omey are a lot more compassionate than the Church. They gave them ground." Grady was getting preachy, but he wasn't going to give ground.

When Mrs. Timmons turned her face away from him, Grady gave Morgan a devilish wink. The topic was closed, at least for now.

Galway City

Reggie settled everyone at Emerald City for the "top of the line" breakfast he had been advertising.

Afterward, Grady and Morgan led the group across the street to investigate Kenny's Bookstore. He, to see a little more of himself displayed in the front window, and she, hoping the owner and her aunt were related. They crossed Main Street balancing mugs of tea and a bag of scones. Everyone seemed to be enjoying one another's company, with the possible exception of Mr. Cyril Matthews. But the label could only be "possible," since Cyril was not a relater—interrogator, maybe, but not a relater.

Morgan had a good sense of Grady already. He was a positive, happy, perennial bachelor. Oddly, she felt a pang of disappointment about that. But without a doubt, he fit her Quiet Man theme.

The whole Kenny Bookshop was painted Kelly green, the name outlined in gold. Baskets of bright red and purple primroses hung every few feet from the façade, giving it a charming air. The street windows made a case for the islands off Ireland's West Coast—the Arans off Galway, the Blaskets off Kerry, Achill off Mayo, Inishboffin—and next to the windows was a life-size cardboard stand-up of the athletic man she was standing next to, in just about the same outfit he had on. Except for a pair of hiking boots, a smoking briar, and a copy of his new book about Omey Island.

"That's pretty impressive," said Morgan, gawking at the window display.

"I didn't know she, her very self, would put such an impressive picture of me in the front window," Grady said with feigned modesty. Then, with typical Irish deprecatory humor, he added: "If only mi mather could see me now," his small blue eyes enjoying it all.

Piles of *Omey Island: Ireland's Grace and Disgrace* by Michael Grady crowded the street window; several of Grady's other books on Ireland jammed the narrow hallway leading from the main viewing room into the back-room stacks. Shelves and shelves of Irish fairy tales, Irish short story collections, signed photos of famous writers "to Maeve Kenny," biographies of Irish writers, long quotes on Ireland. Every patch of wall was hung with photographs of famous Irish authors: Paul Muldoon, Patrick Kavanaugh, signed, of course; and then a few American poets, too. Morgan saw Robert Bly. *Minnesota*, she thought. Seamus Heaney young, thin, before he was gray-headed. The great William Butler Yeats and his patron, Lady Gregory. And then the revolutionaries: John O'Leary, Maude Gonne, the feisty Major O'Brian, Gogarty, A. E. ... "All those beautiful lofty people, never to be seen again."

So it seemed Mrs. Kenny was putting Grady into the pantheon of Irish literary history—in Galway City, anyway.

"Omey? Where is this island?" she asked.

"In Connemara. It's one of those many, many islands on the coast that become islands each day when the tide comes in."

Morgan turned her head, looking at a poster of a foggy strand, the backside of a shepherd dog hightailing it toward the island.

"Oh, I have a plan that you will be coming on one of my tours very soon." Grady smiled.

"Right! I need a bit of time to find out about the grace—and the disgrace," Morgan replied.

The bookstore was almost empty except for old lady Kenny herself, bent over in a black lace shawl with fringes brushing the ground, silver hair combs sweeping up her long silver hair. She was ageless. She had probably looked sixty-five for many years. Her shoes were a giveaway, Victorian lace-ups. *Maybe she's older than she looks,* Morgan thought, *but she is a classy lady regardless.*

An even older petite gentleman stooped beside her, white-headed and frail, pulling out a crate of new books from under the table.

"More books on 'islands,' Mum."

"Good mornin', darlin'!" Grady entered, center stage, gently placing a hand on Mrs. Kenny's shoulder.

"Hello, Grady boy. I wasn't expectin' ye."

Maeve Kenny wore her affection for Grady without embarrassment. The two liked to play.

Morgan envied the old woman's—or maybe it was just the Irish—ease of verbal dancing. She was no mean flirt. *So casual with intimacy,* Morgan thought. *That certainly wasn't a sought-after virtue among "our" Kennys.*

"I want you to meet another Kenny, Morgan. Miss Maeve Kenny. I hope the two of you are related."

After a few minutes of light investigation, Morgan and Maeve found they had no apparent connection, but Maeve Kenny was not giving up just yet.

"I have heard of the Kennys of Castlebar. I am sorry; I have not heard of your grandmother and her sisters ... Lily, Mary, and Aran. No, those names do not fit the frame I know."

Mrs. Kenny gathered books she thought Morgan would "like" or "need" or just plain must have. Her fingers ran across a secondhand, frayed cloth book: *Stories of Biddy Early.*

"Now I know why I remember those Kennys over in Castlebar! One of them was rumored to be a disciple of Biddy Early, the Sightful One."

"The psychic from Clare?" asked Grady.

"Oh, she was the genuine article, Grady boy. The young are unaware of the real craft—only that New Age crap. She was a healer, a witch, a *bean feasa* if you prefer. People went to her for all sorts of cures. I've heard a number of horse and cattle stories. And there's a priest story in it for you, Grady boy," she said with a hearty chuckle.

"Ah, more 'oppressed peasantry ruled over by tyrannical priests' stories," Grady said with a snigger.

He does have a great smile, Morgan thought.

"Yes, the priests were oppressive," Maeve said. "They hated Biddy 'cause she had the power. Didn't Lady Gregory write something about her? You've got to have this book, Miss Kenny. Come back to tell me if your family has a connection. We are not disdainful of the craft here."

By the time they left Galway, Morgan and Grady had two shopping bags full of must-haves, including a few on Biddy Early, signed by Mr. Lenihan himself, a "bundle" for Grady's lawyer friend Padraig from Castlebar, and another for the publican of Moyard. And Reggie had a few more bundles for home delivery along the Twelve Bens.

Grady also had a shopping bag full of his new publication on Ireland's islands. "Gifts for my enemies," he laughed.

"It's a good thing I came in here with you for your 'author' discount," Morgan said, trying to "play" a little, too.

On the R344 again, the twenty-mile strip between Recess and Letterfrak was the "shortcut" Reggie had announced earlier. The road was centered between the Twelve Bens on the left and the Maumturk Mountains on the right. Breathtaking landscape overwhelmed the riders with its sheer immensity—and its solitary drop-offs. Reggie's hack felt like a tiny blue upholstery button being squeezed into a green, cushy couch.

Reggie was picking up speed on this hideaway road sans bikers, hikers, and houses. Morgan had just about hit Zen silence when the wagon began jolting sideways. Grady yelled, "Pull over, Reggie!" Then Morgan heard a flapping sound and the beginning of several prayers—or perhaps they were curses—invoking the name of Jesus and some saints. Reggie pulled quickly off the road and turned off the engine with an expletive: "Flat tire! Damn!"

Grady was the first to jump out and check the damage, with a few more "damns." The atmosphere thickened. Grady, with his "take charge" attitude, told Reggie to get him the spare and jack. To which a long silence ensued. Reggie was flustered.

Soon, three serious men stood around the blown-out right rear tire, offering solutions, as Reggie emptied a canvas bag that held several parts but no tire jack.

"I swear, I had no idea," Reggie weakly protested against Grady's deprecating remarks about his mother. One could not say there were no graces, however—the spare was spotless, there was a small lug wrench, and participation in seeking a solution was 100 percent.

Cyril suggested waiting for a passing car and borrowing their jack. Reggie suggested they find a farmhouse and borrow one—although this was quite lame, since they hadn't seen a house for many miles. Morgan and Grady hunted for rocks to shove up under the axle, and everyone joined in lifting the car onto them.

Everyone except Mrs. Timmons, for whom the tension was too much. She sat by the side of the road, initially working on her knitting from a tapestry bag, but changing to smoking one little black cigarette after another. In an effort to make small talk, she asked Morgan, "I'm sorry dear, what did you say your work was?" Morgan did not want to seem like she was hemming and hawing, but in fact, she was. "I am a nurse. And in spite of everything, I hope I am still working."

Despite the irritation in the air, Morgan felt Grady almost had the tire situation under control. It was a good thing he did, because no car passed the whole time. And in her nervousness Mrs. Timmons never stopped talking.

They weren't hanging over a cliff, but neither were they on flat ground. It was that typical Connemara lumpy road, which made sliding the rocks under quite a technical feat; and the drop-off just made it scarier. "So," Grady impressed upon Morgan, "we have to get it right the first time." Then the three men, on the chanted number "three," yanked up the car while Morgan pulled off the offending wheel and shoved on the spare. It worked, and of course, the men congratulated themselves on a job well done.

Obvious to all were Grady's command and Morgan's interest. "And after everything is said and done, Miss Kenny, I still hope you've got your job because I'm too old to do this for a living." Grady said, with a mouthful of mirth. Morgan smiled at everyone, but there was a real possibility that the Chicago nurses' strike for better working conditions would not work. Only time would tell.

It was only a few more kilometers to Moyard, the tiny burg off N59 that Grady was from, a hair shy of Letterfrack. Grady's eyes narrowed with delight as they reached his house. It was set off a hundred or so feet from the road. The shrubs were so tight around the white cottage that only a sliver of it could be seen. It was situated low, close to the inlet, and a *currach*-type boat lay on the grass.

Grady threw his walking stick and gear over the green gate, onto a pebbly drive, and waved good-bye. Apparently, he had no key. Grady's travel companions last saw him swinging a leg over, letting out a hoot.

They pulled back to the road and headed on to Mayo.

Morgan would have liked to stay and have tea in this romantic little cottage ripped from Beatrix Potter's sketchbook. Grady himself was contagious. *A good spirit*, she thought. The cottage had formerly been the parsonage of the Protestant minister. *It must have been a slender congregation.* Morgan would not have suspected Grady of living in so cared-for a setting, down to the moss-lined basket overflowing with mint that hung from a lintel. *Maybe a woman's hand is at it.* She hoped not.

3
Timmons' Teatime

By the time they arrived in Castlebar, everything and everyone was sorted. Morgan would stay at Mrs. Timmons's B&B, Mr. Matthews at the upscale hotel in town, and Reggie—an old acquaintance of Mr. and Mrs. Timmons, as Morgan had pegged it—stayed in an empty back bedroom (probably in exchange for the ride).

Timmons' Teatime faced Front Street in the town center. Castlebar had been a market town, the "capital of County Mayo," since Norman times, 1235. The two-story traditional red brick building held Timmons' Tearoom on the first floor, the family's apartment in back of the tearoom, and a six-bedroom B&B on the second floor. The many-paned show window was hung with a stiff lace curtain and displayed a table covered in rough old linen and a rose-and-ivy china tea set, baskets of scones, brown bread biscuits filled with ham, sweets of all sorts, and the biggest, darkest whiskey cake Morgan had ever seen. Old Bushmills must have been edified. Eight oak four-square tables with unusually high-backed rush chairs, seats covered in a dusty blue, centered the room. The sideboard held heavy ironstone crockery, ceramic boxes of teas, a variety of jams and cookies, and small silver trays with miniature honey jars. On the top shelf, there were a few photos of family standing in front of a great hill (possibly Croagh Patrick) and Our Lady of Knock in a gilded frame. On the other wall, a glass breakfront highboy, filled with old, old Waterford crystal (to be admired but never used), displayed Mrs. Timmons's treasure.

Morgan had just begun pulling her suitcase into the tearoom when Mrs. Timmons gave a nod to a sleepy-looking teenage boy near the kitchen doors to take the bags upstairs.

"Michael, give the American lady the room with the toilet, lookin' out on the garden." She looked at Morgan now with a bit of motherly care. "Come now, it's time for a good cup of tea." Then laughing, "At Timmons', it's always teatime!"

After a good pot of Brewley's, two plates of ham in biscuits, and a lemon custard tart, Morgan climbed the shoulder-width stairwell to her "room with a view." When she got there, she found her suitcases sitting outside the door. Instantly, she dissolved into a cushy wing chair and kicked off her shoes. *Who wears heels to travel? A leg show-off!* she answered herself. Her eyes scanned the ample room.

A teenage girl's room from the fifties, she thought. Mauve chintz and violet print wallpaper. She felt heavy with exhaustion, but kept up the inner query: *Who buried Mary? Why wasn't I properly informed? Why didn't they wait? Who is "they," anyway?* Lying on the bed, she listened tensely; the very silence of the vacant floor scared her. *Maybe it was that "Irish malarkey" talking Grady did, about the banshee and all.* A strange feeling washed over her, a sense that someone was watching her. Nevertheless, she fell asleep sitting—with all her clothes on.

At about ten o'clock, a loud knocking roused her from a deep sleep. It was Mrs. Timmons.

"Sorry to wake you, dear, but I knew you'd want this message from Mr. Grady."

She tore open the envelope: "Hi. How's the mystery coming? How about Heaney's Pub, Friday night? –Grady."

That's a two-days' wait. Humming, she began unpacking her suitcase into a honey-colored armoire and antique dresser. Then she saw a different envelope, also addressed to her, propped up against the mirror.

"Miss Kenny: Can we meet at the pub next door, around ten o'clock? There is something I want to tell you about your predicament. Cyril Matthews."

Predicament? Morgan threw on her clothes. On her way out, she asked Mrs. Timmons if she'd brought up any other notes.

"One time up those stairs is plenty, dear."

Heaney's Pub

4
Heaney's Pub

Heaney's Pub was one of those old-time taverns that had not yet become a "lounge." It was still a pub, with simple local grub, a place where the locals get up and play their own tunes or jam together. No "name" band, just a melding together of mostly old tunes. Tonight it was a young woman with a fiddle, an older gentleman with a squeezebox, and a young boy of ten years or so playing the tin whistle. A little ragamuffin collected coins in a small box from customers during the set. Morgan was moved for the boy and threw in a few quid.

Just like church, she thought. *Thumbs up to the pubmaster's heart—you'd never see a kid playing like that in the States, nor passing the box either. Instead, the kid would probably have mugged you outside for a few dollars.* That "heart" was the part that Morgan hoped would never change about Ireland, even on its way to big bucks.

A generous peat fire took chill off the damp night. She saw Mr. Matthews sitting with his back to the fire, sipping a pint. He was alone. He stood to greet her and took no more than a minute before rehearsing his insurance company's woes: the enormous outlays Lloyd's had paid to the British Museum and a number of other art collectors, some private, some public, over the last two years. Of course, Scotland Yard and the Dublin heist unit were all involved. To say nothing of the gigantic historic value of the Leonardo. Yes, a famous Leonardo had been stolen.

"That may be, Mr. Matthews, but why are you in Mayo? And why call me?"

"I'm sorry for playing my cards so close to the vest, Miss Kenny. I think it's all right to tell you a bit about this investigation I'm involved in—for the Bank of Scotland and Lloyd's, of course."

His face opened again into a broad smile, making his ears wiggle. He thought Morgan attractive, yes, but "just another American tourist." He personally looked down his nose at Americans and their money. Coming back to Ireland for her inheritance, he supposed. Money motivates. His smile turned to a sneer.

"You know," he resumed, "I almost said this 'mystery' I'm involved in. The newspapers are calling these art thefts 'mysteries.' Maybe it's not so much of a mystery as it is high finance!"

"How's that?" Morgan showed interest. "Isn't it rather difficult to sell a Leonardo?"

"Right. But professional thieves have other options. They know that we're eager to recover the painting—the 'we' being the insurance company. They know that theft alone will increase the value of the art piece. In fact, the more often a painting is stolen, the more valuable in the eyes of the public it becomes. The value becomes inflated. So they know we will pay."

"Some places, it's illegal to pay ransom for a stolen object." Morgan seemed sure of that. "If that's the case, what about Lloyd's?"

"Yeah. Well, what do you think? It's paid anyway, under a different category—'reward for information.'"

"But ransom doesn't always work, does it?" Morgan was staring straight at him.

"No. You're right! We should have paid with Shergar—that was a big mistake. We knew the IRA had him." Matthews slowed to consider the beauty of the great racehorse.

"What happened to him?" Morgan spoke slowly, too, because she could see that Matthews was moved.

"Shergar was … never recovered."

"Destroyed?" she asked softly.

"Nothing like a Peter Sellers movie, where David Niven is the witty cat burglar performing a white-glove crime. No suave Niven here, just some dumb IRA brutes." He took a swallow of his pint, motioning the barmaid for another. "The Irish, my dear, are quite simply made for thievery. They have a history of brigandage that stretches back into the mists of time."

"Really?" Morgan thought he had gone over the top. He seemed to enjoy the theatricality of it.

"Well, what about what the Irish call their *Iliad*? *The Cattle Raid of Cooley*? Isn't robbery the business of Irish royalty? One king stealing from another. Or, in this case, a sexy war queen?"

Interesting, Morgan thought, *Matthews's interest in Irish crime.history. I wish he could have balanced it off with crimes perpetrated on the Irish, like the Viking raids,or the pillaging by the Normans. And what can we say about the English? Genocide? Bloody occupation?*

"It takes so little effort. Just look at the score."

"Score?"

"Sorry. I mean, just look at the number of art crimes in Ireland each year. It's better than a factory job," he winked and attended to his pint. "For example, Wicklow, Russborough House was burgled three times! Thank God we didn't insure them this last time. The Irish police say it was a revenge crime, because the builders back in the 1600s were related to the Prince of Orange! Ha, ha!" He laughed out loud and took another gulp of his pint. "That's what the Irish call 'malarkey.' The Prince of Orange was real all right, but the reason was punt, good old-fashioned cash—not the Protestant Ascendancy. The Irish burgled Russborough because it was a pushover!"

"Is that where the Leonardo was?"

"No, not the Leonardo. But they owned almost everybody else! I mean the classic greats: Rubens, Goya, Rembrandt—even a Vermeer."

"Was it the *Girl with a Pearl Earring*?" Morgan remembered Mary looking just like Vermeer's Girl. She also wanted Matthews to know she knew a painting or two.

"No, it was another one. Something about a woman writing a letter. They've recovered it, though."

"How about the Leonardo? Where was that?" Morgan was genuinely interested.

"It's owned by Scots. In Dumfrieshire. Actually, not far from my own home. Drumlanrig Castle. It's a thief's dream. The Leonardo hung like an old servant pull, next to the main staircase—not even an especial alarm! Its value would be in the millions of pounds—maybe 50 million."

"Leonardo in Scotland? I never heard of that," Morgan replied.

"Well, it's not a very well-known Leonardo. Actually, it wasn't a Leonardo until quite recently." He fumbled his words. "I mean, it's been disputed. But now that it's stolen, the archivists have taken a second look and consider the blue one, at least, to be the real McCoy. You see, that's the big business. As I said, the more it's stolen, the more valuable it gets." He took a big breath and rolled his eyes. "Well, one of them is genuine."

About now, Morgan figured he was full of hot air.

"Do you mean there's more than one Leonardo missing?"

"That's right. There are two, a green one and a blue one. They appear almost identical twins, until you keep on looking at them. Then you see hundreds of differences—they're very different paintings. But I really can't recall now which is the authentic one. I think that may have been the problem, two colors of the same painting. Like Shergar, never recovered. IRA are suspected in that one, too."

Morgan strained to recall the da Vinci catalogue. "What's the title of this one?"

"It's a picture of the child Jesus with his mother."

"Mr. Matthews, Leonardo painted a few Madonnas." She smiled, but she was tuning him out.

"Wait, I've got it." Matthews felt triumphant. "*Jesus with the Ball of Yarn*, that's the title."

Morgan had never heard of that Leonardo, but nodded her head.

"Right now, you could say I am researching a confluence of related circumstances. I mean, the police and Lloyd's are connecting the dots. The thief we're after is not a 'one-medium collector.' He's very catholic in that regard—all media—but he only works in the British Isles." With a smarmy grin, he added, "You're counted out, Miss Kenny. Our prime suspect is Irish."

"I'm sorry, I don't get it. You've located the Leonardo?" Morgan picked up interest again.

"No. But the police do have a prime suspect. A Mayo woman. A museum employee who has been at the scene of several of the missing pieces. The Leonardo is just one precious art piece that's been stolen inside the UK."

"The UK? So not in Ireland, the republic?"

He caught the irony. "Sorry, I meant the UK *and* the Irish Republic. There's definitely a pattern here, Miss Kenny; IRA prints all over them."

"Fingerprints?" Morgan really thought Matthews a righteous so-and-so. His whole superior air bugged her.

"No, not fingerprints." He was fumbling again. "More like dots."

"What are some of the dots? Sounds interesting."

Drawing up closer to her, Matthews whispered. "We've got some substantial dots in Castlebar.

"An Irish maid worked in County Meath in the eighties to nineties at Dunsany Castle, where a number of paintings went missing. She was not suspected. Not then—we paid out. Then a year later, Canadian police recovered a Goya in Montreal, and to their surprise, a cache of paintings from Dunsany Castle. Coincidentally, an IRA man made his last confession in Boston after talking about the heist. Then in 1996, the same Irish woman who had worked as a maid in Meath was on the Dublin Museum employee list as being an office clerk—and a crateload of Celtic antiquities disappeared.

"Was it a coincidence? The Museum insurance was astronomical. And we paid through the ar--" he hesitated for a moment, "through the nose. Perhaps one of the bigger 'dots' has been the suspect's filial association with the IRA."

A bit irritated, Morgan pressed. "Filial 'dots' may be plausible, but why have you asked *me* here, Mr. Matthews?"

"Here is where I must rely on your discretion, Miss Kenny."

"You have it." Morgan was only half-listening. She smiled at Matthews, but now she had definitely drifted from his topic. He was just too talky. She was thinking of Grady and wishing she had invited him to Mayo when they were in the taxi. Then the two of them would be enjoying the evening together, instead of her listening to a long tale about paintings burgled from some rich Anglo-Irish gentry.

"I guess you could say I'm trying to—" he hesitated, waiting for her true feeling to show in her eyes. He was disappointed, but he plodded forward anyway: "I'm trying to recruit you to catch the art thief. I mean, it would probably be in your personal interest."

Frostily, she asked, "How is that, Mr. Matthews?"

"Because our suspect has annexed your aunt's land, that's why."

No sooner had he made his incendiary statement than he raised his gaze and fell mute. A very big man with a very big dog stood over him.

Morgan felt a gentle squeeze on her shoulder. She turned, expecting it to be Grady. Standing there, all six-foot-three of him, was a young Brian Dennehey. Morgan had to take a second look, the resemblance was so remarkable.

"Moore. Padraig Moore, Michael Grady's friend. He said you might need some help." Morgan knew this guy already. In his own wry way, he imitated the 007 star James Bond. He said his name with just that timing. As it turned out, Moore was a star in Castlebar.

Cyril Matthews stood up quickly, addressing Morgan as though she were an old friend.

"Morgan, I'm really sorry to hear about your aunt. Let's talk about my proposal soon, shall we?" He tipped his hat, moved hurriedly through the bar, and was gone.

"Sorry I scared off your Scots friend," Padraig said.

Padraig Moore had the tall, beefy build of an Irish footballer from a few decades past. In his late forties, he was a substantial-looking man, with vintage movie star flair. He had an open, even joyful face. But as Morgan would learn, he was not an easy mark. Still wearing his "court suit" and knitted vest, he carried a *shillelagh* and sported the biggest Irish wolfhound Morgan had ever seen at his heels. He and Morgan fell into conversation as if they were old friends, an ability Moore may have had with everyone he met.

"Thank you for your availability on such short notice," Morgan said. Her irritability had softened, and she almost purred. "Everything has been odd since I arrived in Ireland."

"So it could be. Ireland might do a lot of odd things to people," he said with tongue in cheek. Padraig was giving her a good look now. He liked what he saw.

"I don't know who is doing this," she explained, "but someone has buried my aunt—and she's not here, in Castlebar. I just assumed that she died here and would be buried here. Of course, I thought that Grailside, her nursing home, was here, too. And I don't know what to do about her land and all. I'd like to rely on you to help navigate this whole suspicious affair. Grady says you're the best." She smiled, looking directly into his face and finding the apostle without guile.

"Thanks," he smiled back. "Grady'd better give me good grades. I have a little background on your situation from him. By tomorrow, we should know whether your aunt had a will and what is the disposition of her land. If her body is in Eire, we'll find it. I'm sure we can sort this out. Please drop in, Miss Kenny, to fill out a few papers. My office is down the street." He reached over and handed her his card.

A well-liked local, Padraig was touched and greeted by the usual suspects on his way out of Heaney's. It gave Morgan a good impression of him.

* * *

It was only midnight when Morgan got back to Timmons' Teatime, but the doors were locked. Morgan hated to wake people up. *I should have had a key*, she thought. Then, in the streetlight, she saw the young boy coming to the door to unbolt it for her. He had on a long white shirt, maybe it was a nightshirt, hanging out over his jeans.

"I'm sorry to wake you," Morgan said, only partially apologetic.

"That's all right, Miss. I was just finishing up the cake." He smiled. He had those saucer eyes that always look a little lonely.

"Would it be awful to ask for a tea this late?"

"No problem. Actually your visit has taken on celebrity status."

She was obviously flattered. "I've always wanted to be a star!"

"It's not you, Miss. It's your aunt. Bit of a buzz, but I would like to know more about her sometime." He was polite, but Morgan knew Mrs. Timmons was probably gossiping about Mary's oddness with her kitchen friends.

"We could talk about her in the morning, Michael, is it?"

His face registered the putdown. She couldn't just dismiss him and then think she could ask him to do a few errands.

"No, wait, let's have a tea, and I can tell you a little bit about her. It *is* late."

Michael brought the pot and cups and a leftover chunk of cake.

"Once, when I was ten years old, I stayed with my aunts all summer. Here in Castlebar. I had a wonderful time. I think it's my favorite memory of her. I was pretty impressed, even as a kid, how close to nature she was. And how she could do stuff that nobody else could do—kind of like animal tricks and more. Do you know the English fairy story about *The Princess and the Goblins?*"

"Oh, yes. All kids get it. My father was always the one to read the stories." Michael was attentive.

"Mine, too." Morgan said. "I'll tell the part that describes my Aunt Mary. The story about the king's daughter who found a room at the top of a secret stair. In this room lived a lady with snow-white hair and eyes that were younger than the springtime. Snow-white pigeons flew in to her from the windows and settled in her shoulders. She knew all the ways of the fields and hills—the bees seemed to know her and follow her, and the larks flew out of the sky to her. She knew all there is to know about cows—all her cows had names. My real aunt did not read to me anything much as she recited long poems to me, or ditties you might call them."

Michael nodded. "My father, too. He told me the Irish myths in this fashion as I was growing up."

Morgan continued in the same tone, "And she didn't have charming or clever speech. She wasn't worldly, do you know what I mean?"

"Yeah, I do remember that old woman in the back room in the *Princess and the Goblins*—she was kind of a nature mystic, or somebody like Pan." This seemed to click for Michael, and he put things into a mental perspective now. Mary Kenny was not just some poor old woman on the dole—Morgan had turned her into a kind of lady St. Francis. It worked for Michael; he was into mystery and mythology.

"I heard you're trying to locate where your auntie is buried. I think I could help you."

"That would be great, Michael. Things have changed quite a bit in Ireland in the last few years. I'd appreciate that a lot."

Michael would prove to be a fair guide and an avid student of Ireland's old ways—both points of importance to Morgan and her quest.

Kenny Homestead

5
The Field

Lying in her purple bower, images of the previous day's events floated in Morgan's dreamscape. The odd message from the nursing home … the stagecoach to Mayo … the wonderful scene of Grady sweating and swearing in Irish … that oddball insurance guy, Cyril Matthews … *Is he real, or is he some kind of confabulator? Recruit her for what? … that creak—I did hear it! It's a floorboard near my door—someone is listening at the lock!*

She sprang from the quilt, pulled open the door—and there was Reggie bent over a tray with a pot of steaming tea. Both of them were startled by her swooping action.

"Good mornin', brought this up for ye. Compliments of the house." *Still, he was snooping, no matter how much like Barry Fitzgerald he acts.*

Sipping caffeine helped Morgan plan the morning. One, the cemetery; two, the land; and three, the old people's home, the Grailside. *Another day of rain, but the good news is unmistakable—the scent of bacon frying. Ireland is changing so, but thank God for old-fashioned landladies like Mrs. Timmons. Not anxious about her skirt zipper, she still makes the full Irish breakfast—rashers, sausages, kippers, fried tomato, and a spicy black pud. And of course, country brown eggs.*

Morgan understood her very special status when Mrs. Timmons poured orange juice into one of her Waterford glasses.

"That'll hold you till tea, won't it now?" And it did.

After a bit of negotiation, Mrs. Timmons took the reins and decided it would be cheaper for Morgan to hire Michael as her driver and use Timmons' Teatime's Jeep to get around in, instead of "that cheating Castlebar Taxi." She packed them a good lunch for the ride and sent them to the post office to get the proper location of the Kennys.

Michael referred to his mother's '75 Jeep as "the Green Dinosaur," which was an apt description, clunky and green. Pushing away a month's worth of newspapers with a hatchet laying on top, Morgan got in next to Michael. She didn't ask about the hatchet. He noticed her searching and said, "Don't worry, miss, this tank was made before seat belts."

One day, Michael Timmons would be a nice-looking man. But he was only "on the way" at this point. For a family that made their living on home cooking, this kid looked like a benign Ichabod Crane—a tangled head of blond hair skimming his bony shoulders, a pair of loose jeans hanging off his hips, topped off by a rather tired crewneck Aran sweater. (Morgan envied the skill of the knitter.)

Michael had none of the "quick and witty" one finds in TV teen heroes. As usual, Morgan was trying to place him into her Quiet Man scenario, but he didn't fit. He was the broken-nose type, with big blue eyes. *Maybe a young Nicholas Cage, from Moonstruck,* she thought. *Untapped, volcanic intensity just beneath the surface, but good. Good inside and out.*

They were just a few minutes out of the town when they reached the Castlebar cemetery. It was too early for it to be open, but Morgan went around the gate.

Michael sat in the Green Dino while she walked up and down the treeless rows, searching for the Kenny plot. A half-hour later, Morgan had located seven Kenny graves—Anthony, Wife No. 1, Wife No. 2, three children by the first wife, and Aran. But not Mary Kenny.

Climbing back into the Green Dinosaur, Morgan was shivering.

"She's got to be buried somewhere." Morgan's voice was flat.

"You didn't find her?" Michael was on the case.

She answered simply, "She was not there."

"Castlebar Cemetary, number one, a bust," she continued. "On to number two, the Kenny land. By the way, am I paying you by the hour or by the day?"

"You will have to ask 'She Who Must Be Obeyed.'" Michael smirked on that one.

"Oh," the postmistress advised Morgan, "there were never any house numbers out in the country. Often there weren't even any real lane names, either. One just has to go by landmarks. Your boy there, he'll help you."

Of course, Morgan thought, *if one does not know the landmarks, this is more challenging.*

"Cross the bridge, pass Naughton's farm, you can't miss it. It's got a newfangled energy windmill on it. Go all the way to the top of the hill, get out of your car, look north and you'll see Croagh Patrick, look south and you'll see the Neary farm."

Later, Morgan thought of another landmark herself: *The holy well—it was opposite her farm's entrance gate.* She wondered why the woman had signified the farm as the Neary family's, not the Kennys'.

The dirt lanes were narrow enough and little traveled. Michael grumbled; it took all his concentration just to get the "Green Dinosaur" through them. Brambles grew out of the tops and sides of six-foot stone fences.

"Is this a public road?" he wondered aloud, as the hedges scraped the Jeep's sides.

They were slowly descending from the top of the hill. A gentle slope on the backside away from Croagh Patrick.

Morgan recalled a snippet of conversation she'd had with her aunt— something about travel. "When you go to Dublin—" Morgan had said. Mary had interrupted softly: "I never been to Dublin City in my life, but I climbed Croagh Patrick three times. I done my penance."

Dublin could not be more than a hundred miles, she remembered thinking at the time. That's hard to believe—the aunts didn't seem that isolated.

The sun was on top of the mountain now, outlining the zigzag path pilgrims took to the summit … *to do penance, to erase sin. The great saint Patrick made his climb to imitate Christ. What sin could a saint like Patrick have made? What sin could a simple, good woman like Aunt Mary have made? Her whole life in Castlebar a life of work, with few pleasures … what did she need to do penance for?* Morgan had no answers. But now that she was thinking upon that mountain, she grasped the pride everyone had in climbing it. Mary looked out on that mountain every day … *an eternal meditation of making retribution?*

So much of Irish spirituality had guilt and penance linked up.

"Look, look, Miss!"

Morgan drew a breath, startled as though it were the gate. It was only a badger family strutting across the road. She felt herself a little less tight; maybe she was opening to spring.

Ireland was so different. She was ready for different. At thirty-six, she'd hit "the midlife thing" and was ready for a change in her life. She'd just spent three years recovering from her convent stint. She was ready for a walk on the wild side. Only she had no idea just how wild it would be.

A stand of trees putting out their first catkins drew Michael's attention.

"We should stop, Miss." Michael's tone carried authority. "Those trees can only grow in wetlands—alders, they're called."

"So?" Morgan stared at the trees he was pointing to.

"The holy well, Miss. It's no doubt soggy there."

A flashback moment—Aunt Mary smiling, taking her to the well next to the road when she was a very little girl. Auntie pulled on the ring in the well lid, lifting it off. Her feet had high boots, "wellies." *She blessed me, she blessed me in the water of the holy well, the Lady's Well. Both of us had to scrape our boots from the mud.*

"Michael, this has to be it. There are just too many brambles in the way." Morgan jumped out and stood tiptoe on the running board. Croagh Patrick was still there, but the Kenny farm wasn't. Just open scrubland, stones, brambles. The "landmark" theory was weakening.

"Let me walk ahead, Michael, if you would follow," Morgan announced. A chill was in the air, with a heavy cloud cover. She pulled her suede jacket a little closer. Mud spattered her new tights, and soft clay caked on her fancy ankle boots. The gentle drizzle speeded up.

At the top of the hill, she looked right, and it was there. Not the old wooden gate she remembered, but a fat, rusty chain strung up between two poles, flanked by six-foot solid hedges—a "Keep Out" sign if she ever saw one. Quickly, she looked to the other side of the road for the entrance to the holy well. Nothing but wild reeds and whitethorn bushes. *It must have been there, but is now just grown over.* She saw rags on the bushes, remnants of "petition rags" from long ago. *Apparently no one goes there anymore.*

Michael jumped out with the axe.

"Is it here?" He began chopping through the weeds. "There's nothing here, Miss."

Leaving Michael to clear brush, she inspected the chain.

"Do we have to bash through this chain? We don't have to drive in. I'll just go under and look around." She pulled up the chain and stared at Michael from the other side.

"It's okay," he said. "I can't drive in anyway; I'm out of petrol, I guess. Just be a few minutes, Miss. I'm sure I've got a gas can and so forth." She looked into his eyes and did not believe in the "so forth."

This was the land; she felt excitement well up in her chest. She felt right about it, but there was no landmark. *Where is the house? The barn? The pens for pigs, the garden fence, and … it's simply gone.* Morgan began to have a sinking feeling, identical to the time her car was stolen right in front of a church. A confused feeling, like being lost, robbed. Somehow, she felt that it was her fault.

Morgan had walked about a block from the road. The old drive to the house was filled in with mosses and lichens. Untended chamomile, thyme, and wild mint grew along the old path. *The two aunts used to have an herb garden next to the kitchen door,* she remembered, *and medicinal herbs as well.* She'd been walking with the "ghosts" of her family the whole time.

Arriving at the spot where she figured the house had been, she looked for clues, remnants of the old place. *Stones. Maybe foundation stones?* But Morgan didn't know the difference between one stone and the next. There were so many. Then a dark red half-brick or two; she kicked at the grasses grown over a heap of them. She was sure these were from a fireplace. *This area has been deliberately cleaned of my aunts' house. But they couldn't think of everything.*

One pale yellow rosebush stubbornly maintained, next to what had been a front-door stoop. Morgan bent over and began to scratch the ground around the bush. She pulled the weeds. It was there—the key to the front door! She held it as though it were a long-lost relic. And it did convey power to her. She felt as though her palm were burning. Mary was there in that key. Not unlike Vasilisa, she kissed it and put it in her pocket.

6
Neighborhood *Seanachie*

Hearing shouting, Morgan stood up. A long way off, a man with a slouch hat and high boots was waving his arms at her and shouting. *He looks like he might be a hunter—a poacher on Mary's back acreage? Maybe he's in need of help?* Then she saw his rifle. One shot, then another loud blast. He was aiming at her.

She dropped to the ground terrified. She began crawling toward a higher pile of stones. She was getting close to crying, but instead she began to pray: *St. Michael the Archangel, please help me.*

She cowered behind the wall, if it could be called that. It was a falling-down ruin of the old cow barn, the highest part not measuring a yard high.

She closed her eyes for a moment, hoping this was all a mistake. When she opened them, to her horror, she discovered she had disturbed a snake nest. *But there are no snakes in Ireland,* she thought. A low cry escaped her, but she lay still. They all looked a bit sleepy, like snakes—*snakes. No snakes? Then what the hell are these things?* Her left shoe lay under one's "chin." She found herself trying to choose whether to be bitten by some kind of rodent snakes or shot by a frenzied poacher.

Michael the Archangel, defend us in battle; be our protection against the wickedness and snares of the devil.

Morgan had not said that prayer in twenty years. It was there. where the nuns put it, in the "deep heart's core." St. Michael, he always delivered. No malarkey!

Within seconds, a continuous beep from the Green Dinosaur's horn rang out with more good tidings. Rolling away from the pit, Morgan took her chances that the rifleman would be distracted enough by the horn for her to elbow her way under Naughton's fence. Like Croagh Patrick, the Naughtons had been solid neighbors to the Kennys for generations. She touched the key in her pocket and whispered, "Thank you."

Winded and filthy, Morgan pounded on Naughton's farmhouse door. It was not a shanty like her aunts' had been, but a large fieldstone home of more years than a hundred, with a broad front porch facing the Holy Mountain, Croagh Patrick. Old lady Naughton's great-granddaughter took one look at Morgan and relayed the situation in a few well-placed shouts.

"They're shootin' over at Kennys' again, Granny. Shootin' at Miss Morgan Kenny."

"Jaysus, Mary, and Joseph!" The old woman did not rise to meet Morgan, but looked straight at her with milky eyes.

Morgan embraced her and kissed her on the cheek. "Morning to thee, Mather," Morgan said, in a show of deference and affection from the old times.

"The bastard. The durty bastard!" *Only a sweet old Irish lady could make swearing sound like a prayer!* The lady seemed up for the excitement.

"Shootin' off a gun at a human person. And a nun, too!" she said in a huff. "It's a sin! It's a mortal sin, Sister. The bastard."

Morgan could see all this had upset Mrs. N., in a positive Irish way—and in the midst of it, she had forgotten Morgan was no longer a nun. The old woman's face and arms had become as soft and as wrinkled as brown leather. Her hand began to shake, and then her head.

"The Brit started policin' up your aunties' place from the moment she went to the old people's home, a few years back. He's a sly Brit, he is. Goin' around collectin' old ladies' fields. God forgive me for what I'm thinkin'."

"What's that you're t'inkin,' Grammy?" her little blonde questioned.

"Your gramma's thinkin' I'd like to shoot that eejit in the arse." Laughing a belly laugh, she motioned her teenage great-grandson to bring the tea. He brought in the tea in a plain metal teapot, heavy mugs, a white soda bread with sultanas, and a good chunk of home-churned butter. He set the tea, drawing his grandmother's wheelchair toward the fire.

"Do you prefer a cup, lass? These stone crockery hold the heat longer, you know." Morgan could see now that Mrs. N. was almost blind. Morgan had not seen her in many years.

"Mrs. Naughton," Morgan began, "what has happened? Everything is gone. House, barn, gardens … my auntie." Morgan began to cry and sat at Mrs. Naughton's feet, her head on her lap.

The old lady's white eyes held years of loss. Still, she felt Morgan's sobs. She was touched by the American lass's tears for her auntie. She remembered her as a summer child, a child everyone prepared for with cakes and new pinafores.

"What happened to Aunt Mary? I don't know where they've laid her." Morgan choked out words she had been trying to form for a few days.

"And so it was with Jaysus." The blind old lady's hands trembled as she lifted her cup. The blonde girl child came noiselessly into the room and arranged Mam Naughton's knitted shawl about her shoulders, smoothing the tartan lap blanket in ritual fashion. The old lady was composing herself for the "telling." She knew her duty at a wake, and whether they had the body of Aunt Mary or not, she had her part to play. The head of her clan began her narrative of Mary Kenny with the formality of the old-time *seanachie*. And Morgan gave her sacramental attention.

Michael had slipped in the back door. The children knew that Mrs. Naughton was a serious storyteller herself, and they beckoned him to sit on the floor to hear her.

"Fado, fado." *Long, long ago.* That is the way fairy tales begin in Irish, and so it went with Mary Kenny's life as told by Bridie Quinn Naughton in the Year of Our Lord, 1999, Mayo, Eire.

"I remember Mary Kenny as though she had come to our house yesterday. Mary came to our house when I was seven or eight. She was older, a teen she was, but she was closer to me in age than to any of the rest. So the two of us played, ran the fields, churned butter, danced at the fairs together. She helped my mother in the house … cooking, laundry, gardening for the six of us laddies. My mother loved her. And she was good to her. We all loved her.

"She was modest and meek. 'Musha,' says mi mather to me, 'be of good cheer as Mary is.' No school did she have, but possessed of the virtues, you see. She was moderate. Everyone in our clan wanted the biggest chop on the platter. Do you understand? Mary cut her meat and gave half of it to the shameless beggars at our table. 'No cryin' in this house,' she'd say. 'With the plenty you have!'

"Mary Kenny did not impose. She had feelings—she must have had them—but she never showed them, Mary didn't. You knew she had them when she sang. She sang all the little ones to sleep with them tunes of old. Sure, she would make mi mather cry whenever she sang the old tunes in Irish. All your family still spoke the Irish, you know. I suppose it's because she never went to school. No, they didn't beat it out of her.

"I think it always made my mother think of the times she lived with her family in Clare. When she was young and …"

She turned her face away. The great-grandson set a jar of porter on the table, seeming to know they were entertaining "mighty things." She sipped her beer from the stein as though it were hot soup, slowly blowing on the foam, savoring the flavor of the dark draft. She continued seamlessly like the storyteller who had received his portion.

"Mary's mother had died some years before. I think she wound up with us because Ol' Man Kenny couldn't care for her, and then when she was in her teens, he died. I really can't remember much about her father, except that he was dour and married twice, and Mary and Aran were the children who survived of his second wife. Your own grandmother, Lily, must have been the living child from the first wife. No one ever knew where Mary's mother came from. She said Clare, but no one from that county knew her. No one knew and no one asked—she just arrived. But she were different from the get-go."

Mrs. Naughton took a breath, rolling her eyes, adding, "Some say she came from the *cailleach* of Clare, the wise woman Biddy Early, because she had the "sight." No one knows. She taught her children the old language and the old ways. It was my mother taught her the beads. After Kenny died, Mary's sister Aran came back from Dublin to manage the farm. Aran was the most prudent with the punt."

She sat up straight, lifted her head as though she were seeing someone, and continued her narration.

"I can see Mary Kenny crossin' the fields again to go back home. She stayed home, too, until they took her to the old people's home in '89. They'll be takin' me there too, one of these days." She laughed.

Morgan hesitated to interrupt; but when the old lady paused to sip her beer, she asked, "But didn't she have even one outside work?" Morgan spoke softly so as not to change the flow of her narrative.

"Now wait a bit—she did serve the priests over there at the parish for a few years. What a sour place for a young girl! No wonder she never met some nice young swain." She pronounced it *shawin*. "Servin' old Father McGinty, he who wouldn't give his piss to the crows. And then spendin' her Sundays dodgin' Horsey Neary in her own home, the old devil."

"You mean Aran's husband? Mr. Neary?" Morgan asked.

The old woman took a deep breath and blew out the following words like filling a balloon.

"Mishter? He had a gob on him like a horse, and the horse in the field was smarter than Neary. Disgrace was he to his parents, worse to a decent wife, your aunt Aran. Was he not after every clerk and Sally in the town? Did he not run after Mary as well? Her stayin' at the rectory, just to keep a step ahead of him."

Now Morgan was confused. "I didn't know Neary was this much of a cad. Well, if he was so, why did Aran even marry him?"

The old lady raised her wispy white eyebrows. "Sure that shouldn't be such a secret? You have to remember, everyone had very little then—and on top of that, options were few for girls. Marriage or the convent! Castlebar is thriving now, but then ..." Her voice trailed off in remembrance of those times. "I myself had to spin and wind yarn for my mother till my fingers bled. A whole wagonload of yarn would collect very little back then.

"Nearys' farm was next to yours. They weren't very rich, but his family had airs, you know, and a big house, horses, and a water closet! Emet was never up to his family. I only knew him as a town drunk. I know for a fact he was forbidden to drive, so one of his brothers would go into town lookin' for him." She gave a nod for her grandson to fill her stein. "In truth, it was a merger. The two fields together were a good piece of land. Aran plowed for potatoes and turnips and barley. Mary had an herb and flower garden, selling them at the crossroads. They had *caffeen* like us." Mrs. N. slowed a bit and petted her little blonde great-grandchild.

"I never saw her much when she went to work for the church. From time to time, I would see her in the butcher's, Dolan's, shopping for the priests, or walking with bundles up the hill to the parish house. Let the saints forgive me for what I'm thinking." She muffled a curse under her breath. "She did all the work in that house for the three of them, the priests, serving them back then. Pluckin' geese and ducks for stew and then makin' quilts with the feathers. She was quick with a stitch. She laid all the fires, too. I canna' imagine how many fires she kept goin' in a house that big. Finnegan brought in dried turf from Newport by the load. Whenever she laid our fire, sure she said a prayer. She was probably sayin' the kindlin' prayer at the priests' house, too. She used to sign us, too, from the Lady's Well near her road.

"There's only one priest there now, over at Transfiguration Parish. The young ones don't go in for the monastery anymore. With all the stories you're hearin' about them. Holy Mother of God, the young ones canna' get themselves into a church except for their wedding." She lowered her head and her voice, leaning over the table.

"Just a soft bit of gossip. It's not really gossip, 'cause I know it to be true. The old man Mr. Kenny got by in hard times by makin' *potcheen* in their barn. Back then everybody made it. My own father went to Kennys' from time to time. My father always said that Aran Kenny made the best *potcheen* in Connacht. She must have learned how to make it from her father, and I believe that she and Mary was able to survive by its help, too. Sure they couldn't keep flesh on the bone with the few *caffeens* they raised."

Morgan tuned in on this one. "I thought there was kind of a liquor police that was always sniffing that production out."

"Right, right, there was … there still is, but the two sisters had a baking business for more than a few years. Delicious brown bread, soda bread, the old-time hearth-baked oatcakes, and didn't they sing the old-time prayer when she blessed the dough?"

"I know it was so long ago, but do you remember that blessing song?" Morgan loved the ancient Celtic invocations.

Mrs. Naughton began, a soft chant, more spoken than sung:

I put food for her in the eating-place,
And drink in the drinking-place,
And music in the listening-place,
In the Holy Name of the Trinity.

She blesses meself and mehouse
Me goods and me family.

And the lark said in her warble
"Often, often, often
Goes Christ in the stranger's guise,
Oh, oft and oft, and oft.
Goes Christ in the stranger's guise."

Morgan made no mention, but the blessing, although haunting, was not the bread blessing. The old woman had obviously forgotten and had sung another of Mary's prayers. One could feel in it the old religion mixed in with the Christian religion, but the mix felt right.

"But what difference would a baking business make?"

"Well, I always thought that they never catched her buyin' all that yeast for the *potcheen* they were brewin', because she had a wee bakery. And you got to have somethin' to heat up that potato mash."

She used her handkerchief to muffle a laugh. Just that lightness inspired Morgan to continue on the sleuth, even though less than an hour before she would have easily abandoned it.

"But what about Horsey Neary? I've heard of him but rather little," Morgan asked.

"Well, that's a story for another night," Mrs. N. was quick to respond. "He went to Dublin lookin' for work, and he never returned. Let us say, Aran was well to be rid of the lazy oaf."

Morgan bid Mrs. Naughton and her kin good-bye and promised to see her before she returned to the States. As they stood at the door, the blind old lady, whom she would never talk to again, said, "You'll find all of this out, lassie. Don't forget. You have your auntie's blessin', and you have mine, too." The old lady held Morgan's face and made the sign of the cross on her forehead.

Then Michael and Morgan climbed into the Green Dinosaur. Morgan felt squared away. *Even saved … cleansed … and other warm thoughts.* Michael gave her a quick look.

"Right. I'm more worried about my mother seeing you with all your clothes ruined than tellin' her about the bullets and snoots all over your land."

Hungry and exhausted, it was back to Timmons' Teatime.

As they passed the neighboring farm, Morgan wondered if they were the ones who "annexed" the Kenny land Cyril had been talking about. *Talking about Cyril Matthews, it looks like him stepping out of a police car right in front of that farmhouse.*

"Michael, I'm too tired and dirty to take a ride to Connemara to visit the Grail place." She waited to see if he would catch the joke, but he didn't get the Grail reference. "How about tomorrow? After breakfast? I think now, after all this about my aunt's estate"—she paused—"or the lack thereof, well, I think I have to get that lawyer, Moore, the solicitor friend of Mr. Grady, to tell me what to do about it."

They pulled up to the garage in the back of Timmons'. Michael's face went into a bit of a wince. "I was hopin' you thought it 'propriate to share a little more about your Aunt Mary."

"When I was about ten years old, I stayed the whole summer with Aunt Aran and Aunt Mary."

The pink fading sun shone on Croagh Patrick. They were hushed as the monastery bells tolled the six o'clock Angelus.

"You were *my* saving angel today, Michael." Morgan spoke softly.

Moore Hall

7
Rebellion of 1798

In 1798, a band of determined Irishmen rose up in County Mayo against their English rulers. The French, fresh from their own revolution, came to the aid of the Irish against a common enemy, England. Early victories under the brilliant command of French General Humbert in the summer of '98 gave way to inglorious losses in the autumn to superior British forces under Lord Cornwallis. Yes, the same Cornwallis who lost to the Americans in their Revolution of 1776. Recalling his colonial defeat, he became a vicious adversary in Ireland. The Irish were doomed. This failure at a freedom uprising by a people brutally oppressed was not to be the end of a bloody dream that refused to die. For a very brief moment in time, one month to be exact, John Moore, thirty-one years of age, of Moore Hall, Mayo, became the first president of Connaught in the Year of the French.

Timmons' Teatime was bustling at breakfast. More than a few Irish visitors, as well as American tourists, gave the place a cheerful air. Michael was tucked away in the corner near the swinging kitchen door. He sat hunched over scones, tea, and an open schoolbook. Morgan sat down with him and motioned to the serving girl, who held a teapot in her left hand and a coffeepot in her right, to "fill 'er up."

After the first sip, Morgan asked, "Have you recovered from that wing-ding of a day?"

"Is that American for 'We almost got our heads shot off'?" Michael had exaggerated the brogue. And he was laughing. "Almost."

"Right." Morgan mocked him, rolling her eyes. "I have an appointment with a local solicitor, Mr. Padraig Moore. Do you know him?"

"Moore? Yeah. He's a big fellow. Old footballer. Mayo. Heritage family. How'd ya get him?"

"He was a schoolmate—rather, a football mate—with Grady."

"The guy from Letterfrack that fixed the taxi flat?" Michael said it straight.

"Right. The anthropologist guy who rode with us from Shannon."

"Another old footballer, eh?"

The world was full of old people over thirty in Michael's mind.

"See you after school, yah?" Morgan liked this kid.

"Do you need the Green Dinosaur?" Michael asked, searching on the floor for his book bag.

"I don't know yet. Let's find out what Moore has to say about the gun guy. And we'll go from there."

"Right. I'll check in with you after class. Also, I'm supposed to be thinkin' on what I should be doin' in college next year. So?" Michael was out the door.

Morgan made a mental note: Give Michael a little airtime about his studies. He's a smart aleck, but he's smart, too. Needs to be around a man somehow, like modeling.

* * *

The antique carved doors to a curbside office should have given Morgan the first clue. Padraig G. Moore was something more than a solicitor.

The secretary in the outer office, an older woman in a dark suit, spoke softly, as though she were in church. The half-lit waiting room had the feel of a parson's parlor, with comfortable furnishings of an earlier era. Miss Ryan helped Morgan off with her damp jacket.

"We were expecting you, Miss Kenny. Expecting. Mr. Moore is on his way back from court. He's on his way." She emphasized in a slightly higher pitch, "Could you take a cup of tea, a good hot cup?" She spoke while simultaneously hanging up the jacket and opening the inner office door.

The inner office was, in fact, a revelation. If the outer office appeared rather drab, the inner one impressed Morgan as Byzantine, a richly designed museum. Shuttered in Spanish-Arabic screens, the long, narrow room was dominated by a massive armoire filled with very old law books. A long oak library table fronted the bookcase; it was piled with cream-colored files and a marble ashtray, filled with half-smoked stogies. The walls on either side of the desk were covered with paintings, drawings, photos, certificates, and blue ribbons, awards of every stripe. Morgan simply gawked at it all. And the muchness was not a mess. It had to have been put together by an artist, someone who understood collections and dimension, color and big art. Among the hundreds of pieces displayed, a small heavily-framed photo of Grace of Monaco standing with her Irish relatives—and probably members of the Moore family—caught Morgan's eye.

By the time Morgan reached the desk, Ms. Ryan had entered with a clattering tea cart. Morgan was impressed with the beautifully arranged tray, especially the pink rose and the lace napkin. Ms. Ryan poured a cup for Morgan and was compelled to mention "Timmons' scones." Morgan smiled.

With a cup in one hand and a Timmons' treat in the other, Morgan perused the walls. *A mélange of really great stuff,* she thought.

Moore Hall, or rather the fantasy of what Moore Hall might have been if it hadn't become a ruin in a swamp in the nineteenth century, was artfully interpreted as a pastel on wood. It was by far the largest of the paintings, two feet by three. Another large piece that drew Morgan's attention was a wood carving of the Black Madonna of Monserrat, mounted on a backdrop of yellow and blue Spanish tiles. At the other end of the scale were a series of colorful miniatures, paintings of red soldiers and blue from Mayo's Rebellion in the Year of the French 1798. The most intricate painting was of the French commander, General Joseph Amable Humbert, at the battle of Castlebar. *Humbert cut quite a dashing figure riding a chestnut stallion, with a crimson coat and hat and gold-trimmed blue breeches, brandishing a sword above his head, almost saying "Into the breach" or some such*, Morgan thought.

"This Moore has to be an interesting guy," Morgan sighed. She looked up to find a barrel-chested man around her own age standing with his hand stretched out to her. He seemed larger in every measure than the man strolling through Heaney's Pub the other night.

Silently, from the other side of the armoire, a large animal lumbered out. It startled Morgan.

"Oh."

"This is Fand. She is my mistress from the Other World and Great Companion," Padraig announced. Smiling. Stroking the top of the dog's long gray head. She almost reached his waist. "Miss Kenny?"

"Irish wolfhound?" Morgan asked.

Within minutes, the two "strangers" had struck a harmonious chord, as had the hound, which took a liking to Morgan and laid down in front of her. Padraig had that natural gift of connection that unleashes confessions. Perhaps his profession gave him assurance; perhaps his family's status gave him a bit of swagger. Whatever the factors, a warm starter relationship began between the two.

Another person in on the hunt is not a bad idea, especially a solicitor, she thought. *Michael will approve.*

And so Morgan "confessed" the events of yesterday's visit to the Kenny field.

"It all seems surreal now, to find the old house totally gone except for a few stones—a moment of disassociation. I began thinking, 'Is this some kind of a bad dream?' Thank God I found the old rosebush, and the house key buried next to it. It saved the day—or at least, it saved my mind, a kind of proof of my aunt's existence.

"Then, a man at the back of the field began shooting at Michael Timmons and myself, in live rounds! Total disbelief. Even now, it is hard to believe it's all gone."

"We have to report this to the police, Morgan." Padraig walked toward her.

"Not only have the house and gardens disappeared, but the field has some kind of madman on it. I was able to escape to my aunt's neighbors, the Naughtons. Mrs. Naughton says they tore down the house the minute my aunt went to the nursing home. That was more than five years ago!"

"Sounds like they didn't want you or anyone else in your family to move back into the family home," Padraig said.

"Torn down, Padraig. That's hostility!" She broke off. Just saying this had put her on the verge of tears. "Home and hostility."

Morgan surprised herself—she called Ireland her "home." And when she said the word "hostility," it seemed to be the first time she realized someone didn't want her here. Maybe Ireland was not in her horoscope.

"Wait, Morgan … there may not be a house there, but this is *your* family business. The spirit of your aunt is still here. You are here for a reason, love."

Morgan stood and addressed him.

"This is the thing, Padraig. I have come to Ireland to bury my aunt. And I can't find her. I have come to take care of her home and the land of my ancestors, and there is no home." Flashing through her mind in that instant was the enormous ruin of Moore Hall in the woods of Castlebar, compared to the few remaining stones of the Kenny cottage. "I thought that being her last and closest family member, I would be inheriting the farm. I'm not quite sure I would have known what to do with it, but I assumed that. Vaguely, I thought some possibilities would be in Ireland for me. I guess all the 'supposed tos' didn't happen."

A bit coolly, Padraig asked, "The Naughtons say that the aunt's neighbor Welch tore down your aunt's cottage five years ago. How is it that you did not know this?"

"I am afraid my great-aunt has not been on my radar for a number of years. When I entered … the convent, that is, everything related to family fell to my mother. I'd visited Ireland every summer. When I entered the Order my visits ended. My mother visited Mary in the home, and even in the nursing home, when she came back to Ireland.

"I just assumed that Grailside Home was in Castlebar. I never questioned. I suppose I let my mother 'carry' all things about Ireland for me. Then my mother died, and the links to Ireland went with her." Morgan sat quietly, reflectively, a bit disturbed, wondering what happened to all the years.

Padraig sat down with her, on a blue velvet love seat next to the fire. He placed a notebook from his desk next to her and opened it. This was the first chance he'd had to take a longer look at her. *She's quite pretty in the firelight,* he considered. *One of those long-legged, rich California blondes.*

"Let's look at these reports I've found out since last night," he said.

Padraig told Morgan he hadn't yet located her aunt's body, but that she was definitely not in Mayo.

"My regular investigator has combed funeral homes and grave sites in Castlebar and the rest of Mayo, so we're sure on this county. Not everyone has the computer, yet. We have learned that Grailside, her nursing home, *is* in the County of Galway—the area of Connemara and the town of Claddagduff, on the sea."

Padraig looked at Morgan's face, and it spelled confusion, like the signposts—five arrows, with various names, going to the same place ...

"Lots of new names for you, Morgan, I'm afraid, but what I'm suggesting is that some of the rubrics for one county may not apply to another. Listen, I hear the Timmons' boy is your chauffeur-about-town. He'll get you to Connemara. My man cannot get out to Claddagduff until Monday. So, I advise you to go to Grailside Nursing Home with the Timmons' boy tomorrow. Be proactive, Morgan, and you will feel more hopeful about the case. If you dig around, you might find out more than he could. Positive."

"I was planning on doing that."

Padraig was still thinking of Timmons' "tank." He smiled broadly, recalling the green World War II Jeep. "Bucko Mike, he's a nice lad," he said, sounding a wee paternalistic.

Morgan's face questioned him.

"The nursing home must have a 'Cause of Death' certificate at least." He recovered his lawyerly tone. "Find the doctor, the doctor who signed that document. Someone made arrangements at the home for her burial, someone.

"The second thing, Morgan, is that your aunt *did* make a will. Fifty years ago! Grady helped me out with that one. He has a Dublin friend or two at the English firm of Browne & Brandeis. Of course, he's bringing a purloined copy to me. I'm going to call them as soon as I can read it over.

"So, let me comment about what I know right now, even if something might change later on. As to your aunt's two properties, her own field and that which accrued to her on the death of her sister Aran, from her late husband Emmet Neary ... both fields in Castlebar were made over to a neighbor-man named Welch, Angus Welch, when Miss Mary Kenny was twenty-six years old. That would have been 1950. So let us see how this unfolds. For now, we have to discount the theory that she was too old or too ill, and hence incompetent, to have made such a decision. Still, the big question I have is, 'What twenty-six-year-old makes a will?' Especially, what country girl with little education? And why would she need to make one? Do you catch my meaning, Morgan? Something is not right here. It is not just some mistake.

"We have to find out more about Welch, who owns the property now, and why he got both your aunts to sign it over to him!"

"Well, we know one thing about Welch," Morgan said with flat conviction. "He's scared of something, or he would not have a guy running around with a gun guarding the property. Of that we are quite certain."

Padraig stood on that note and offered his hand.

"When is Grady coming up?" Morgan felt a little more energized.

"He'll be here tonight, actually. I'm going to meet him at Heaney's. I should have said, '*We* are going to meet him.' He asked me to tell you he'd be there around ten." Padraig swept up the papers on the love seat and walked to the desk.

* * *

On her way out, Morgan passed an oil portrait of a handsome young gentleman in a ruffled shirt and a green armband: "John Moore, President of Connaught, 1798."

8
Heaney's Pub

Padraig and Fand led the way through a rowdy dinner crowd at Heaney's, with Morgan following, to a back bar glowing and spicy from a peat fire—and a Celtic harp. Fand stretched out in front of the fire. Without a word, a young barboy brought them a couple of porters and plate of oak salmon. Padraig was a regular. They knew his favorites. The original Heaney had worked for the Moores almost a century earlier.

They had just settled in when Grady arrived. He looked a bit perturbed, seeing the two of them in easy laughter as though they had been old friends forever. He was expecting to find Morgan alone. He thought he had indicated a date, just the two of them. "Don't be greedy, Grady Boy," he thought. "That must wait."

"You two are really working," he offered in vague jest.

"Grady, you can't marry me for my land," Morgan mocked. She took a sip of the porter and lit a cigarette. "I am no longer an heiress."

This caught his attention.

"Forget about a farm in Mayo." Grady waved a dramatic gesture. "I'm really out after the crown jewels, meself." He laughed.

"Padraig assures me the field was disposed of before I was born! Point of fact, the Kenny mother-house is gone, too—literally. There is not even a ruin, not a shell. Every stone has been carried away. The old cattle barn is still there, but the roof is gone." As Morgan spoke, her chin jutted forward.

"They demolished the house, I suspect, because they don't want the Yanks comin' home to roost," Padraig explained.

"What happened?" Grady looked at her sympathetically.

Padraig cut in: "Morgan is lucky she didn't get killed. Some bloke shooting a rifle scared her off the land yesterday."

Padraig's emotion revealed a growing affection for Morgan. Grady, who had staked no claim, began to feel a jealous ping.

"My aunt left the field to a neighbor, a British one, no less. So, legally at least, Michael and I were trespassing."

Grady was beginning to get it. "Who was the guy with the gun?"

"Morgan, was that the Brit owner?" Padraig asked, and then answering himself, "Ach, he was probably a caretaker. Bloody brute." Padraig stroked Fand as he spoke.

Grady gave Morgan a worried stare. "You've got to be kidding!"

Padraig leaned toward them.

"There's something odd about this whole thing." He spoke directly to Grady. "The will is fifty years old. Thus, the aunt made the thing when she was little more than a girl!"

"Why in the devil would you make a will at that age? There's some kind of coercion here." Grady turned to Morgan, touching his head with his index finger. "Was there something *wrong* with your aunt?"

"I don't know if she was 'touched' in that sense. I knew her as an eccentric and kind country lady. She was a simple woman, as they say, but not mad." Morgan was staring into the blaze. "I really wish now that I had come home during those years.

"Our neighbors, the Naughtons, told me agents of the Welches razed her place when she went into the nursing home, about five years ago." Morgan continued. "But my aunt never mentioned it in any of her letters."

"Your aunt knew, Morgan," Grady said.

"She signed the will," Padraig added. "But maybe she didn't want you to know."

"Something's fishy," Grady shot in quickly. "I'd like to go out to your aunt's field. Maybe there's something on her land that Welch finds valuable."

"Precisely!" Padraig said.

"Mrs. Naughton told me something that adds to the mystery," Morgan said. "About the time of the will, 1950—her brother-in-law, one 'Horsey' Neary, went to Dublin or London looking for work. Work! That sounds suspicious in itself, since he never worked a day in his life. But the point is, he never returned."

"So you think there could be a connection between Neary's disappearance and the will?" Grady asked.

"What I know is that Horsey and my Aunt Aran married to meld fields. Like so many marriages in Ireland, it was a merger. So his field would go to Aran upon his death, and both fields would go to Mary when Aran died. Aran died sometime in the eighties."

"You know how many guys 'disappear' with a pint?" Grady was still thinking about Horsey.

"My Aunt Aran was as good as a widow after that, but she never spoke of a letter coming from Horsey. In fact, she seems never to have spoken of his absence. It was as though he was still there, as though he never left Mayo."

Padraig leaned forward. "And at that point, the ownership of both farms would have fallen to your Aunt Mary. That's a good packet." Turning to Grady, he asked, "Did you bring that will from Browne's?"

"Indeed." Grady handed him a dun envelope. "Let me tell you, they're a snooty bunch at Brown and Brandeis. I can't imagine a young girl from Castlebar hiring them, not fifty years ago!"

"I'm with you," Morgan said. "I think someone pressured my aunts. It's got to be Welch. He's the one who's got the land."

Grady sat higher in the chair. "Yes, Morgan, but he seemed to have been patient enough for fifty years. Doesn't that sound odd to you, too?"

For another hour, the warmth of the fire, the Irish love of *craic* (Irish chat), and an extra draft of Guinness carried the three of them like a wave out to sea. The excitement of it all made Morgan a bit heady.

Padraig Moore's mind had not gone dull from the fire. He began in mid-thought, "But that leaves us with the third party?" He spoke slowly as though waking from a dream.

Morgan sat up in the cushions, "What do you mean, Padraig?"

"Both your aunts signed these papers, but where is Horsey's signature? He was part owner, too." He had pulled the papers out for another look.

"Last call before closing."

Grady stood to hand the bar boy his stein. "Maybe, Horsey was a bit farther away than Dublin."

On their way out of Heaney's, they saw Mr. Matthews and Reggie sitting at the front bar in convivial conversation. Touching Matthews's coat sleeve, Morgan whispered, "Mr. Matthews, I caught your meaning about my rude neighbor at the end of a rifle."

"What, what?" Matthews gasped.

"You were right: my aunt's land has been *annexed.*" She drew out the word.

"Miss Kenny, we've got something, we've got some proof. We must talk. Please add three letters to the pot—IRA." Morgan noticed that Matthews had changed his brown felt hat for a plaid porkpie. He really wanted to blend in.

Reggie was still smiling at the three of them as they left Heaney's.

When they were on the sidewalk, Padraig turned to Morgan and said, "You know, your friend Reggie is an old IRA man. There are more than a few old guys left. Maybe just a runner, but still in the game."

Padraig, Grady, and Morgan walked to Timmons' B&B arm in arm. Buddies in brew. At the door, for just one awkward moment, Padraig stood with the two of them until Grady put his arm around Morgan. Quietly, Padraig waved and crossed the street to his office. He decided he would read through the will before midnight. And he did.

Morgan and Grady stumbled through the darkened tearoom, weaving through tables. Grady touched her hand and looked into her eyes seeking silent permission for a kiss or perhaps an invitation to her room. Permission was more than waiting. She closed her eyes, thinking, *He is a perfectly beautiful stranger. I've never even dated him, and I don't care. And Rose, take the night off.*

He looked down at her and pulled off the barrette that held her braid. Unbound, her hair fell below her shoulders. *She is so close to what I've been looking for,* Grady thought. He seemed to have been thinking about her all day, and now he took hungry kisses, wet kisses. In some way he had opened her suede jacket and was fingering buttons on her layers of sweaters until he could feel her breast. They were small breasts; he smiled. *They are chaste like her. Yes, chaste … the right word.*

Something new was emerging in Morgan's life, and she was not going to stop it.

In their embrace, the two of them heard breathing and then sniffling and wheezing in a corner of the tearoom. Grady's "animal alert" pulled him away as though he were being held at gunpoint. Morgan's eyes widened, and she steadied Grady's arm. Someone was in the room with them.

"Oh my God, Michael, you scared the bejaysus out of us," Morgan whispered loudly.

"Sorry, Miss. My mother wanted me to stay up for you to lock the front door."

"You mean we have to get permission for a late night?" Morgan felt a little overprotected.

Grady squeezed her hand and said, "Another time, Bucko!" He got in another kiss, even if it was one he could have given his sister.

Michael locked the front door behind Grady. Morgan was lingering at the stairwell in the hallway. Spontaneously, she walked back into the dining room to have a parting word. Michael was grazing through the leftover cookies and cake crumbs on the sideboard.

"Michael. Tonight, Cyril Matthews, the Scottish gentleman who rode with your mother and me from Shannon, added a new piece to the situation. What do you know about the IRA? Paidraig indicated that Reggie is an old IRA guy."

"Yeah. That's probably true. I heard it somewhere that he was called 'Fingers,' 'cause he was a pinch for the IRA."

Morgan felt Michael was just on the edge of a big laugh. She smiled. "Are you kidding me? That is such a corny name."

"Yeah, yeah. I agree." He snorted a few chuckles. "Yeah. He wasn't working for 'the General' or anything. He wasn't a killer. He's just a low-level guy who was a 'mover.'"

"A mover?"

"Yeah. When the Garda was on to the location of some loot the IRA had stolen, like ransoms, Reggie—or guys like Reggie—would move the stuff somewhere else."

"Okay, now I know it's time for me to sleep. See you in the morning,

Michael. Will you be ready to roll after breakfast?" He didn't look eager, but his smile was affirmative.

She was just too tired to make out the whole crammed bag. *Anyhow, my Irish inheritance is down the drain. It wasn't so much the money, though a few quid would help. It was to have someplace like Timmons', where I could climb into my own four-poster with the cabbage rose quilt and remember Aunt Mary's stories.... I guess it was always a dream. Ireland, always the place we came home to. It was always part of the dreamtime. But then there is Grady—and Padraig. Maybe all is not lost.* "Maybe," she sang half-aloud, "I should *Praise the Islanders, Lucht an Oileain,* and 'be grateful for seals when God withholds pigs.'"

9
The Church of the Transfiguration

Castlebar

Morgan awoke with the stirrings of Irish spring. She drew Grady's new book on Omey Island into her fluffy-down violet bed with her. He was smiling on the cover, and she smiled back at him. *Ireland's Holy Ground, Our Grace and Disgrace*. She skimmed the pages.

Not all Irish faults can be blamed on the British, she thought. *There's plenty of intolerance among us Irish, plenty of religious hypocrisy. We were all brought up this way in the Irish Catholic home. Be generous of spirit, but disdain things carnal ... constantly covering up. Personal fraud. With the right hand, he works as a field archaeologist and lover of native habitats. Expected. With his left hand, he's a moralist exposing Irish "sexpocrisy." Riskier, in Connemara.*

> Tiny Omey Island, on the most westerly tip of County Galway, has been in use as a cemetery for a thousand years. The unforgiven found ground here, too.

Who are the "unforgiven"? The church seems to be finding the unfit everywhere. Women, basically—the bloody clerics are women-haters. I'll bet that island buried miscarriages and abortions and babies the families couldn't afford a casket for.

Morgan put the book down. She felt a good day ahead. She loved this room. It was so retro; it reminded her of her attic bedroom in the old house. Mrs. Timmons probably did it up for her daughter a long while ago. She decided that her Purple Bower was the best place she'd been in Castlebar.

Today was a day for Grailside, the retirement home, and maybe a chance to visit Nurse Shanahan and find out a bit more of Mary's life. As long as Michael was available, Morgan would keep on truckin'.

Her bed faced a pair of casement windows. She parted the lace to see the face of the day. She found herself looking directly onto the back porch of the Victorian row house across the way. There, standing in a white nightgown, was a fragile old lady, hair flowing in all directions, cocking a hand telescope up to her eye. She knew Morgan was staring back at her. The old lady started waving. Morgan waved back, tentatively.

The thought of another "Mrs. Rochester" locked in an attic flashed across Morgan's mind. She felt compelled to run downstairs and find out from Mrs. Timmons if the old woman were really in trouble or just a "case" of some sort. Mrs. Timmons assured her the lady was just old. A "case" all right, but only "a soft dementia." Her name was Goodchilde Walsh, from a very old Castlebar family, descended from rich "publicans."

"That's a good one," Morgan smirked out loud. "From kings, maybe, but from publicans?" Silence. A mistake. Mrs. Timmons didn't smile.

Morgan decided Goodchilde had been trying to signal something to her; she needed all the help she could get, even from the "daughter of a publican." She imagined the stout Leo McKern, with his roving glass eye, playing the Irish traitor-informer in David Lean's film *Ryan's Daughter*—well, he *was* a publican, after all.

Mrs. Timmons could not let Morgan go without a sly whack. "Oh, I remember your great-aunt, now that I've been inquiring from some of my friends."

Morgan turned around from the door with interest.

"She was not from my time, you know. But there were always rumors about their hill, that the Kennys probably practiced the craft."

"What craft is that, Mrs. Timmons?" Morgan thought she'd ride her out.

Mrs. Timmons was blushing. She lifted her drying cloth to her face, whispering, "The old religion, you know." She began to throw cloths over the tables.

"She was a practicing Catholic," Morgan said, irritated. This exchange felt like more of that Irish phoniness she had just been thinking about.

"The thing of it is, she and her sister possibly helped a number of people with illnesses back in their time. That's what I hear. I dunno, maybe they had the 'sight' as well." Mrs. Timmons rested her case, for the time being.

* * *

Morgan kept her focus and went in pursuit of the "publican's daughter."

Goodchilde Walsh's home was a short skip across the alley. By the time Morgan lifted the door knocker, the housekeeper had appeared and motioned her to the back door. Stepping down a few steps, she entered a vault-like kitchen. She expected to be ushered into the front part of the house, but the housekeeper motioned her to sit down here in the working kitchen. She sat, waiting for Miss Walsh to appear.

The house of a publican, Morgan thought. *Monied enough to have a housekeeper, a KitchenAid, and seven chimneys.*

Pie dough had been rolled out on the heavy wooden table, and chunks of lamb were piled in a wooden bowl. Vegetables lay scattered about like a still life in process. Lamb stew in the making. Rows of pewter pitchers hung from the front of the fireplace. Two chairs were poised before the cooking fire.

Miss Goodchilde Walsh appeared, her snow-white hair gathered into a tidy bun. She was subdued, even composed. Perhaps Morgan was going to get the "Good Child" side now. Someone had dressed her in a long, dark, flowered robe. The housekeeper didn't ask Morgan into the drawing room, but silently served tea and hot cross buns on heavy ironstone china next to the fireplace. Morgan offered a few pleasantries, but passed on to the main query in a matter of minutes: Did Miss Walsh know Mary Kenny?

"Did we know Mary Kenny?" Morgan noted the papal *we*. "All too well, and not at all." A singsong reply. "I made First Communion with Mary Kenny. I saw her at the church for Mass. She was a servant there, *fado, fado*."

Morgan recognized that Miss Walsh really was frail, her voice quavering.

"And at Bridget's Feast, when Mrs. Walsh and I were out that way, we brought them a spring lamb from my brother's farm or an Easter cake." She sipped her tea, reflecting on those muddy Lenten visits a half-century ago.

"How is it that you brought them food?" Morgan asked.

Miss Goodchilde Walsh replied, "'They're more to be pitied than censured,' as Mrs. Walsh, my mother would say. 'Kennys never take the dole. We visit all the tenants on Easter morning.'"

Morgan would have liked Miss Walsh to speak in regular English instead of literary quotes, but the old eccentric was as interesting as she was irritating.

"My brother—long gone, God bless his soul—tried to give a 'shine' to Miss Mary Kenny, she with ruby hair to her waist. 'A good looker,' he'd say." She winked at Morgan, underscoring her meaning. "She always held her head straight up—and her nose too, if you take my meaning. My mother, Mrs. Walsh would say to him, 'Mary's only a *cailin rua;* you needn't come *down* to her.' He didn't. But then he pined after her for fifty years."

Cailin rua only meant "the redhead," but the way Miss Walsh said it, Morgan could feel Mary was of the servant class to the class-conscious publicans. Morgan smirked at the implication.

Miss Goodchilde Walsh whimpered, obviously taken by her own testimony.

"He blamed the priest for not gettin' her. He said the priest had his eye on her himself. She's over there," she said, pointing down the street to a church ruin. "That's it."

The old woman got up and stood at the window. The church's garden wall and iron gates were just visible from their house.

Morgan was puzzled. "Whose garden is that?"

"It's a graveyard."

"Do you mean Mary Kenny is in that graveyard?"

"So be it."

"How do you know that?" Morgan pressed.

"I watched 'em put her in there."

"Who's 'them'?" Morgan's throat was dry; her words sounded shrill.

"My people, the Welches." The old woman saw Morgan's disbelief, and so she added, "My cousins."

At that, the housekeeper chided Miss Walsh, suggesting that the "visit" was over. "Now, now, Mum, we don't know that, do we?"

Trying to hold onto the moment a bit longer, Morgan directed her next question to the housekeeper. "That ruin inside ... is it the wall of a church?"

"Yes. The church was taken by a great fire more than fifty years ago." The housekeeper glanced around, as though she had just said something incendiary.

Looking again at Goodchilde Walsh, Morgan asked, "Was that the church where Mary Kenny worked?"

"Yes, she's over there." She pointed out the window. The old woman looked oddly at her housekeeper and made the sign of the cross. "Pray God they took their bad luck with them."

"What bad luck was that?" Morgan pressed.

"Why that horrid death, of course. Father McGinty died in the fire. He's been in there fifty years. Father O'Toole died tryin' to help him down from the third floor. Father Sean O'Toole. A chip off the old block." She gestured to the heavens. "So God punished all of them."

Morgan could not sense any feeling in the old woman's statements. She seemed canny and cold.

"Thank you, Miss Walsh. I am most grateful for your remembrances. My great-aunt never spoke of the fire, but she did speak well of you and your family." Morgan had to cross her fingers on that line.

Miss Goodchilde Walsh looked up with childlike innocence, the innocence of a cold, old psychopath. "Come again, Miss Kenny. We don't have many visitors anymore."

"I'm sorry, Miss Walsh, I must ask one more question. Who was the priest that so angered your brother?"

"Father O'Toole. He was the one with the 'eye.'"

Morgan felt no Catholic guilt for her little lie to Miss Walsh about her family. Aunt Mary had never spoken of the Walshes. Nor the fire ... nor the priests, for that matter.

It seemed Aunt Mary didn't speak about a lot of things. Morgan wondered just how much of all this was true. She promised herself she would get into that graveyard just as soon as she could get Michael to climb the wall.

But for the moment, she thought, *I may just have found out where my aunt is buried.* She couldn't wait to tell Michael. Only ten o'clock in the morning, and she had a royal flush!

grailside

10
Grailside Nursing Home

From Castlebar to Claddaghduff

The motor of the Green Dinosaur was running as Morgan jumped in. Even before they reached the main thoroughfare, she had slipped into her sleuth mode. And Michael slipped in right next to her.

She excitedly relayed her visit with Miss Goodchilde Walsh, the story of the church fire, and the possibility that the old church graveyard could be where Aunt Mary was buried. Morgan almost winded herself in the delivery, but she was charged.

"Michael, would it be hard to get into that graveyard?" Morgan swayed against the door as they maneuvered to avoid a truck.

"It'd be very easy to ge' in there, because it's a Mayo Trust garden. I mean, tour people go in to visit the flower and heather collections. But the graveyard thing? Very doubtful. Nay, I've never seen more than a few graves. Most of them are very old."

"But Miss Goodchilde said it was a graveyard." Morgan felt she was losing her royal flush.

"Yeah, well. She is a very old lady, and a bi' out-of-date at that. No disrespect to her family and all."

Michael's lead foot was on the pedal, and they sped past the graveyard, prompting Morgan to think they'd be in Claddaghduff before noon.

"Have you been in that graveyard often?"

"Yeah. But it's not a graveyard at all. They always hire lads in the spring to dung the delphinium beds layin' 'longside the church ruin. Some say the ol' abbot was a Scot with a thing for Queen Mary, so he copied her Falkland palace in Fife. Aye. Y'know, there's lots of pookah-y stories linked to th' church."

"How's that?" She kept her eye on the road as he looked at her.

"I think the biggest reason is the first bishop had the architecture people put the foundation directly over a pre-Christian worship center of Danu."

"Danu. You mean a fairy hill?"

"No," he paused to put together a defense. "Maybe Danu stands for Diana, the famous goddess. And maybe it was one of the 'mother religions' before Patrick. But for sure, it was a powerful worship site, bigger than a fairy fort, Miss." Michael felt brilliant.

"You know, you're the second person to talk to me about religion 'before Patrick.'" Morgan was feeling a bit put-upon, but couldn't show it.

"There were lots of fires in that church before it finally burned down in the fifties. Mi mather told me about them."

"So you're saying the Christian clergy shouldn't have built on that spot because of the rights of the 'old religion'? So now the old souls haunt it?"

"Right."

"I thought Ireland was solid Catholic."

"Right. But there are layers of beliefs and stories underneath. Let's face it, the old folks of Mayo didn't even want to work on the buildin' of a new church there. They wouldn't dream of goin' there at night ... alive with *siogi*, fairies, they say."

"You mean like the pookah and the banshee?" Now Morgan was being a bit of a smart aleck.

"Right. Everyone knows about the death bringer, the *banshee*. But I mean other things, too, like people layin' on the grave of their dead loved one so they receive their spirit, to share communion with them. You never hear the church people tellin' ya that. Sure, the priests don't knock heads anymore. They've lost the power. But they made the people even more frightened of such spots by talkin' 'bout bad spirits bein' there, so then the people put up a wall. Do you see what I'm intimatin'?" Michael looked long at Morgan. A little too long for their safety, running along the "chippings," the stones of the shoulder.

"You have a big problem, Miss Kenny," he said solemnly.

"More than I've already got?"

"What are the means and the motives for your aunt's supposed burial in such a ruin?"

"The means and motives? Right. That sounds like a mystery," Morgan said. But she knew Michael had a point. "This is the church Aunt Mary worked at when she was a young woman," she added feebly.

"Well, it must have been a great job, for her to want to be buried in its walls—and even have people bust in there to bury her? I challenge, Miss Kenny. Aunt Mary was just a 'molly,' no offense. The church was burned a long, long time ago. You've got to have more interesting proof than employment." Michael was so into the mystery game that Morgan had a silent chuckle.

"You're right. The job theory by itself does seem a little weak, especially in view of the *siogi*. We'll get to the bottom of this, Michael."

"Maybe we can hit Transfiguration's ruin when we get back from the old people's home, if it's not too late." Michael was smiling.

Morgan unfurled her map and began plotting their path through Connemara's narrow roads. She felt a little like Reggie.

Leenaun and Killary Harbor, Kylemore Abbey, Claddaghduff.

But Grailside Home's location was not on Morgan's map, and Michael only had a Mayo guide.

In Clifden, they stopped at a tearoom to get an orientation, again. On the glass window, etched in eternal youth, were the red-haired Maureen O'Hara and a plaid-capped John Wayne, hand in hand, walking over the town's famous three-eyed bridge from *The Quiet Man*.

So they did make that movie here, Morgan thought. Her image of the rural West had come from seeing that film over and over at home.

"Do you know where Omey Island is?" the young woman attendant asked. "No? All right, then. Don't go the Sky Road. Take the next road left. It goes on the north side of Streamstown Harbour. Stay right on this road, and you'll come to Claddaghduff." She pointed on the map to a finger peninsula edging into the Atlantic.

"If you get lost, ask anywhere how to get to Sweeney's Bar in Claddaghduff. Folks might not know the old people's home, you know, but everyone knows Sweeney's. And Sweeney knows everyone and everything. He'll tell you where the home is, and he probably knows all the folks in it, too.

"And give yourself a pint of patience," she added. "That's a wild and beautiful part of Connemara. You might as well enjoy it."

One needed patience on these stone-cluttered one-lane roads, with their soft shoulders and confusing signs. Claddaghduff was one of those earth fingers sticking out into the Atlantic that received all its weather extremes—wild sea, wild sand-and-salt storms. The people on this sliver of peninsula took gales in stride. Even with her borrowed "mac" and wellies, Morgan put up an umbrella to get to Sweeney's Bar.

After she'd stated her case to Mr. Sweeney, he bid her come outside in the mild blow. Pointing directly up to a hill on the right, he asked, "She has a commanding view, has she not?" The white stone Grailside Home perched above the bay, overlooking Omey Island and the roiling ocean. A bit of a roar outside, so Morgan thanked him at the top of her lungs and thought how this land might be the last before the end of the world.

"Grailside had the most auspicious setting in all the west of Ireland," Morgan told Michael as they drove through the peat hills and soft Connemara pines, up through an entrance gate of twisted iron, and right up to the edging stones of the huge white house.

Grailside had once been a Georgian Great House, a substantial old Irish property with its back to a mountain and its front facing the ocean and the bay of Claddaghduff. Now, in spring, the back hills were purple in heather. Faded pink and white old roses framed the long white mansion. Residents had a clean view of the ocean, one hundred meters of frontage on the bay. The grasses were everywhere set with white deck chairs facing the western sky. It was truly majestic; celestial blue meeting azure blue, accompanied by the purring bay and a wide swath of dazzling white beach below. And there was wind. Atlantic wind. And sea salt on your tongue.

There's truth to be found here. Mary, you spent your last days well, Morgan thought to her aunt.

Some chatty old ladies were sitting in lawn chairs, swathed in shawls and crocheted afghans, enjoying the brief noonday sun. Morgan walked amid the chairs until one resident asked her name.

"Kenny from Castlebar?"

It was thus she met Caitlin, an unforgettable witness to Mary's life. Caitlin was on her last legs herself, carting around an oxygen tank on a wheeler. But she had an audience, and could she talk!

"I met your mother one time. Rosie, the rose of Tralee she was, a grand girl, she was. She came out here to visit your auntie, dressed like a million punt. A great brimmed hat she wore," raising her hands in expanse over her head, "a brown Borsalino from Arnott's in Dublin, no less. Sure'n, the nurses ran to get *her* tea. They knew she had the class. I told Rosie, 'I like that Dublin hat you're wearin'.' When she was on her way out the door, she came right over to my chair and put it on my head. 'You look better in it than me, Caitlin, baby,' she said."

The old woman, remembering better times, looked out to the water and then back at Morgan.

"I knew your Auntie Mary. I saw her yesterday, too." Irritated, she yelled, "They say there are no more banshee in Ireland. What the hell do they know? A lot of people here say they've never heard one. How ridic'—*all* of us here heard her the night before your auntie died. No wonder! Your aunt was a Flannagan, and don't banshee always visit that clan? This one sounded like a bird screechin' or a cat fightin'—but I knew it was for her immediately, peckin' at the window, waiting for Mary Kenny's soul. When she died, we opened the window for her soul to go home, and I'm sure the banshee flew away with it."

Morgan didn't think local people really believed in the banshee anymore, but Caitlin ended her story with a long oratory on the banshee coming for most of the people dying there. Though the staff never heard them, because they were not in "sanctifying grace."

"You say you've seen my aunt?"

The old woman pulled her shawl up over her head. She put a finger to her lips.

"I am telling ye the truth. Let God be my judge, she was as close to me as you are. I'm not the only one. Clare saw her, too. Yesterday. First I saw her down below, walkin' the strand."

"You're sure it was my aunt?"

"Aye. I just thought it was a handsome young girl from the house. Then she turned around and looked straight at me. She was beautiful and wild as well. She had those 'silkie' eyes, dark and lonely-like. No. She wasn't an ordinary girl, no. I knew she was from the beyond. I wasn't afraid of her—it was your auntie. It was Mary Kenny. I'm sure it was her.

"'Mary Kenny,' I said, 'what is it you want of me?' Only two words she said. 'The murder.' Mind you, she said '*the*' murder. Then she walked straight into the sea. 'What murder?' say I, but she do na' answer.

"Long ago, Mary Kenny was cryin', and I asked her what she was cryin' for, and she said those very words: 'the murder.'"

"Do you have any ideas?" Morgan didn't expect a straight answer.

"No. But you know the saying about ghosts. They'll keep comin' until you give 'em what they want. When they get the right thing, they'll stop. So maybe you have to find out about 'the murder.'"

Morgan stared at the total belief in this old woman's eyes; for a moment, she believed, too. Her mind was reeling—or more likely, clogged.

Murder. Another chunk of the puzzle. *My God: Her house razed, her land willed away. I'm not sure where she's buried. And now, there's a murder in it.*

"Did Mary ever say *who* was murdered?" Morgan whispered.

The old woman stood, her long white hair flying in the wind, holding her hand out to the ocean.

"She told me she had to be here. When she was on earth, she had to be in the West, in Claddaghduff. It was important for her to be near the sea, she said. Someone she loved was buried out there, on the islands, she said. She always took her walk and prayed facing the islands. Every day. She was faithful to her love."

Morgan was so grateful for the tender witness of Caitlin that she kissed her gnarled old hands. Still, she had not a clue as to who was murdered or, more essentially, whether any of this talk was true … *better said, "real."* As for her aunt having a "love" out to sea, Morgan was happy if she'd had a love over her long, long life. It was odd, of course, that she should have kept it hidden from her family.

"Is there anything I can get for you, mather, before I leave?" Morgan was sincere.

"Can you get me a bottle of beer?" Caitlin smiled without compunction.

"You're in luck, my dear, we're packin' a Harp," Morgan said, trying to reprise her mother's natural earthiness.

She went on to the administration building and sent Michael to Caitlin and the ladies with bottles of stout and some ash cheese that Mrs. Timmons had given her as a gift for Nurse Shanahan. Morgan's last peek was of Michael popping caps, as long-robed old ladies gathered around him.

Grailside's administrator, Sister Philippa, informed Morgan that only one person was mentioned in Aunt Mary's official papers at the home: Mr. Welch, from Castlebar. The home knew who he was, since Miss Kenny did have a visit from him last Christmas. Recently, Sister Philippa added, he'd passed away. "He was quite an elderly gentleman, I am told."

According to the Grailside papers, Mr. Welch was to officiate at the burial, at a place of Miss Mary's choice.

"Obviously, someone other than Mr. Welch came for your aunt's body. A woman, I believe. I was expecting the cemetery from Castlebar. I took it for granted. But they didn't come from Castlebar. A white van came for her. I didn't speak to the driver. I thought it was taken care of by Nurse Shanahan." The nun looked a bit puzzled, but her interest went no further.

Mary Kenny came with nothing and left with nothing. That was official. Sister Philippa was not accustomed to leaving loose ends.

"Would you like to see Mary's room? We haven't yet reassigned it."

She took Morgan to a room on the second floor. It was a dreary place, not a picture, not a color. *It could use brighter paint,* Morgan thought.

"There is one thing I am sorry about," Sister said at the top of the stair. Morgan stared at her. "What's that?"

"Your aunt mentioned"—and here the nun seemed surprised at how emotion caught her unawares—"asked her nurse for a harper, 'to take her over.' Oh, we told her a harper in this neck of the woods was not an easy thing. And of course, you know, we have not a ha'penny for that kind of a thing. When we couldn't find a harper, she said she'd take a fiddler. Well, we found her a fiddler. Nurse Shanahan found one, anyway. Miss Mary told Shanahan, or the fiddler, that her *anam cara* would take her across when the time came. I asked later, but no one came for her."

Sister Phillipa looked reflectively out the long, curved window, adding no further comment.

I will leave you to your thoughts of what you might have done, Sister, Morgan judged her silently.

It was a large, gray room with a bed, a side table, a lamp, and a radio. Bay windows and a pink window seat. The iron bed was facing the ocean, the islands, the horizon.

Today the sun-dappled sea is content, Musha. You are part of the great sea now, Mary. You are part of the islands you loved, Morgan prayed.

She then asked after Mrs. Shanahan, the nurse who'd taken care of Mary, with whom Morgan had corresponded for a number of years after Mary's handwriting became shaky. She found that Nurse Shanahan had been up for retirement for a year, but stayed on until Mary Kenny died.

Someone loved Aunt Mary here.

"She lives right down the lane, in one of those seaside cottages," Sister Philippa said. She extended a hand in farewell, thinking perhaps that she could forestall an embrace. Morgan felt her remove in her stiff arm, so she turned and avoided touching her altogether.

To Morgan, "down the lane" meant a block or so. *Not much of a stretch of the legs,* she thought with Maureen O'Hara determination. Michael followed alongside in the Green Dinosaur until she was really too cold to walk. He opened the door, and she jumped in. They drove together for another half-mile before she saw smoke curling out of a tiny stone cottage set into the side of the hill. It could best have been described as a hobbit house. *This,* she thought, *would have to be Winnie's house.*

Morgan had long wondered what this woman, who never interjected herself into their years of correspondence, was like. By the time she tipped the knocker, her fingers were red with cold.

A big-bosomed woman with an apron to the floor answered the door. Whatever Morgan was expecting, this woman was just a little rounder, cheerier, and shorter than she could have imagined. She embraced Morgan, her head neatly tucked under Morgan's arm. Morgan released a heavy sigh, as though she had been in some compression chamber. Guinevere Shanahan was the kind of woman you had always hoped your own grandmother would be. The whole house smelled of something delicious.

"Call me Winnie, my dear." She led Morgan in. "I have heard so much about you, and now you're here. Are you still Sister Julia?"

Morgan smiled and shook her head. "So you do know about me."

The one-room house was bright and moist, with a peat fire and a line of clothes drying near it. An ironing board held napkins and a black iron. Morgan had interrupted ironing day. She didn't think she had ever seen an iron—or a cat—so big. Winston (Churchill), the size of Timmons' dog, dozed on a quilted footstool next to the fire. He was one of those cats with a flat face, out of *Alice in Wonderland.*

The Irish god of the hearth was always appeased by a whistling kettle and a pan of oatcakes. He would not have been disappointed. This was a true Irish home of old. Morgan had come to a person and place with soul, Irish soul.

Winnie scurried around the kitchen putting together tea, chatting about all the changes in Grailside and Ireland. It was as though Morgan were visiting an old friend. Oddly, she felt more at home with Winnie than she had ever felt with her Aunt Mary. There was a generational difference, yes, but there was also that thing of chemistry and a sense of immediacy. With Aunt Mary, there had always been courtesy, but a filter as well.

"I liked her," Winnie said, bringing the tea tray. "It wasn't hard. She was a pleaser, you know. As old as she was, she loved to sing, and could she sing in the old Gaelic, too." She averted her eyes for a moment with unexpected emotion.

"Your auntie was from the old Ireland, my dear. She said her beads every day. And she knitted for the poor, as she'd been taught as a child. Can you imagine that, she being poor herself? And she failed not to say the evening prayer—on her knees, mind you, next to her bed. 'The Lord loveth a humble heart,' she would say."

Winnie began to sing the incantation that preceded the prayers:

"God with me lying down
God with me rising up
God with me in each ray of light,
Not a ray of joy without Him,
Nor one ray without Him.
Christ with me sleeping
Christ with me waking....
Spirit with me strengthening, forever and for evermore,
Chief of Chiefs, Amen."

Winnie had a good voice, herself. The visit was bringing her back to Mary's life, and perhaps to the old ways now departing her sister, Ireland.

"She was a pious maiden lady. Yes. She had that wonderful mix of the old world, you know. She knew the Other World as well as this one. Do you know? She could hear the banshee. She was a diviner of sorts. She was so much a part of the nature all around her; when she would die, she bid me to poke a hole in her thatched roof to let the bees know of their sister's passing." Winnie sighed. "It's passin' away with the likes of Mary Kenny."

Morgan realized now that Winnie signaled a double loss with Mary's passing. They called Ireland's newly booming economy the "Celtic Tiger," but it also meant the end—of living the old myth, of the innocent mind.

"Did you say 'thatched roof'?"

"At the end, you know, she was spiritually in her old house back in Castlebar. It was as though she'd gone home to the cottage where she was born, and to the church she toiled long in, the land her people settled in, Castlebar. And her holy well."

"Yes, that's a strong memory I have of her," Morgan said. "Taking me to the holy well to say good-bye and blessing me in its water."

Winnie's eyes lighted. "She told me she was taught a ritual of walking around the well three times and praying from her mother, who certainly sounded like a *bean feasa*. I don't know if you've ever heard of that term, *bean feasa*, a wise woman who speaks to fairies and has the gift of 'sight.' They were far more common years ago than you'd think."

"What is that like, the 'sight'?" Morgan asked.

"Well, it can be knowing something before it is going to happen or recognizing one's true nature. So many saints possessed that."

"Like a hunch or a feeling?" Morgan was zeroing in on her own gift.

"Yes. She told me it's like having a very good idea. It seems illuminated to you, or at least that's the way it presents itself to the mind."

"Was Mary a *bean feasa*?"

"Truly? No, I think not. But she had some gifts; she knew of their ways. I think one of her sisters may have been, and as I say, from what others say, her mother was."

It ran in the family, Morgan was beginning to think.

"She spoke often of the family's holy well. The Initiator, she called it. I think most of her spirit was in her land, and when she came here, she might have lost some of the 'gift.' She spoke of her sisters and of a young man she loved. She spoke to me like I was her priest, asking for forgiveness for her sins. Sure, she had some different points of view. She believed Jesus always forgave."

Not like some of the nuns that ran Grailside, Morgan thought.

"She was certain. 'He came for love,' she'd say, 'you can be sure of that.

Or for what reason did He come here at all, at all?'" Winnie stopped to search for her hanky.

And I'm sure that's a quote from Julian of Norwich! Morgan's mind was shadowing Winnie. *So Julian is my compass now? Maybe Mary in Julian?*

"I'm just so happy that someone came to know her." Morgan squeezed Winnie's hand in gratitude.

"I was with her when she died," Winnie whispered. Then, adjusting her apron, "I found her a fiddler to accompany her to the Other Side. God gave me a gift that time. Of the many dying people I've attended, your auntie was the happiest. Believe me, she was happy. She wasn't afraid. She asked me to push her bed to the window." Winnie sat down closer to Morgan.

"It was as though she'd had a vision. She looked out to the ocean. She saw the Other Side. Aye. She was talkin' to someone, seeing someone she loved from the beyond. His name was Jack. Truly, she opened up her arms to receive him. Her last words were, 'I knew you would come, Jack. O, Jack, I'm coming.' She looked so beautiful then, and peaceful. Really, her face was radiant. That fiddler stayed long after she left us."

"He kept on playing?" Morgan asked.

Winnie and Morgan cried, and had tea staring into the fire.

"Oh my god, I forgot about Michael!" Morgan waved him in.

After he had warmed up and had his tea and cakes, Morgan stood up to go.

"I have a couple of things for you, Morgan," Winnie said. "As soon as I came to Grailside, five years ago, your auntie gave me a green box. She said it was her personal papers, and she didn't want the home to have them. She wanted me to give them to Rose, your mother; but as time went on and your mother died, I took the box home. Later, I asked Mary who should I give it to. She said, 'When Sister Julia comes home to Mayo, give them to her.' So you're the one in the family to carry her story for the Kenny family. I give you her box."

The two went to the kitchen, where Winnie pulled out a green metal box from behind the sink curtain. It was a metal fishing-tackle box, with a rusty padlock. It felt quite light when Morgan received it.

"One more thing." Winnie left the room for a moment and brought back a painting, a Madonna and Child. It was an unusual picture. The two of them sat in a plain with a greenish brown background, and the chubby-cheeked child was holding what appeared to be a pencil-thin cross. There was a "cozy" feeling about this painting. Morgan felt she'd seen the Madonna's face before. She couldn't think of where, but it would come to her later when she was not straining to remember.

"Last Christmas, your aunt had a visit from a neighbor man, Mr. Welch. Do you know him?"

"Never met the man, but I met his land agent," Morgan replied, wondering what that greedy guy was doing visiting her aunt after such a long interval.

"He did not look well. He had a driver. He was well-bundled. They spoke privately. He didn't stay long, but he gave her this picture as a gift. Shortly after, she gave it to me. I didn't want to take it, but she really wanted to give it to me as a Christmas present. You should have it, Julia—sorry, Morgan—to remember your aunt."

"*Au contraire,*" said Morgan. "I know it will always remind *you* of her. You must keep it. It is a lovely piece, really."

Morgan said good-bye to Winnie and Churchill after promising to visit her once more before leaving Ireland in a week. She saw her waving a handkerchief at the doorway, and it clicked in. She knew where she'd seen Winnie before: as Mrs. Tiggywinkle, in Beatrix Potter's work.

They left Claddaghduff, Winnie, and Churchill at twilight.

Twilight in Ireland is like none other. It's the time of fairy merrymaking, as glimmering lights from celestial auras play over the hills and glens, giving a surreal moment to the senses. It plays for hours, a liminal moment for reflective musings … or maybe it's just being in the West of Ireland.

11
The Green Box

Darkness fell in the west. Silence had fallen on the weary adventurers as they made their way home to Castlebar by the Westport Road.

The only thing Morgan said in the last hour was half spoken to herself: "What a blessing today was, eh, Michael? That incredible ocean view from the Grailside Home!"

She had thought of asking Winnie about old Caitlin's visions of Mary and "the murder," but the right moment never presented itself.

"You made it, ol' girl," Michael whispered to the Green Dinosaur. Earlier times may have had highwaymen, but the present age had potholes. The green old Jeep pulled through without a flat this time.

The two of them sat motionless in the garage behind Timmons' Teatime, too tired to think of the next move. Clouds scudded past in an ink-black sky, throwing moonlight in odd and scary shapes into the alley. Morgan looked down at the green box. She hoped to find more of the meaning of Mary Kenny's life in its contents. But regardless of what they would find, at the moment she seemed content enough to believe in the simple Mary described by Winnie. Maybe after a bag of fish and chips, a pint, and a hot bath, things would get clearer.

Michael seemed to intuit her sentiments. He cleared his throat to make a pronouncement: "Listen, Miss, I think ye should be doin' this on the sly. You read me?" He nodded toward the inn. "*She* shouldn't get her nose into this—yet. You think?"

He was definitely still on the quest. Morgan was just tired.

"Aye," she smiled, "but we've got to get this hasp off. How can we do it so she doesn't hear?"

Morgan probably shouldn't have colluded with Michael against his gossipy mother, but she knew that "murder," an old beau "Jack," a landgrab, a stolen body, and a "secret" fishing-tackle box would reap the whirlwind among the tearoom crowd.

The two entered Timmons' basement on the alley side, Michael leading the way. He lifted a squeaky wooden trapdoor, releasing a hundred years of stale beer smell. Giggling, he offered *sotto voce*, "This used to be a brewery! They ran barrels down here."

Descending broad stone stairs in utter darkness, Morgan hung onto the back end of Michael's sweater, him saying, "Step," "Another step." *There is no doubt, Hades lived here.*

Michael was dauntless in the dark cellar. It was his childhood hideout, a junkyard feast for a boy's imagination. But Morgan was so worn from the journey that even the talk of ghosts—her aunt's and whoever "Jack" was—did not scare her as much as the thought of rats, old barroom rats.

He pulled on a light chain in the hallway, casting elongated shadows of their crouched shapes, like thieves, or cops attempting a bust. The basement was a rabbit warren of "rooms" cramped with cases of empty beer bottles, old wooden beer kegs, pallets and old brewing vats, stacks of newspapers, hanging laundry, and trunks and tools from all ages since "the Year of the French," about the time this public house was constructed.

"Don't worry, Miss Kenny, we're almost to the toolroom." To scare her a little more, he added, "I've heard tell the Irish hid some bodies of Brits down here in Humbert's War, threw them into the foundation." He was enjoying her horror.

Michael approached the massive eighteenth-century workbench with the solemnity of a priest at an altar. With focused deliberation, he grabbed an outsize hammer and whacked the lock off in one blow. That blow let energy out of the balloon. They exhaled together, erupting into spontaneous laughter.

"If this thing is full of old Irish punt, I'd better get a fee!" Michael grinned. He stooped over, and the two began another wave of convulsive laughter.

Staring into the box, Morgan assured him there was not a quid. It looked like a fisherman's tackle box full of crinkled, black stuff; it even smelled fishy.

She grabbed a newspaper from a yellowed stack next to the bench and dumped everything from the box onto it. Rust from the metal box clung to her fingers and the heel of her hand.

The thing is decomposing as we stand here, she thought. She poked the black stuff. It felt like tea.

Mrs. Timmons must have heard them laughing, because the door at the top of the stairs creaked open and she yelled, "Michael, Michael, is that you down there? For the love of Jaysus, don't be smokin' down there! Michael, do you hear me? Come on up here! Your supper has been sittin' in the cooker for an hour!"

Michael yielded to the situation. "Just wait down here for a while before you come up. She'll be watchin' the telly in a few minutes."

Morgan was sorry he had to go. The boozy place was creepy. She was ashamed that she only talked fortitude—real virtue in the face of rats had to be cultivated.

The toolroom had a plethora of carpenter's tools from down through the ages, hanging in haphazard fashion. Morgan took down an awl and began gently teasing each object in the box onto its own space on the newspaper. Everything was thoroughly dried out, even crunchy. She was hoping the fresh air would not have a Shangri-la effect, decomposing things before they could see the light of day.

Under the black crunchy stuff were a number of things. This box apparently wasn't used for fishing. Three faded blue cards, about the size of a narrow hand. Two were copies of Castlebar baptismal certificates—Aran Kenny and Mary Kenny. The third was a copy of a Verification of Birth for the two sisters—"Arianhood" and "Meredith," handwritten by the person who made the delivery, both names on the same card. In truth, Morgan had never heard her aunts ever called by these names. *They're lovely-sounding, even a little fancy. I wonder why they never used them.*

The next item Morgan delicately separated was a black-banded Funeral Mass card with the picture of a young priest in his collar. Father Sean Fintan O'Toole, Assistant Rector, Church of the Transfiguration, Castlebar. Born 1913, ordained 1945, died May 1950. Scrawled on the back of the card, "*Anam Cara.*"

May 1950—wasn't that the date of the church fire?

Morgan turned self-consciously, as though someone were watching her.

This must have been the priest who died in the fire Goodchilde talked of. The parish Mary worked in. Was he the same priest Goodchilde's brother was jealous of, the one who "took a shine" to Mary? There was a lot to process here.

Morgan was tired, and her thoughts moved slowly, as though she were clomping through water.

There is no other man in this box, not even her father. "Anam Cara"—this is a very specific title in church life. Morgan hazily recalled the term to mean a spiritual mentor. In the convent, your spiritual director could be called *anam cara*, one who leads the soul in the matters of prayer, a "soul friend." *Maybe that's all Father O'Toole was, a soul friend.*

On the other hand, the priest's name was Sean ... *anglicized, "John." Could this John be a "Jack" for short? The Jack to whom Mary had called out when she lay dying?* Maybe Morgan was reading too much into the name. Father O'Toole was pretty good-looking, though. He had the looks of the black Irish—thick jet hair, deep-set laughing blue eyes. *An intelligent air about him, too.* This was getting complicated.

Morgan picked up a dirty envelope. Then a door scraped closed. *Someone's come in the back way, the alley entrance we used!* Fearful of being discovered, feeling vulnerable, she quickly rolled up the newspaper with everything in it and made for the stairwell to the kitchen. She got to the first step by the time she heard a man's voice: "Can I help you with something, Miss Kenny?"

It was Reggie, standing so close to her she could smell his cigarette breath. It was the first time she'd ever seen him without a cap. Now, his few hairs plastered to his head made him look tired, old, and sinister.

"Oh, no, Reggie," Morgan's heart beat faster. It was eerie, him coming up on her back like that. "I must have taken the wrong turn in the hall."

She looked past his shoulder to the bench in the toolroom. The open green box was sitting on it, the black "tea" scattered all over. A bit of moral sweat rolled down her soul. She pretended to be absorbed in finding her way up the rickety stairs, to keep his attention away from it. She'd have to retrieve the box later.

She headed straight for her Purple Bower, grateful for a cozy room and a deep bathtub. Pouring in a vial of bubble bath, she turned the faucets on all the way and called downstairs on the in-house phone.

"Hello, Mrs. Timmons. Yes, we had a big day today. I want to let you know I'll give the jeep a petrol fix in the morning. I'm so grateful for Michael's help in driving today. Is it possible to send him for some takeaway? Thanks so much. Could I buy a beer off you, too? Thank you again....

"A call from Grady? A trip to Omey Island? That's funny; Michael and I just got back from Connemara. Thank you, I will join the bus in the morning."

Michael arrived in several minutes with a greasy bag of fish and chips. They smelled wonderful.

"Michael, *you* are my white knight," Morgan said as she opened the chips.

"Yeh, yeh, yeh. Is that an English knight or an Irish knave?" The two laughed. They were becoming buddies. They were "working" this case together.

Morgan found a couple of glasses for the beer, and they shared some fries. It was a treat at day's end.

Michael asked for an update on the green box.

Pointing with a fry to the contents of the box on her bed, Morgan told him, "Take a look. I need a consult with you on what this stuff could mean. I had to leave the metal box downstairs because I was surprised by Reggie, the cab guy. But everything's in the newspaper."

"Reggie helps out now and then, and mi mather gave him a room down there. I'll get that box back for you, don't worry." Michael's forehead wrinkled in seriousness. "Can I open the envelope?"

"Sure," she answered, forking up a piece of fish.

The first envelope was a wax-paper sandwich bag, with a scrap of a lined page with a handwritten list on it. *Barrel fresh rainwater, 6 stone sugar,— [blurred]—pail yeast. Stir until dissolved. Lower barrel into barn hole. Loose top until heats up, cover with tarp and carpet. Test daily.*

The handwriting was quite small. Could it be Mary's?

"What is this supposed to be?" Morgan looked puzzled.

"Oh, man, tha's a lotta booze." Michael was impressed. "That's *potcheen*—Irish white lightning. Blow your head off! Just the old-fashioned stuff, without any chemicals, too." Michael was thinking this was going to be fun. "The Kennys were chancy lassies, all right. You'd be 'flyin' with the birds' sure with a dram of this stuff." Michael grinned, referring to Morgan's Pollyanna description of her aunt as a "nature mystic" from *The Princess and the Goblins.*

"More than I imagined," Morgan said almost to herself.

"Here's another envelope." Michael looked to Morgan for permission.

On the outside of the brown envelope was a caret, or inverted "V." Then the numbers "41 R + 13." Gingerly, he shook out a very dry compressed flower, with just a faint rim of an orchid tint on the edge.

"Wha's this?"

"I'm not sure," she said. "It looks like a flower that's been pressed in a book for a long time. Maybe an iris?"

"Yeah, tha' could be right. There's plenty of that kind about."

"The little black stuff looks like tea," she said. She then added, "But it doesn't smell like it."

"What about the numbers? A safe number maybe? Like 41 to the right plus 13? I like that scenario."

"It'd be pretty neat if it was a safe with a secret last will and testament in it," Morgan smiled.

"Maybe the stuff in the green box is her last will and testament?" Michael spoke reverently. "But it's in code."

"Yes, it might be the testament to her identity, too. And whether it was intended or not, it's for me." Morgan wasn't quite sure where inside her that came from.

She picked up the last item from the box, a picture.

"That's her. Mary." Morgan held up a formal black-and-white graduation photo of her aunt. *It really was,* Morgan thought, *Vermeer's* Girl with a Pearl Earring.

"Well, she *was* very pretty." Michael sounded surprised.

"It's late, Michael. 'She Who Must Be Obeyed' will be on your case."

"Is there anything interesting in all this?" Michael nodded toward the pile of dusty articles on the vanity table.

"If this is her last will and testament, it's all interesting. But as you said, it's in code, and we need to figure it out. What is she really trying to tell us?"

Michael shook his head. "This is a bit like detectives figurin' out the clues. What I think is that she had a secret life no one knew about. Like the 'inner life' stuff they talk about."

"Michael, I need you to do some private-eye work. For starters, who is the priest on this burial card?" She handed it to him. "Sean O'Toole. Was he the priest in the fire? Was he buried in the church's graveyard across the street? His dates are right. And could that be where my aunt is buried now, too?"

"I doubt very much that your auntie is over there. Not unless she gave them, the priests, some *big* gift or something." Michael rubbed his fingertips together.

"Miss Goodchilde knows something, but now the funeral card is in the box, and that ratchets up the importance of it. Where is the archdiocesan office, anyway?"

"Right here in Castlebar."

"Could you go to the office tomorrow and find out something about him? Because I'm going to Omey Island. A-a-and … can you get into that graveyard tomorrow, too?"

She looked up to see resistance on her partner's face.

"Wait a second. Omey Island? The Omey in Claddaghduff? We were just there! What do you need to go back there for?" Michael was bugged.

"Right," Morgan demurred. "It's a tour Grady's conducting."

Michael appeared offended. "We didn't *tour* it," he whined, "but you must have seen it from Sweeney's Bar. It didn't look like much to me." He was sounding tired.

"Grady's written this book on Ireland's islands, and …" She paused, wondering whether she should confide in a kid. "It's a way for me to spend some time with him. I like him."

There. Morgan had said it out loud. Even to herself.

She attempted to switch the subject.

"And the green box. As soon as you can retrieve it, I'd appreciate it."

Morgan ushered Michael out for the night. Before getting into her lukewarm tub, she gently shook the tea off objects from the green box, blowing dirt and dust from each one onto the newspaper, and then gingerly placed them in her dressing-table drawer.

Staring back at her from the news sheet was the face of a big brown horse, with a bold caption: SHERGAR VANISHES, IRA SUSPECTED.

Shergar vanishes, she half-whispered. *That's the famous racehorse that was insured by Mr. Cyril Matthews's company.* She glanced back at the yellowing paper. *1983. What does Shergar have to do with anything? I don't have an answer for that. But as dear old Caitlin would say, "We don't get the right answers because we don't ask the right questions." Maybe the right question I should be asking the universe is, "Why have I found this old news now? What's it meant to tell me?"*

A few paragraphs down from Shergar was the photo of a mummified male found in the bogs, "Ireland's Tollund Man." The torso of a young naked boy in one perfect piece, considered "a Celtic sacrificial victim." He wore a torque, and hair to his shoulders. *I wonder how old this mummy was and what he was sacrificed for.*

Five seconds later, there was a knock at her door.

"God, Michael, what do you want?"

"I want to go over to the church gardens, right now."

"But wait, Michael. First, what about Shergar?

Seeming irritated, Michael huffed, "Shergar? What does a horse have to do with it? He was stolen, 'kidnapped.'"

"That's not it."

"All right, he was a priceless horse who probably won every big race in Ireland, including the Derby … more? I think the bloke who owned him was the richest man in the world, the Khan or somebody like that."

"Was he ever found?"

"Nah, he's long gone."

"Why would anyone want a famous horse that everyone knew?" Morgan couldn't figure it.

"Pretty simple, I'd say," Michael smacked his lips matter-of-factly. "The money … the ransom."

"Wait, Michael, wait for me to get my jeans on."

* * *

An hour later, sitting on the Timmons' front steps, Michael proffered a filter-tip cigarette, and she took it.

"This is a filthy habit, Michael. I just want you to know, this is an exception." She took a long drag of very stale Luckies. "Some things we found out from all of this graveyard snooping. Number 1—O'Toole is *not* buried there. There's only a place plaque, and the same for Father McGinty, the pastor. Number 2—Mary Kenny isn't buried there either, unless she's under a hedge somewhere. So-o-o, Miss Goodchilde Walsh was either very mistaken, or—"

Michael interrupted, "Wait, Miss, this isn't that far out. We didn't waste our time. Miss Goodchilde saw a burial ... but maybe she saw it somewhere else? Maybe she got her burials mixed up. What do you fancy?"

"I fancy the mixed-up burials, rather than deception. She has no reason to lie. I think she saw someone burying *something* from her window. If it wasn't Mary Kenny, it's got to be someone else. But the main thing to me is, *she was there*. We need more leads to figure out who was buried—and maybe where."

"We definitely need to tease some more facts from Miss Goodchilde."

"A more crucial question is—will there be anymore hot water if I run another bath?"

In another part of that same yellowing paper, there was an article by a church lady that read: "Whoever heard of the *Madonna of the Yarnwinder*? A gold star if you know that this Renaissance masterpiece is by Leonardo da Vinci. But whoever heard of a yarnwinder, at all? Have the knitting machine and the sweater factory dulled your imagination to what a hand yarnwinder is? Hmmmm, a double gold star if you have one in the shed. Light in weight, in the shape of a cross.

"The Madonna of the Yarnwinder, a masterpiece of Renaissance art, often thought to be a faithful impostor of Leonardo da Vinci, has been stolen— again—leading some art critics to believe it may be genuine. Stay tuned." By Minerva Mac.

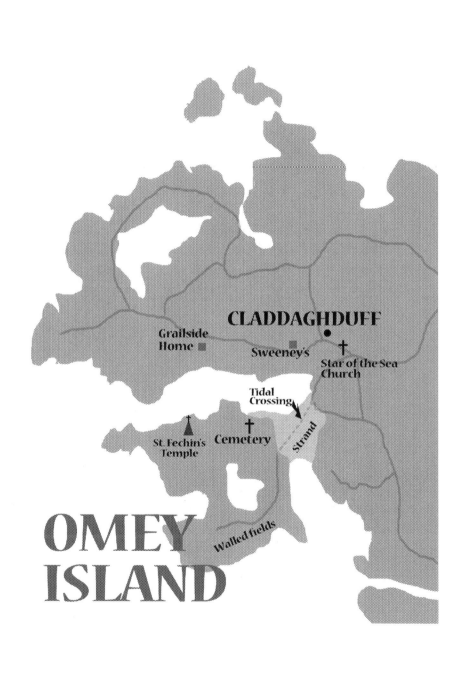

CLADDAGHDUFF

Grailside
Home ■

Sweeney's ■

Star of the Sea
Church

Tidal
Crossing

St. Fechin's
Temple

Cemetery

Strand

OMEY
ISLAND

Walled fields

12
Omey Island

PITY THE ISLANDERS, *LUCHT AN OILEAIN*
for they dwelt on a rock in the sea and not in a shining
metropolis
and lived off the pick of the strand, the hunt of the hill, the
fish of the sea
the wool off the sheep, and packets full of dollars; for they
ate black pudding,

drank *sleadai* squeezed from seaweed, treated themselves on
Good Fridays
to tit-bits from the shore, and thought a man rich if he
possessed two cows;
for they stuffed their pillows with puffins' feathers, and the
sea roared

... for they were full
of sunlight and mist, wind and stone, rain and rock, but the
Atlantic Ocean

would not pay them a regular salary; and they did not fret about tumble driers

or grouse about the menu, for the wind would not let them strut, the rain
made them meek and the waves kept them low; for they feared vain-glory
and the evil eye, chewed bits of seaweed and prayed to the mother of God;

•••••

Praise the islanders, *lucht an Oileain*, for they were a fair people
who pelted the stranger with blessings and the bailiffs with volleys of stones;

for they were gentle people, who twisted puffins' necks, patted babies' heads
and split the skulls of seals;
for they were a quiet people, who never

stopped talking, full of malice and affection, whose delights were tea
and tobacco, a big ship on the waves, a donkey on the loose, a battle
of tongues, a boatful of rabbits, a dance, a story, a song in the dead of night;

•••••

for their stage was not the city, nation or world, but the village, the island and the
neighboring parishes, which are about the right size for a human being.

When they strolled beneath the Milky Way their laughter did not pollute the
night, for they kept their boats high on the waves and their roofs low to the ground
and were grateful for seals when God withheld pigs.

—David Quin

Connemara

By 9:30 a.m., twenty tourists and Morgan met one another in the Kylemore Abbey car park. They were a pretty average tourist lot, mostly women, mostly American, and mostly middle-aged. A few introductions, and they were on their way to Omey Island, a tiny island on the Atlantic fringe of Connemara out of Clifden.

By ten o'clock, the "soft day" had worked itself into a downpour, but the bus driver, a Connemara man, slogged on with more than a little cheer and a few old-time tunes. The tour group sang along, defying the odds of a spoiled day.

Morgan was seated next to a gap-toothed woman with large, strong features and flame-red hair. She must have been six feet tall. She reminded Morgan of an old hippie, with cowboy boots, a longish skirt, and a stunning silver wrought necklace of oak leaves and acorns circling her throat. She was from the States. Albuquerque, she said. Morgan thought of what her mother might have quipped: "She sure is a Western woman, a take-charge woman few men in this country could handle."

They quickly fell into sharing "why I came to Ireland" stories, Irish poetry, and their favorite Irish films. Morgan told how her three great-aunts could have been the models for the three sisters in *Dancing at Lughnasa*, Brian Friel's play. All of them were stuck in Mayo. And like Ireland herself, they were a paradoxical bunch. They were virgins wise and foolish, sisters isolated yet gregarious, generous "spendthrifts" with barely a pence in their pockets.

"And your Aunt Mary, which one was she?" the Western woman asked.

"I think she was the simple girl. As the poem says, she was satisfied with 'a dance, a story, a song in the night.'"

"Yah, I remember that poem ... the paradox, 'They were a gentle people who twisted puffins' necks ... and cracked the skulls of seals ... were glad for the shipwrecks yet prayed for the corpses.' So it was, the harsh life on the Blaskets. That's where I live every summer now, and I rely on my transistor radio for the weather."

Morgan found she had revealed to a stranger what she could hardly tell herself. It was a bit like being in the old-fashioned confessional.

"Mary was the last of my family in Ireland." Silence for a minute.

"The last of them all?"

"Yes, all."

The woman put her hand on Morgan's hand and said, "Yeats wrote at the end of the Irish Revolution about his friends, who had become his family … they were the 'beautiful lofty people, never to be seen again.'"

"Yes, that's perfect. 'Never to be seen again.'" As Morgan said the line, she thought of her mother and father as well.

"Yeats had his melancholy. It's as though the Irish Revolution made 'those beautiful lofty people' great. Maybe they would have been just the run-of-the mill types, you see, but through some heroic grace, they rose to the occasion. Maybe *want* played its role in your aunties' greatness—and smallness."

"I suppose. I came to know them through the stories of my grandmother, Lily. She was the oldest sister. And of course, my mother's stories about her own mother, and her mother's sisters left in Ireland."

Somewhere in the conversation, the Western woman told Morgan her name was Donna, and then laughingly said, "My mother named me after the conjunction of two Irish Gods, Donn and Ana, so I have an advantage in miracles."

"Miracles," Morgan said, a bit mesmerized by Donna's words. "Yes, I believe in miracles." There were many wishes in Morgan's heart. She had prayed for miracles. A miracle to heal the rift between herself and her parents before they died. It didn't happen. She had prayed for discernment about leaving the Benedictines. Here her prayers were answered.

Morgan sat silently in her seat, playing the "old saws."

They protested me entering the convent, and then took an "I told you so" attitude when I came out. She felt she couldn't win for losin'. *When I tried to please them, those were the worst encounters. I could never figure out what they wanted from me. Then, the inevitable. Cut off. Cut out of their hearts. Cut out of their wills, cut adrift.*

Then, as though Morgan had been speaking out loud, Donna said, "So many cutoffs in life. What a waste! So many people who love one another wind up letting the small stuff get in the way."

"Small stuff," Morgan repeated. "Right. That's what happened in my family. Every little thing got in the way of our friendship, our love."

"That's why you're here, in Ireland? Yah, to step out of the negative family patterns, yah? Doing something that's very *you*. Not so much trying to please *them*." She turned her head and looked at Morgan with smiling eyes. "You can choose love, not just fall into it. Maybe that's the good thing about your search for your aunt. You're choosing to know her, to appreciate the mystery of her being, even if she's in the great beyond. And even if she was not perfect."

The mystery of her being, Morgan repeated to herself, and then said aloud, "Yes, it's a mystery all right. That is good, 'the mystery of her being.' She seemed to have kept a lot of her life a mystery."

"Maybe she felt she had to. Maybe she felt she would be criticized or ostracized if she revealed too much. But isn't that the orphan archetype? Having to do it on your own, going it alone?" Donna's voice sounded tender and wise.

"I think that's right. She was a motherless child." Morgan went on: "Ireland is still full of deception, because of the 'religion thing.' A kind of false righteousness was a necessary facade. Maybe the 'sin' about Aunt Mary was that she had to pretend she was as cute as everyone wanted her to be."

"Well, we Irish—whether we're the 'blow-ins,' as they call us, or born in the sod next to the well—have the gift of memory. You'll be able to carry it." Donna smiled and meant it.

Morgan could not believe a total stranger could grasp what was in her heart in one hour—and yet, Donna had. Did she reveal her aunt's situation so much? How could Donna know that carrying the memory of all of them was so important to her, even a sacred task? She had only just figured it out herself.

Irish Island Tours pulled into Sweeney's Bar in Claddaghduff at exactly 10:55 a.m. A warm and steamy Irish snug it was with a peat fire. The "usual suspects," a few silent old men, were sitting at the bar "nursin' a pint," observing the tourists the way tourists observe chimps at the zoo—curious, furry, foreign.

Mrs. Sweeney served up gallons of tea to help the travelers bear up against the chill, and plates of biscuits to prove her generosity.

"Don't worry," she said, setting scones and butter pots on the bar. "Don't be discouraged, lassies. 'Tis a soft day. It'll be clearin' shortly. Trust me. The strand will be ready for ye to cross by 11:15, no later than 11:30. Right, Grady?"

Grady had been sitting in the corner, talking to a local and waiting for the bus to arrive. He was a natural glad-hander. You felt sure he had talked his way out of every tight spot, and the tour group did not expect him to disappoint now. Rain be damned. He wended his way through the group, welcoming each one. Some seemed to know him quite well from other tours.

He opened his arms to welcome them like a conductor at the Met. He had grandiosity and contagious energy.

With deprecating humor, Grady introduced himself as "a Saint Francis of the bogs." Morgan was so drawn by him, his playfulness and humor—two virtues true of her dear father. Grady said he felt his work uncovering the "stones and bones of Ireland" to be a lot like being a detective, keeping an eye out for clues, the love of the search. Research in the West of Ireland was "both a calling and an obsession." Another time he called it a work of "singin' over the bones," bringing to life Ireland's past.

He turned his attention to the weather then, telling of the great sea storms that had taken so many ships and men in this area of Connemara. Cleggan, which lies next to Claddaghduff and the isle of Omey, was named after a storm in October 1927. The storm took everything in its coastal path for two days. It was so horrifying that it became an event carried in collective memory, passed down as though it were a family experience.

He told of coastal sounds. Winds that drove men mad with their eerie pitches and ceaselessness. The lucky were driven off the islands. That would not be difficult to imagine. A steady whine could be detected whirring through every crevice and lock at Sweeney's, scattering ash from the hearth into the room.

"You know the Greeks sacrificed Iphigenia just to get a good wind for their journey to Troy. Let the sacrifice begin!" He lunged toward Morgan, grabbed her around the arms, and said, "How about our journey to Omey? Do we think the ancient Celts would sacrifice, let us say, Miss Kenny to the gods for a few rays of sunshine today?" Everyone laughed.

"Only if you're a virgin, Miss Kenny," he whispered in her ear. Morgan laughed, too. In a way, she liked being paid a bit of attention by him, for fun and a hug. Now everyone knew she was special.

"Mrs. Sweeney is correct as usual," he intoned. "The tide will recede in just a few minutes. And like the Israelites of the Bible, we will walk dry-shod across the strand to the other side." It did not sound likely, listening to the gale. "Meanwhile, 'Sweeney's on the Strand' will be our classroom."

Grady held forth on the history of Omey, including the fact that before and after Elizabeth I and Cromwell, Irish "royalty"—such as the famed O'Flaherty chief and the O'Malley clan (Grace O'Malley's son Owen)—used the island as a way station before heading out to farther islands for the summer.

"Together with their women, children, priests, servants, dogs, and cattle. All walked the same strand for more than a thousand years.

"Of course, there is a saint who has walked on every square inch of Ireland, but Omey had the honor of the rather famous St. Fechin, who founded many abbeys throughout Ireland but died in Omey. Today, gone are the chiefs who came with their kin. Fewer living inhabitants on the isle every year, but Omey is still thought of as a special isle, a holy place to the Irish and the Irish who return from all over the world.

"People come to the island who are not Catholic, who don't have a favorite saint, and yet they, too, feel its grace. Some would call it 'good vibes.' They feel a concentrated energy here, as in a force field. As T. S. Eliot said, 'It is where prayer has been made valid.' There have not been holy monks on this isle for hundreds of years, but holy it is. See for yourself.

"The main thing now is that it has become this holy island, not because one saint lived here and built some abbey now in ruins, but because there are many, many saints residing here. They are the holy innocents of Ireland— the stillborn, the miscarried, the SIDS infants, many children of the Great Hunger, and yes, that forbidden word, the aborted. Yes, the aborted baby is as holy as any baby. Holy, but the Church finds them all wanting. They may not be buried in the church confines. So tell me, what would you do? Over the many decades, women came here, often alone, without the approbation of their fathers or their church. Holy Mother of Jesus, what courage these mothers who'd lost their own must have had!

"So what's the status of these holy innocents, where are they? The church would have us believe they are neither in heaven nor hell, they are in some in-between place theologians strain to justify, limbo."

As he spoke, the tide sucked the waters of the strand out to sea. The waters separated as though Moses himself had raised his staff. The group began to move slowly over the strand, still wet but maneuverable. And pilgrims from the island began appearing out of the fog to pursue their various chores on the mainland.

Two young men in bright yellow slickers came whistling out of the fog, carrying extra-long pointed shovels.

"Turf cutters," Grady said. "The last of a dying breed. An honest profession."

"Out to make a few quid before noon," the man next to Morgan elbowed her. "It used to be a sign of manhood. Cutting turf by hand, you know. If you could cut, throw the bloody clumps on a dray, and get it home by nightfall, you were a strong man, indeed."

A dog followed the cutters to the mainland. Then a few milk-chocolate cows cleared the mist, bells clinking, herded by a "cowboy" on a vintage green tractor waving a long reed over their heads. One cow seemed to want to go out to sea, walking into the waves.

Grady pulled on Morgan's sleeve and pointed to the eastern hills, dotted with bright yellow gorse. "The white house up there? 'Grail something,' the retirement home," he said.

She stared at the blurred outlines of the white house and then back at the island.

Yesterday, at the Grailside Home with Michael, Morgan had not even seen Omey Island … it was so foggy. She noted how in a clearer light the island was only a stone's throw from Grailside's hill. The white strand they were treading must have been the beach where Mary's old lady friends saw her ghost.

So, she was out here all the time. Omey was the island she faced when she said her prayers. Omey was her spiritual container, not some church. Omey was her Holy of Holies. Mary's love was out here then, on Omey.

Hugging the shore were hundreds of graves, grading up a slow hill. Grady commented on a famous few. The group followed him, filing singly through the wider aisles, absorbed in the names and dates, taking rubbings.

"The oldest ones are closer to Fechin's Temple and Well. In the dale beyond this ridge, they are ninth-century," he told them, bidding the company climb higher on the slope. He stood at the top, pointing with an umbrella to a large indented blur of deep purple flowers three or four hundred yards forward. A stand of pines, the only trees in this windswept area, preceded another section of graveyard fairly sunk into sand.

"To give you an idea of this place's extremity—the gods who refused Agamemnon a 'sailors' breeze' lifted up this Connemara bay and its sandy bottom and dumped it on St. Fechin's church and abbey!"

Now they were looking at where St. Fechin's Well was buried from the storm, the bell tower protruding from sandy scrub.

"The O'Toole graveyard," he said, raising his voice above the wind. "The O'Tooles were a great clan, the loyal agents of the O'Flaherty clan. You can see that the place is still in use by them, a number of graves from this century. It's their land, and any O'Toole from anywhere in the world has the right to be buried here. They say the actor Peter O'Toole, of *Lawrence of Arabia* fame, has family out here. He was born in Clifden, you know."

Morgen heard "O'Toole," and all she could think of was Father Sean O'Toole's Funeral Mass card from Aunt Mary's green box.

A few chanced the steep, lumpy hill to the burial ground of the "chiefs." Morgan steadied herself near the edge of the half-sunk wrought iron fence marking the O'Toole graveyard. Windswept grasses amid lichen and rare flowers grew in abundance here, the last vestiges of a lost wood.

There were many O'Tooles from the seventeenth and eighteenth centuries, one grave after another, as though they were a regiment. *A few generations before the famine*, Morgan thought. *Maybe O'Tooles of Connemara fought with the White Boys of Connaught in the Year of the French, 1798.* Her eyes scanned the names and dates on every O'Toole stone as though she were looking for a friend. "It was Father Sean O'Toole, died May 1950, wasn't it?" she murmured to herself. He wasn't there.

The wind died down. Morgan thought she heard music. Then, Donna reappeared. She stood next to Morgan and said, "Are you looking for someone out here?"

"Yes," Morgan muttered. "I heard music. Is that possible?"

Donna smiled and said, "Every island, like every poet, has its own music. They say the music of what happens is the finest music in the world."

Morgan did not know what the maxim meant. In that moment of silence, she could think only of the priest's name on the funeral card in Aunt Mary's green box. The next question was scarier. *Could Sean—the Irish for John, affectionately termed Jack—be the person Winnie said Mary called out to with her last breath?*

Was the person she loved a man of the cloth? In love with a priest? O my God, Mary—that might have posed a very, very big problem in 1950!

Donna answered as though Morgan had asked her what the epitaph meant.

"The story is that the poet king of Ireland, Finn MacCool, ate a certain fish, which had eaten a certain salmon in a nearby well, and that salmon's flesh gave him wisdom. And so, being the wisest man on the island, he wanted wise men for his *fianna*, his fighting men. And so he asked them this riddle: 'What is the finest music in the world?'"

Kylemore Abbey

13
Kylemore Abbey

Coill Mor: Kylemore: The Big Wood

   *Kylemore Abbey, originally Kylemore Castle, dominates
this magnificent glacial valley, a private estate of thousands
of acres of woods on the Dawros River and lough. Without
doubt, it is the most romantic estate in the west of Ireland. In
fact, Mitchell Henry recreated the kind of castle one finds in
fairy tales, for fairy-tale reasons—a wedding gift to his bride,
Margaret. Incredibly, it was built during the famine in 1865.
Had it not been for that fact, the Henrys might not have had
such able and available workmen at every level to accomplish
a castle, church, and Victorian gardens. Mrs. Henry died only
six years after Kylemore was completed, and Mitchell Henry
honored her with both a minicathedral and a family vault on
the property. Kylemore was later purchased and sold a number
of times, until the Irish Benedictine nuns returned from their
European exile and purchased it as a school for girls.*

Dusk at Kylemore Abbey

The tour bus emptied quickly as each passenger had yet another ride to her lodgings and hoped to get home before dark hit the hills. Donna squeezed Morgan's hand, saying, "You've only scratched the surface of the ol' sod. I hope you stay longer. Ireland is still talkin' to ye. Stay in touch."

Morgan felt a link with her. She was an American. You could say they read the same newspapers and laughed at the same jokes. In addition, there was that whole "vision thing" she seemed to intuit like Morgan. She wondered if Donna had the "gift," too.

Staying longer in Ireland was probably out of the question. And yet, if she could find Aunt Mary and figure out some of this green-box stuff, Donna would be the first person she would look up. She was a free spirit, someone who had taken a walk on the wild side and didn't have to brag about it.

"Tell me that over again," Morgan called out after her as she was beginning to drive away. "You stay on the Blasket Islands all summer?" Morgan's voice was drowned out by the motors revving for takeoff. Who knows, maybe Donna had a few tips on how Americans survive here. She tried to remember if there was any electricity on Great Blasket.

Grady waved the last of the tour good-bye and caught up with Morgan, who was talking to the gate attendant to get a pass into the abbey grounds before it closed.

She asked Grady if he wanted to make a short visit to the abbey church with her. She had never been there, and it felt fitting in such a magnificent setting to throw in a few *Ave*'s on her old name day.

Past the parking lot filled with smoking tourist buses, a trendy Irish shop, and a tearoom, another world opened—the big wood of long ago. Unhurried pace, unlimited space overhung in oaks, a hillside banked with about-to-bloom wild rhododendron, occasional waterfalls spouting out of the cliffs, mirroring lakes, and languid air put Grady in fantasy mode.

Morgan felt the direct intention of Mr. Henry, Kylemore's original owner. It could not be mistaken. Mitchell Henry had planned an Englishman's notion of the Garden of Eden as a gift for his bride. Morgan and Grady drank in his plan. Something new between them was "in the beginning," too—that intoxicating moment called "falling in love."

Under its spell, Grady took Morgan's hand, and the two walked the garden path to the miniature Gothic church.

When they were in sight of it, they encountered a long line of nuns recessing away from the great doors, signaling that Vespers was over. *This must have been a big event*, Morgan thought. The pious faces of the young nuns brought her back twenty years, to her own days of solemn feasts.

Many sisters wore the full, long, black Benedictine habit. Morgan recalled her old heavy woolen cape, "thick enough to repel bullets," the French nun who sewed it told her. And years later, on the day she left them, her sister nuns folded that great gray cape, placing her ordinary garments on top of it. They had carefully clipped out her religious name label, "Sister Julia."

It would not have been too heavy in this climate, Morgan thought.

The Benedictines were chanting in Latin, "*Veni Creator Spiritus, mentes tuorum visita imple supernos gratia.*" Even now, she still loved the old Gregorian chant. "Come, Holy Creator, and from heaven shower us with the rays of your light." That warm ray of light had flickered now and again in her life. There are some things that inspire us only once, yet stay with us for a lifetime. And Morgan could feel some small sparks right now, on this Eden-like path. *It is true*, she thought, *God is love.*

The church was a half-mile from the monastery/girls' school, treelined with a river running alongside it. Another group of chatty nuns were coming from the other direction, returning from the mausoleum of Mrs. Margaret Henry and a small graveyard addition of Benedictine sisters.

"What feast is it?" Grady asked. "So many nuns gathered."

Almost as if in response to his question, one of the sisters dropped a holy card.

He picked up a slender red cardboard cross with the picture of a red rose centered in a saffron-colored flame.

"Dame Julian of Norwich, Saint and Visionary, May 13, 1353.

> *And all shall be well*
> *All manner of thing shall be well*
> *When the tongues of flame are in-folded*
> *Into the crowned knot of fire*
> *When the fire and the rose are one.*
>
> —T. S. Eliot

"It's my old feast!" Morgan said, on the proud side. "I knew there'd be something special from her, because it's our feast day," she whimpered, daubing her face with the handkerchief he proffered.

"Your mother told you something about Julian? Or T. S. Eliot?" Grady was straining to be empathetic and still keep his own thinking clear. He was beginning to sense an emotional flood coming that he could not hold back. He felt he was on loose chippings.

Morgan smiled back weakly.

"No, no, my mother probably only knew of Julian because of the name the nuns had given me. Aunt Mary didn't know anything about Julian either, except what I had told her. But she loved my name, Julia. She kept a scapular of Julian of Norwich I gave her sewed inside her camisole. She felt Julian had a lot of spiritual power."

Grady raised his eyebrows. This was the first he had heard about the convent. He'd felt that there was something unusual about Morgan, just a little "off," as they say. Her pursing her lips when Reggie had said "friggin'." A nunny thing, he'd thought at the time. He was just hoping she wasn't still in the convent. His mind was racing ahead to the evening. He didn't quite have that scenario worked out yet.

The two of them passed through a gaggle of nuns at the chapel doors. Grady removed his cap. They sat down in a sunny end, next to a plaque inscribed by Mary Robinson, the president of Ireland who rededicated the church.

Morgan felt peace in this place. Sitting next to Grady, she felt she could stop thinking of all the "Mary questions." She could let down with him. Grady could do the thinking for a while, and all would be well. Grady was a man who took things as they came, something Morgan had yet to learn.

"They did a grand restoration," he whispered, taking in the corpus of Jesus suspended above the stone altar by invisible wires.

Sans cross ... sans all our weight, the burden lifted. Christ is now free to be in the universe, Morgan mused.

Late afternoon light shafted through the yellow, green, and blue stained-glass windows. Some mood change had taken place. Tears streaked down Morgan's face, gathering around the corners of her mouth.

Grady held his breath, waiting for a wave that was swelling up in the core of the place to land—somewhere safe, he hoped.

"She is giving me counsel, too, about my trip here," Morgan whispered. "She's like an *anam cara.*"

"You're talking about Julian, right? Well, I do know what an *anam cara* is, since that guy O'Donohue's book took off. Soul friend, right?"

"Yes, a spiritual adviser. It's like Julian is giving me ghostly counsel now, here in Ireland. Since the plane, she seems to be leading my movements to find my aunt. 'Stay in Mayo and follow her lead.'"

"How is she doing that?" Grady pressed her hand as though requesting the answer.

"It's really just intuition. It comes through my imagination. My imagination becomes a little 'perky,' you could say. But also it starts concretizing, like in clues. I'm finding them everywhere, like a mystery.

"Of course, I am trying to find my aunt's body. But then again, I think Julian is leading me to find *her.* Julian, prodding my imagination, is hinting that there's more to my aunt than anybody understood. You know, I still haven't found out where she was buried. I'm beginning to think maybe I'm not supposed to find her—until I find *her.*"

"The local authorities have no knowledge of where she is either?" Grady was half in and half out. The half in told him that he had met more than a few Irish psychics and they were all sane, if weird. The half out told him he had to be sure this wasn't a nutcase he might be falling in love with.

Morgan shook her head. "But I just feel Julian is leading me on this. I think she led me to take your invitation to Omey Island today. I had planned to go to the chancery office with Michael, but then your invitation arrived. I think there's more there—at Omey, I mean—but I need some time to think about it."

"Morgan, how does a ghost 'hint'?" His Irish eyes were smiling.

Then, without any warning to himself, Grady picked up Morgan's palm and kissed it. They faced one another, a little startled. One nun turned ever so slightly to give them a faint knowing smile.

Morgan liked the kiss, but she thought she was going to cry again.

At forty-five, Grady thought he finally had a bit of experience, enough to figure out women—but now, with this weird American looking up her dead aunt by holy intuition, things were beginning to unravel again. He didn't need a transatlantic love affair, much less a long-term one. But something was drawing him forward. *Maybe Julian is doing it!* he laughed to himself. He would have to maintain his boundaries, he decided.

A few young nuns seated themselves in the pew across from Grady and Morgan. He thought they should move to a quieter place in the chapel.

"I'm not quite sure where you're getting all this," Grady said in a steady, reassuring voice. "But it's some kind of Irish 'sight' thing, is it?"

"Yes, 'sight,' but no. It's more like a voice in my imagination."

"I'm takin' you to Kildare, kiddo." Grady winked.

"What's in Kildare?" Morgan looked at him mystified.

"A racetrack." He took one good look into Morgan's eyes, and it was clear she didn't know what he was kidding about. "I'm sorry, I was going to make fun of this. I do that, you know. If something is beyond my comprehension, into the scary zone, I keep it at bay with humor. I make fun of it until it goes away."

"Do you want me to go away?" Morgan looked hurt.

"I don't know if it's you or God. I've been on the run a long time." Grady was surprised that he revealed his run from God. But did he just admit to Morgan that he was on the run from women and commitment, too? *My old racetrack hunch is that maybe Morgan and God are connected in me, now.*

"Well, did Julian have visions?" Grady was not kidding this time.

"Yes, she had a number of visions of Jesus. She also had a vision of God holding the universe—which was about the size of a hazelnut—in His hand, and loving it. But she saw him both in her mind and actually, bodily. I don't have any visions of Jesus." She laughed. "But then, I'm no Julian."

"Was T. S. Eliot a visionary?" Grady was on the hunt.

"Oh, I see—the poem." She took a breath. "Eliot was a convert to Catholicism, rather pious I think, but not a mystic." She shook her head thinking of Eliot smoking his endless cigarettes.

"So what is he saying in this poem that might link up Aunt Mary?" Grady was warming up to the whole visionary idea.

"Right. The fire, first of all, that's right on. I think Aunt Mary may have been involved with a priest who was in the Castlebar church fire of 1950. She worked for that church at the same time, too. That's just a holy hunch, though. No proofs. Michael is in town today, trying to find out more about him. But I guess you could call it a transgressive love affair."

"Transgress—what?" He couldn't help the smirk. "I'm not making fun. I just have to be the devil's advocate here. Even in church."

He's contagious, she thought.

"You know what I mean, Grady. I think they crossed the line, the church being the big fat celibate institution!" She was not on a fun note.

He did know what she meant. But "crossing the line" suddenly gave him a very different picture of Aunt Mary.

"Everything at Transfiguration Parish was consumed by the fire," she said. "The buildings, the people. And somehow everything as far as my hunch about Aunt Mary is concerned was consumed, too.

"Eliot's poem is speaking about love, how love burns through, transforms, transfigures everything. Really eats them up, burns them up; real love consummates everything and everyone, too. Completed. Not something half-done or half-baked, but total." She was speaking with a mature depth he had not quite heard yet.

Grady offered, "I'm sure the love Eliot speaks of in Julian consumed her. Right? Wasn't she a nun? So then, you could say she was married to Christ—He was her lover. They consummated their love in the visions he allowed her." Grady understood this poem and its links between Julian and the mystery of Mary. What he was amazed at was that there was a small flame in him still lit.

Morgan whispered, "Julian said, 'That's what Christ is all about. Love. Divine Love. Christ is not about punishment.' Maybe love consumed Aunt Mary, too. Straitlaced as I thought she was. 'The fire and the rose are one' … the consuming and the consummation. There is a lot of sexual innuendo in the rose image. It's the passionate self, the unfolding of the perfect-petaled yoni—and maybe how we 'connect' with God."

"Wow." Grady spoke in almost a whisper. "Did you ever think that Julian was trying to teach you about love, too?"

"That's good, Grady, really good. Yes, I have thought that. The new part is that you are teaching me, too."

"Your aunt's mystery could be teaching you. My holy hunch is that your Aunt Mary's love was consummated, too."

She took in a great breath and released a soft sigh. "Right." She couldn't stop the tears from flowing. Some truth was being touched upon.

Silently, he led her from the last bench in the chapel to the nave, where there was a darkened side altar to the Madonna and Child filled with pink peonies and candlelight.

Almost against his will, Grady felt compelled to hold her, to inhale her simple goodness. The believing girl in her had warmed the long-forgotten believer in him. His soul had been thirsty for such extreme belief. He touched her cheek. She held his hand on her face and covered her eyes with her other hand.

At that moment, Grady realized there was no going back. He knew he had fallen in love with her because he could feel her joy-pain. And she was in both, now. Tears gathered in his eyes, too. They both shared in a mystery and a mystic's love. He cleared his throat and said, "And maybe this kind of thinking is just perfect for you and your Aunt Mary. You couldn't figure her life from the outside, so …"

"There didn't seem to be that much there. Whenever I came to Mayo, she was just the simple old aunt on the farm."

"But now you see her differently. You've uncovered a hidden life, a secret life."

"Yes, a secret. I know the rose is the perfume of love she had for someone who died in that fire; the crowned knot of fire was like Jesus' crown of thorns. She experienced love pains and loss pains, like in the crucifixion, the terrible pain of losing someone who is perfect for you."

Grady's mind strayed for a minute. He was struck by Morgan's clear intelligence in the midst of emotion. For a split second, he envied her devotion to her aunt. He always came to the same place. He always thought he loved someone, but "out of sight, out of mind." He had never experienced the loss of a true love. They just moved out of his vision. Then, without mourning, he was on to someone else. He had burned a few.

"It seems that love can burn right through you." Morgan plucked the thought from his mind. There were so many nuances of the word "fire" and the word "rose."

They both stared at the card. He put his big rough hand around hers.

"You're very different. But I like you." Grady had to stop himself from saying, "so I think I might keep you, too."

The abbey guard tapped Grady on the shoulder. Kylemore was closing. They had been so engrossed in their sharing, they had not noticed the chapel was empty and only one candle was burning before the Madonna and Child.

Newport House

14
Newport House

When the judges judged by Brehon-law,
when tribe was your fealty and lineage,
when chieftains ruled the tribes
O'Donel's band stretched from Donegal to Sligo,
When Cromwell exiled the O'Donals to Connaught.
O'Donnel, O'Donal, O'Donnell rode to Mayo on a white stallion,
Built Newport house, O'Donnel of the bloodline of Red Hugh O'Donnel
of the Nine Hostages.

Morgan awoke from her catnap as Grady was pulling into Newport House. To say she was shocked as she looked up at the stately cedars would be an understatement. She had assumed Grady had a roadside tavern in mind when he mentioned taking her to dinner. This was a great house. Built by the O'Donel clan in the late 1700s, Newport House was a Mayo manor house turned restaurant-hotel. Generous pebble drive, its broad structure covered in vines, with a raft of chimneys, an entrance like a cathedral—and all Morgan could think of was she had to get off these muddy wellies before anyone saw them.

Grady, on the other hand, was always prepared. He pulled a clip-on tie from the glove compartment and a suede suit-coat jacket from a duffel bag. Grady was a man comfortable in his own skin, in manor houses or tinkers' caravans.

The Edwardian dining room sat about forty people, filling it with a light conversational buzz. As she entered the candlelit room, she was greeted by a larger-than-life painting of the clan leader, Red Hugh O'Donel, in his plaid wraps, sword, and battle gear. The room could have been reminiscent of an English gentleman's club, with lots of dark wood and Oriental carpets, if it were not for the emergence of a bright maypole in the center of the room—pale streamers tipped in small, white flowers flowing out to the walls.

Ciaran, the host, was a boyhood classmate of Grady's and appeared delighted that they'd come, on a last-minute invitation. He met them in the dining room, seating them as though they were coming to dinner at his own home—and in fact, it was his family's estate. He carried a bottle of champagne to accompany the first course and introduced himself to Morgan as "Ciaran, son of the Laird of Newport Manor."

"The maypole—how perfect! I love your home and the spring theme." Morgan tried not to gush.

"Beltane. We try to give a little honor to the old Celtic calendar," Ciaran said.

"This guy is an old pagan. Druid stock, really." Grady patted Ciaran's sleeve. "Actually, we bonded in third grade, when Ciaran's brother took us to Burrishule, the old Dominican monastic ruin here in Newport, and taught us how to cast—and pee—standing on the graves of the holy monks. I know that was probably a 'transgressive' act, but I was able to give a truthful answer to mi mather when she asked if I had gone to church." He winked at Morgan. "All the Thomases keep winning the fly-casting trophies. They have walls filled with them. Well, how can you beat them, when they start fishing in the womb?"

Ciaran opened the bottle with a grin from ear to ear at Grady's flattering remembrance.

"The fact is, Newport House has been a retreat for fishing gentlemen, British or Irish, for generations," he said, proffering the Perrier Joet and then pouring it.

"Make that about two hundred years," Grady added.

When they were quite young, the two of them shared Ciaran's older brother, Brendan, and his father through the contemplative art of fly-fishing. One learns a lot about another man in the practice of this art. Their friendship helped raise Grady, whose own father was not available to him or his sister because, as their mother told them, "Your father was taken to the otherworld by spirits," the kind of "spirits" the two of them were presently imbibing.

Ciaran handed them each a small yellow card, with an "All Fish Selection" at a fixed price, and an arm-length menu.

"I recommend the card," he said. "They are all our catches." He meant the Newport House fisheries.

The yellow card held the wonderfully debauched Newport House May Menu—Appetizers: trout pate, gulls' eggs. Soup: lobster bisque. Entree: scallops in Irish Mist, accompanied by snipe pudding, and new potatoes in black butter. Salad: Cresses dribbled with fish roe. Dessert, in the reclining bar: rhubarb and strawberry bread pudding or peppermint ice cream.

"This is my composition," Ciaran said proudly.

"You're a genius, Ciaran. But how the hell did the snipe get in the 'All Fish Selection'?" Grady attempted a mock attack.

"I justified the snipe because cook pressed me into showing off his pudding and told me, 'Well, the snipe runs around on the Atlantic shoreline, doesn't it?' I caved!"

"So he was *close* to the fish, is that it?"

The back-and-forth bantering was a male mark of their mutual appreciation, even affection. Morgan could see how Ciaran's docility could mesh with Grady's alpha male. The two had not quite settled into middle age, but they'd made a lifetime commitment to their friendship. Maleness was a mystery Morgan knew little about, but she always knew she liked being around men, especially men who could make friendships with other men.

"Thank you, Grady," she said. "This has been an amazing day. Today: Omey, the Abbey, now Newport House. It makes my stay here this time almost like a tour of the Best of the West."

Grady looked pleased. As he observed Morgan, he did not find the typical woman on the husband hunt. He wasn't quite sure who she was, but he was willing to take the risk of no return in knowing more of her.

"Well, if I'm not getting in too deep here, wherever did you get such familiarity with a remote figure like Julian of Norwich?"

"Truth? She wasn't so remote in my former life." She started to answer him, but wanted to make sure he was really interested, not just curious. He was interested.

"I was a Benedictine nun for fourteen years—and then spent three years in recovery."

"I knew you were a bit off, you know, when you told Michael the 'no F-word rule.'" He chuckled into his vest as he cracked a green speckled gull's egg. "I don't mean not *doing* it, just not *saying* it." Her face flushed, but she laughed with him.

"Right," he couldn't help himself for one more comment. "Hey, I like the rule—I just don't know if I can keep it." He finished the champagne and served her the trout pate on square crisps.

"Ambrosia," he purred. "What was it like? Not the 'no fuck' part—let's stay on Julian." She looked a little startled. Still adjusting to his "quick and witty."

"I was exposed to a heck of a lot of jam recipes ... and a few good women, too. Even wise." She looked reflectively into her wineglass. "One nun in particular was very good to me. She was a holy feminist, the novice mistress. She fed me the best."

The waiter arrived with the bisque in a small white tureen and two soupspoons.

Grady, smiling, "Like?"

"Feminine mystics. She really liked the Germans—Abbess Hildegard von Bingen was her favorite. Anyway, these mystics became my teachers, my life guides."

"You know, I was an altar boy, but I never met a mystic," pouring himself another. "But the Mass back then, in Latin, made me feel like I was in a secret society. Coming into the sacristy early mornings from the fog, the candlelight in the darkened church ..."

"Yes. I loved that, too. We were in another world in *that* church."

"More about Julian," Grady insisted.

"Early on, Sister Timothea gave me Julian of Norwich to study. Partly because Julian wrote her visions in English, and partly because she was my namesake. I was at home with both of them, the fourteenth-century wise woman and the twentieth-century one—Dame Julian and Sister Timothea."

"Dame?" Grady sat up, seeming a bit offended. He began to address a round hot covered casserole of steaming shrimps in whiskey cream sauce.

"Julian was not formally a nun, and she never became a saint. Not canonized, anyway. She was more like a lady hermit who had a cottage attached to St. Julian's church in Norwich, England, and wrote a big fat book about her visions."

Grady was dishing up the scented shrimps and potatoes.

"She was an 'anchorite,' anchored in one spot. No one even knew her name. They just named her after the church she was attached to, but she became famous anyway."

"So, what was *your* name?" He had a bit of cream sauce on his chin.

"Sister Julia."

"I like that name. Well, Sister Julia, do you think we'll go to hell for committin' one of the seven deadly sins?" By now he had moved his napkin into his neckpiece.

"What?" She still was a novice at "playing."

"Gluttony, Sister!"

"It's all right, Grady—I got a dispensation." Her first return lob.

"So, you are out now. But you are still drawn to the arcane," he said, passing the snipe casserole.

"I must be—I'm eating snipe, aren't I?" She lifted her fork in mock salute. "Yes about the arcane, and yes, I still like different things. The old nuns wove a medieval fantasy for us novices. We became spiritual pilgrims of the holy Isle of Iona. We were tutored by Columba, *Saint* Columba."

"Holy Isle of Iona—have you been there?" Grady listened.

"Well, only in books, you know. Convent life back then was a little like living in a historical novel. I wore twelfth-century clothing and sang ancient chants. Pretending I was being taught to be a monk by St. Columba wasn't that far-fetched."

"Let's go," he said with energy.

"You mean to the real island of Iona?"

"Yah. It's still a holy place, of course. I've done a number of gigs there. We aren't that far from crossing for the Hybrides. Besides, you might not have a job anyway."

Morgan was swept up by Grady's enthusiasm. She hoped it wasn't from the cups.

"Okay. I must find my aunt first. I also need your help in figuring out some of her papers from her 'treasure box.'"

"All right, so that's the plan. Find Aunt Mary, and then find the holiness of Iona. Or perhaps, if you find holiness, you will find your aunt Mary? Whoops, back to the musty mystics!" He was high but still clever. "So, I see: Julian and some of the others became your companions."

Morgan nodded. "If it were only the mystics, I probably would've stayed. The problem was the real live nun down the hall!" She was smiling, practicing "playing."

Grady gave his first smile since Sweeney's.

"Let me play devil's advocate for a minute. Okay, so what is Julian's pitch?"

"Pitch?"

"Yeah. What might Julian 'say' to you that's pertinent right now, in the twenty-first century, while you're trying to figure out your old Irish aunt?"

"That's a valid question," Morgan sighed. "I don't know."

A waiter opened another bottle of wine, showing the label to each of them: May Eiswein. He said softly, "Compliments of Mr. Thomas."

"Come on, try! If Julian is supposed to be leading you, there's got to be something from her own life that's relevant to Aunt Mary. Otherwise, I'm going to give up on the saint theory."

"I'll try. Julian lived during the plague, the Black Death … and yet she had an understanding of God as essentially forgiving and loving."

"Okay, okay." Grady was a bit impatient. "But don't all the saints say that? What is she saying to *you*? 'Forgive your aunt the way God forgives you?' 'Love her the way Christ loves her?'"

"Yes, I suppose you're right."

"Well, what are you forgiving her *of*?" Grady pressed.

"I don't know—yet."

"How about the guy in the fire? 'The fire and the rose are one.' Does that pertain?"

Morgan sat forward. "You know, that might be a real possibility, Grady— because one of the pictures in her box was the funeral card of this priest, O'Toole. He was pretty good-looking, too. If our hunches are true, then Aunt Mary was loved, at least."

"*Our* hunches?" For some reason, Grady felt jealous of Morgan sharing this with someone else first.

"Oh, Michael Timmons."

"Your driver, in Castlebar?" He underscored the rank.

She decided to let that "control" crack go. "The forgiveness I'm thinking of has to do more with her hiding herself, not trusting any of us to share in her life."

"Do you think maybe she couldn't share because she was doing something illicit? Or because she wouldn't find family agreement?"

"Maybe."

"Maybe the 'leading role' of Julian as your *anam cara* is that she got you here to Ireland, to Mayo, to find the real Mary Kenny—*and* the real Morgan Kenny."

"That's good. I heard you were a digger." She hoped he received it as a compliment.

The food came in waves, punctuated by wine pourings, and now the final course—"Salad: Cresses dribbled with fish roe."

They talked and ate and talked. They seemed to have an immediate interest in everything in each other's lives. She in his work excavating mountains, bogs, and shorelines of the West and its isles, seeking Ireland's ancient past. They shared a passion for literature and politics, and both had been addicted to Patrick O'Brian's sea novels, with the hero of grace, wit, and a bit of trickery, Captain Jack Aubrey.

"I was actually inspired by Captain Jack," he said, "to take up my fiddle after many a year." Morgan changed her mind on Grady's type: he was closer to "Lucky Jack" (aka "Goldilocks") than to the Quiet Man.

Grady thought she'd been pretty plucky in her political gamble with the nurses' strike. He loved her oddball faith, even in fairies. And she loved the way he talked about "listening to the very stones of Ireland."

Coffee came. Most of the dining room had emptied.

"Here's another 'odd thing,' Grady. Aunt Mary's nurse from Grailside gave me a lockbox with a few of her papers. You'll love this. She's got an old recipe for *potcheen* that begins, 'Take one barrel of fresh rainwater.'"

"God love her, those old-timers," he smiled, and then added, "Any other will in the box?"

"No other will, but a number of ambiguous documents. Both aunts had birth certificates with different names than their baptismal records. No one ever called them by the certificate names. The baptismal names were the only ones we all knew, Mary and Aran. The old-time birth cards, registering the midwife, witnesses, dates, and so on had names I'd never heard: 'Meredith' and 'Arianhood.'"

Grady's brow raised. "Let me think just a minute. These names sound so familiar. I know who they are; they're Celtic names. No, they're not Celtic, but they are from legends or something. I was just in a field in—where was it? Yes, yes! I was researching the water cults, British and Irish water cults that grew up around wells."

Morgan stared. "Wells? My aunts have a well."

"You mean a holy well?" Grady countered.

"I believed it was. My aunts would take me over to their well when I was a kid. It was among trees and bushes—other people came there too, apparently, and left their prayers on the bushes."

Grady was excited. "This is the gift from Julian! Connecting Aunt Mary with Irish mythology!"

"What do you mean?"

"Well—pardon the pun," Grady continued with some energy, "I've been plodding along for years with the grail myths in the back of my mind. All that Arthurian stuff. I'd been fascinated from boyhood with the knights questing to find the grail. That was Thomas Malory's Christianized version, you know—in his story, the grail is the chalice that Jesus used at the Last Supper. It had been lost—stolen, really."

Ciaran quietly joined them and poured himself a glass of wine. He picked the story up while Grady wet his whistle.

"Malory wrote his version around 1500, emphasizing 'worthiness' and 'purity.' Not just any bloke could get a crack at the grail. After all, this is the vessel that truth itself comes from, having touched Jesus' lips. So Malory has the knights performing all sorts of feats first, to prove their worthiness.

"Remember the *Wasteland*, T. S. Eliot? He's talking about finding the grail, too. But in the modern world, it's become virtually impossible—because the spiritual environment has become impenetrable. It's overgrown, a wild barren, from our neglect of virtue. Sin and arrogance overflow—producing a wasteland where people can't be nourished by truth."

"Yes," Morgan concurred. "But my aunts had a well—not a grail."

"Ah. Ciaran, get to the Irish version, the archaic stuff." Grady was getting antsy.

"In the Celtic stories," Ciaran complied, smiling, "the *graal* was a life vessel—not a metal cup. And that life vessel was often imagined as a holy well. Round, deep … a life source. A living thing, not a static metal object."

"Right," Grady was back in, "and in the Irish version, the well is open, free for whoever—"

"It's not about being pure," Ciaran cut in, in full tilt. "It's about *being there,* catching the wisdom when it comes. So, in the main tale, the druid's been fishing for years in this pool—a well, actually—trying to catch this salmon, who's been swimming around eating all the nuts of knowledge. The angler achieves his dream—he lands the big one—and *poof!* The kid who's his apprentice is cooking the salmon and burns it. He pulls it out, singeing his thumb, sucks the burned spot—and *he* gets the whole of the knowledge, by *accident!*"

"Now, *that's* Irish," Grady laughed. "The wrong guy gets the prize! Or, more deeply, you can't control who gets the gift. The straitlaced path from A to B doesn't work in old Ireland!"

"But what about the names—what do they have to do with the wells?" Morgan sounded pushy.

"In the Christian telling," Ciaran said, "as the focus moved from mystery to virtue, you had to earn your way. Which is why Malory set the knights on their terrible quests—and why he stuck in grail ladies, guardians, to hold the grail secret and protect it from the wrong guys, the unworthy." He was proud of himself.

"Righto," Grady nodded to Ciaran, reflecting his pride. He turned to Morgan. "And the names are the kicker. The names of Malory's guardians of the grail are *Meredith* and *Arianhood!*"

"Wow." Morgan was humbled.

"Your aunts were supposed to be guardians of the grail," Grady concluded. "That was to be their MO, their life's work. They were 'vessel virgins,' just like the Roman vestals. And like the Roman maidens, they had to be pure."

"And *that* was the only thing my aunts took real pride in—the holy well on their property! But why did they use the other names?"

"That's pretty straightforward," Ciaran said. "Arianhood and Meredith are pagan names. Someone—their parents, I'd guess—figured that would cause difficulty getting them baptized in the church."

"Your Aunt Mary was Meredith," Grady concluded, shaking his head. "And at her birth, someone gave her a spiritual task—guarding the sacred well. Her mother, probably."

Ciaran cut in. "Come on into the bar for dessert and coffee. I've got a good fire going."

"We have to have a Brandy & Benedictine," Grady insisted. "This lady helped make the stuff."

Grady had been right about the wall full of fishing trophies. Morgan stood, B&B in hand, looking at the cases. Ciaran came up beside her and said, "There was a guy who won year after year. Maybe seven times. Finegas MacCahill. Funny we should be talking about the grail stories tonight—the name of the druid who fished for the wise old salmon was Finegas too, or Fintan. Anyhow, Finegas Mac. He was the rector of St. Anne's, on the back of our property."

The fire was indeed mesmerizing. Morgan only had room for a bite of the rhubarb bread pudding. She wasn't sure about a mortal sin, but she felt she had definitely committed a calorie crime. Grady grazed through both desserts, coffee, and both of their B&Bs.

The three of them sat shoulder to shoulder in a high-backed velvet booth, staring into the fire. It had been a long day for Grady, who was the worse for the wear after drinking with every course. He was nodding off now, in the warmth. Morgan had an ounce of energy left, yet she could not figure out how they were going to get back to Castlebar in the utter dark. One thing for sure: Grady could not drive.

In the spirit of brotherly friendship, Ciaran found a room for the two in what he called the "Henry the VIII suite—which only means it's been out-of-date for a few centuries." There was some truth in his remark, but gratitude was Morgan's response as she and Ciaran assisted Grady up the winding servants' stairway in the rear of the house.

The room actually had been a suite, furnished in the grand old style. Decades of castoffs from refurbished rooms wound up in Henry VIII. A colossal four-poster bed with a dusty rose coverlet and canopy dominated the room, punctuated with wobbly French furniture and a silent fireplace. Under the circumstances, it looked like heaven.

Grady excused himself for the bathroom. Morgan pulled back the quilt and slipped in, leaving on her socks and sweater. When next she looked up, the gray dawn had arrived, and Grady was not there. Pulling a bed shrug around herself, she moved to the bathroom. There in the tub, without any water, lay Grady, naked and content. A tipsy fellow who undoubtedly got into the tub and fell asleep.

Morgan did the only thing an American girl would do. She called the kitchen for pots of coffee and scones, extra butter, and extra jam.

On the return to Castlebar that morning, Morgan attempted "play" with one who, in the masculine mysteries, was a bit vulnerable.

"We committed a sin, Grady." She kept a stiff upper lip.

"We did?"

"We wasted a perfectly good Henry VIII bed at Newport House."

white thorn & the Lady's Well

15

The Excavation

On Wells

*Long before the Church employed water for baptism,
the whole Celtic world understood water to be the
amniotic fluid of the Great Mother, who gave birth
to the world.*

*The druidic priesthood taught that the well was
the natural entrance into the supernatural ... the
otherworld, Tir naOg ... the beyond, or, in Christian
parlance (a mite paler), heaven. It was the vessel of
initiation into the new life, the afterlife. Christianity
took up that proposition, and the baptismal font became
the container on earth for the Church to initiate her
new recruits, neophytes, "new plants" needing fresh
water. The Irish, with their natural love of spirits (of
all kinds), intuited the well to be the repository of their
key beliefs.*

On the Number of Holy Wells in Ireland

There are probably thousands in the Republic alone. In County Mayo, in the Newport, Westport, Castlebar, and Ballina area, there are at least:

St. Anne's (southeast of Westport, near Knockrooskey)

St. Barbara's or Tobarnasul *(a mile and a half from Newport, on private land, near Burrishoole Abbey)*

St. Brendan's (northwest of Westport, off the Westport/Newport Rd., Kilmeena),

St. Brendan's (unmapped, half a mile from Newport, Killeen, Tienaur, off the main Newport/Mulranny Road; covered at high tide)

St. Dominic's (Newport, Kiltarnagh, a mile from Newport on the Newport/Achill Road; not far from Burrishoole Abbey)

St. Marcan's (on Rosscleve Inlet, not far from Newport)

The Well of the Lord of Sundays (ten miles from Westport on the Louisberg Road)

As Morgan stepped from the Green Dinosaur, she looked over her shoulder to her family's land, where the stone cottage, barn, coops, herb boxes, and kitchen garden had lain long, long ago. *Grandmother Lily told me the Kennys owned it for five hundred years. I guess that really meant "a long, long time."*

Now, she was greeted by a number of uniformed garda with spades and a Caterpillar with a winch dredging earth, crunching rocks, ripping open the family's well. Her well, the Lady's. What was happening to her family?

Someone took away the house—and now, on the other side of the road, the well? What did all this upheaval mean? The bulldozing of her soul? Excavating memory? In her memory, the Lady's Well was a place of blessing and the locus of many of Grandmother Lily's sentimental stories about herself, her sisters, and Ireland's Catholic faith. Although Morgan had not been to the well in many years, this wrecking scene flooded her with emotion.

The sacred wells were understood as a whole "complex." A typical well was often surrounded by rocks, overhung by trees, with a surround of brambles and brush. Morgan's aunt's well was typical—with the addition that the well itself was sheltered by a bonnet of bricks (giving it the appearance of an outdoor bread oven), which was closed off by a short, Victorian-style wrought iron gate, whose lock never locked. At its mouth, one could step down a broad stone stair or two into a circular pool, which then dropped off to a deeper water source.

As far back as Morgan could remember, there was a lid on the well. It looked like it had been taken from a vast beer vat with wrought iron hinges, in the Tudor style. There had been a hidden stair shelved under the bonnet that led to a hillside spring, but decades of farmers draining the nearby fields had sucked the well almost dry. It had been a muddy basin for a long time.

The whole well complex was a hundred feet from the road, and it had become overgrown by hedge and bramble, thick with whitethorn scrub. It was impossible to detect from the road, except in winter. While it had lain in neglect, as the fairy tales would tell, a forest of spindly trees and evil had grown up all around it.

When Morgan was a girl, the kids on the nearby farms told her that the whitethorn shrubs were the sign that the fairies truly lived there. In other words, this was a protected spot. Aunt Mary's "wild woman" image encouraged the children's description—and their fearful respect.

It seemed that half of Castlebar now stood on Aunt Mary's road, watching the Caterpillar crew dredge the field next to the Lady's Well. The Naughtons and other curious neighbors had gathered in a tight little knot on one side of the garda's cars. A reporter and Cyril Matthews stood on the other side of the road, in full view of a clay-caked skeleton and numerous clay-covered objects heaved by the machines onto outstretched canvas tarps. Reporters huddled around Cyril, who appeared to be giving an interview.

In the immediate woods, only the caps of the local garda could be seen above the matted whitethorns as they tromped forward, poking the ground with long sticks.

"Here, sir, here!" one yelled. Another policeman came forward with a stick topped by a colored flag. After only a short time, the flags in the dozens, each indicating a found object, created a pattern encircling the well.

Morgan pulled Mam Naughton's long-necked grandson aside. "What the hell is all this at the Lady's Well, Liam?"

"A robbery, Miss. An' maybe a murder." Just the way Liam put that soft Mayo "th" on the "d" in "murder" tripped her memory to chatty old Caitlin at the Grailside Nursing Home repeating, "*The* murther. She was walkin' the strand below, and then she said, 'The murther.'"

Pointing to a trim-figured, white-haired man who had the swagger of one in charge, the boy continued, "We heard 'im say the bones with the mud on it was some screw—you know, some English copper, missin' a long while."

"What's a long while?" Morgan was gentle but insistent.

"Maybe a hundred years, they think. They're checkin' for sure. Callin' up Dublin or London. A skeleton specialist."

His little sister added, "Maybe it's an Englishman who came to kill us, but somebody kilt him first."

"Who told you that thing?" Morgan asked.

"The man in charge told me, 'Somebody did 'im in a long time ago,'" the child reported faithfully.

"How did they know he was murdered? I mean, it's a skeleton." Morgan was repelled by the whole business.

Liam was uncomfortable, too, but he answered. "They really don't know who it might be, nor for how long he lay here. They figured this man was shot in the head and then buried next to this well, because no one would disturb holy ground."

Was this a trite end for a 007? Morgan wondered. *How ironic: Mary left her land to a Brit, and now some Brit winds up buried next to her well. Maybe there is a higher justice.* Morgan made an unconscious smirk.

The thin-lipped, white-haired man with the clipboard was Francis X. Mahoney, chief inspector from Dublin. His primary task over years had been the recovery of art the IRA used as "fundraisers," heists for ransom. Bodies, dead ones, were an inevitable bonus.

Francis Xavier Mahoney was not the beloved Irish policeman. He did not have the human fallibility of an Inspector Morse, of British mystery fame: F. X. didn't thirst for a pint for lunch. Nor was he the portly Sicilian Carabinare Salvatore Guarnaccia, fantasizing his perfect pasta and a romp with his wife for lunch. Francis Xavier (no relation to the saint) was a narrow paragon of chilly virtue and steely efficiency. His men fancied him a teetotaler.

He stood now over the cadaver with the forensic specialist from Dublin, talking the lingo of the long dead, pulling on plastic gloves over his small hands.

Cyril Matthews, "Mr. Insurance," was in his glory. Morgan noted that he'd dressed for the media, with a snappy checked hat and tie and scarf to match. He was talking, heatedly gesticulating to the reporters, citing a long list of stolen Irish antiques and museum artifacts—undoubtedly some of them showing up here in the Mayo countryside.

After an eleven-month investigation and a three-year hunt on behalf of Staunton and Staunton, Ltd., a United Kingdom insurance agency, he had finally tracked the IRA operative Miss Barbara Welch (aka Martha Halber) on a robbers' sojourn from the British Museum to private wealthy Irish estates, thence to Castlebar, and finally to Kennys' at the Lady's Well.

Even after all the photo ops, however, Cyril would not be on the front page of the Castlebar morning paper. The hundred-year-old "screw" would.

One of the reporters told Morgan that most of the recovered goods were not, in fact, of museum quality. They were common housewares, cast-iron goods in use at the turn of the last century and before.

"Do you think so many metal things, pans and such, give evidence of a hideaway for tinkers?" another reporter asked Morgan.

"I'm just an American, remember? One of the 'blow-ins.' But think, guys. Just consider such a theory. The tinkers are called 'travelers.' Doesn't that mean they spend most of their time on the road? Does it make sense that they'd leave all this tin stuff lying about the woods for so long and not come back for it?" She surprised herself with her own anger. *Wherever did this hostility come from? It must have been silently building since I arrived and became a casual witness to smart-aleck remarks about tourists and Irish-Americans—and tinkers.*

She spotted a big man sporting a gray mac, field hat, and walking stick, with an Irish wolfhound.

"Padraig! How long have you been here?"

"An hour only." She saw his worried eyes. "I knew all this wreckage of the holy well would hurt you." He smiled softly and touched her shoulder.

He continued, "This is going to be a pretty deep mess. Your aunt's old place appears to be a minefield of stolen articles. Very old pieces, some museum pieces, and a truckload of new ones, they say. Most are not buried that deep. The media, of course, are delighted with talk about evidence of 'the craft' and 'the old religion.' The police are saying the dead guys were probably murdered."

"There's another one?" She put her handkerchief to her mouth.

"Yah. This gentleman, who was in the well, probably got stuck under a rock ledge. They may have more information now."

"Which is it—was my aunt a thief, a witch, or a murderer?" Morgan was on the edge of tears.

"Calm, Morgan. No one is talking about your aunt."

Michael appeared from nowhere and stepped up next to Morgan, facing Padraig.

"You better believe they'll find some big stuff the IRA stashed in these woods. Isn't that why the British screw was murdered? Maybe he was onto where they were stashin' stuff. And isn't that why me and Morgan almost got blown away? Them bullets wasn't witchcraft. They wanted people to stay away from here."

Padraig interrupted, "But there are numerous objects, Michael, hundreds. More than the IRA were interested in. And some have been here more than a hundred years, the expert is saying. Indeed, we may find out that some are four hundred years old!"

"So what? Look at most of the stuff! Old iron pots. Almost like a couple of tinkers got mugged in the woods." Michael couldn't resist sticking it to the overrational Padraig. "Just kidding, mate."

Padraig bristled. He was not a "mate" of this know-it-all kid. The wonderful thing about adolescence is that Michael could not have cared less … and yet he did.

"Okay, the point is," Michael continued, "they're just common votive offerings that superstitious people left behind for petitions. The wishes they prayed for—and maybe received—at the Lady's Well. Let's face it, the Lady is not the Blessed Virgin Mary. These are whitethorns, man, not lilies!"

Padraig was trying to follow him. He looked in earnest at Michael. "Are you saying *not* Our Lady? Then whose lady is it?"

"There are lots of names for Her. The Divine Lady, the Great Mother, who gives power to the *bean feasas*, the wise women. We've got a hunch Morgan's great-grandmother was one of them." Michael passed a glance at Morgan, asking her permission and forgiveness at the same time. "They were the ones who got most of the gifts, the wise women. Payback for gifts received."

"Michael, Michael, wait a minute." Morgan could see that this was hard for Padraig to process. "It's a theory, Padraig. So far, just a theory. But it makes sense now, does it not, with the two classes of objects?"

"So you're making the case for two separate sources of these objects?" Padraig scratched his head and replaced his hat. He took his pipe out of his pocket and began to stuff it. "Of course. I'm looking for the wrong thing."

"Right." Michael nodded.

Padraig was in direct dialogue with Michael now, even if he considered him a smart-ass. "You think the IRA is probably responsible for the demise of the Brit *and* for the museum pieces—but the local people of the craft are responsible for the household goods left over the centuries?"

"Brilliant." Michael patted Padraig on the back, as though he were a child who'd won a spelling bee.

The gray-haired inspector had silently moved in next to them, with a recording device cocked. In a gesture of irritation, Padraig waved it off.

He had no idea how much Michael knew about Ireland's old craft, but the chief inspector was about to get an earful.

"Right." Michael took charge. Still wearing his stretched-out fisherman's sweater hanging below his rump and his threadbare gym shoes missing a lace, he was the man of the hour—not counting the corpse. "The household stuff wasn't stolen by the locals. No. It's their stuff! It was either a gift to the Lady of the Well or … or maybe payment to Mary Kenny or to a *bean feasa* in her family.

"And for the IRA, this is really the perfect place. It's mostly been abandoned."

Morgan opened up now. "Don't you think the real thieves had to live around here, too? They knew about the people's fear and respect for the holy well. The locals wouldn't touch an offering, or anything that might appear like one." She'd learned a few things, too.

Padraig looked at them quizzically. "What do you mean?"

Michael seemed older when he talked. "I mean that there were *cailleacha*— wise women—who lived near here, and who both blessed and healed people at this well. Maybe they even gave 'ghostly counsel.'"

"Ghostly counsel?" the inspector put in.

"You tell him, Morgan. What you told me about Julian of Norwich. It's the same thing." Michael was proud that Morgan was so brainy.

"Norwich? Are we talking the UK now?" The inspector spoke with interest.

"Let's forget Julian right now," she said. "Suffice it to say that 'ghostly counsel' is a good thing. It's spiritual advice."

Padraig entered the fray. "Is Julian a good—that is, reliable—witness?"

"She was reliable, but she's been dead awhile. She was a Christian mystic. What we're trying to tell you is that some of the work of these Irish wise women was quite similar to that of a Christian mystic."

"So the Holy Ghost was advisin' these wise people to be leavin' their possessions at the well, was He?" The inspector was tight.

"This well was in use for hundreds of years," Michael said. "Don't you think the locals paid Her in gifts as well as punt? Why do you think so much of this stuff was left out in the open? People just dropped things close to the well. And took off. They didn't wait for change."

"Because?" Padraig could barely believe he was talking like this.

"Because the people were afraid of *siogi,* the fairies, ghosts—as well as the priests, the cops, and everybody. I don't know if Morgan's auntie was an authentic wise woman," Michael slowed his speech. "But everyone around here says her great Aunt Mary's mother surely was."

"People don't do that kind of thing anymore, do they?" Padraig questioned.

"Indeed," put in the inspector.

Michael answered quickly, "I don't hear of it. But they used to, for centuries. Here in Ireland, as Morgan says, 'Belief has layers.' People tell you they don't believe in the banshee anymore. But then you go to a farmhouse after a funeral, and there is always someone in the house who has heard her. Lots of people have done this for lots of years—and then they went to Mass!"

"Michael has a point, Padraig."

Michael jumped back in. "Look at all the people who *still* go to Mass at the wells! Some priest was sayin' the rosary at a well on the Newport Road for the beginning of May—Beltane, for godsakes."

"Okay, Michael. Enough." Morgan turned to the inspector. "Shouldn't Barbara Welch be out here making some explanation about some of this? It is her land."

F. X. had an answer for this one: "Conveniently, Miss Welch has disappeared. There are stolen goods, and there is a homicide. Possibly two. As the crime writers say, she's on the lam. But if she's in the area, someone will give her up. The Welches are not that well-liked in Mayo, I hear."

Padraig appeared more animated, squeezing Morgan's shoulder. "It may be *her* father's tie to the IRA shall present *us* with some grounds to reopen your claim to the land, Morgan. That is, if we can find out where your aunt is buried."

Michael turned to the inspector, smiling, "Has anyone mentioned that the Welches are related to the Walshes of Castlebar? Maybe someone should speak to Miss Goodchilde Walsh. Maybe she knows where Miss Welch is, since she is her cousin."

Crazy Miss Goodchilde! Morgan watched Francis Xavier write down the names, "Welch-Walsh." She wondered if the relationship between the Welches and the Walshes was real or just part of Michael's one-upmanship. Padraig and Francis Xavier were wondering the same thing.

Cyril Matthews waved to Morgan. She took the opportunity to walk over to him.

"What did they come up with, Cyril?" she asked, like an old friend.

"Well, my hunch about Welch's daughter panned out!" He grinned, offering her a throat mint. "I told you. Everywhere she worked, every home or museum, something went missing. So many pieces. Of course, the Leonardo is the *pièce de résistance*, the item that triggered all this investigation. Now we have a line on everything!"

"Did you—?" Morgan asked, knowing the answer.

"No. They didn't find the Leonardo yet. We're positive she's got it, though."

"Do you think it's still in Ireland?"

"You bet! Somewhere in Mayo. I can almost smell it. So far, we've recovered a number of the insured antiques. And let's not forget the bones, whosever they are. Another theory, but I'll bet this stiff is just another rich Irish bloke. One they didn't raise the ransom for. Look what happened to Shergar."

"So, this Mayo wing of the IRA was very busy. Horses, murder, and great art."

"So Irish." He winced, and then lifted his hat, smoothed his hair, and replaced it. "The horse obsession, I mean." Cyril waved to a new reporter.

"We don't have Miss Welch, though," he added. "She was more than just a runner for the father. She raised real cash. We paid out big-time. I'm told the old man, A. Welch, was the big man here in Mayo. The Mayo boss, before the General. Well, the police won't let up now, you can bet on that. This is going to be solved. Pray they find the Leonardo." He crossed his fingers and turned back to the reporters. They couldn't get enough of the excitement; he couldn't get enough of the attention.

Just then, the excavation was yielding up another "large entity, partly held together in a shredded hemp-type bag, still moist." The onlookers moved back to the well. Morgan and Michael stood shoulder to shoulder. He was much taller.

Someone was yelling from the well complex.

Padraig lumbered in the direction of the yelling, taking Morgan with him by the hand, to avoid the machinery—and to hold her hand.

"An arm, no, a foot, sir!"

Chief Inspector Mahoney silently turned in the direction of the well and raised his hands over his head, motioning for them to stop. Two men, in hip boots and rubber gloves, stood over the well pulling a rope.

"Be careful, lads. For the love of Jaysus, do not yank at that bundle. This could be very old." Even as he said this, the hemp bag tore apart, and a brown, shriveled, mud-soaked leg connected to the knee by a thread fell from the bag. The observant gathering had moved closer, and now emitted a gasp as some recoiled at the sight of dangling body parts.

"Shamus, a pallet. Lay the bag gently. I said, gently." He raised his voice above the crowd. More of the disintegrating bag fell away, and a much-disfigured head rolled out.

"Holy Mother of God," the Chief Inspector gasped through his teeth. Once it was on the stones, he gave permission to cut what was left of the bag open. Miraculously, much of the body—mostly bones, and some shreds of clotted flesh and cloth—clung on. When the field adjacent to the well had been drained, years ago, the water in the well had been siphoned off, and this body's clay hardened. The bog-like mud had sealed parts of the victim like an Egyptian mummy; but recently, air disintegrated cloth and flesh. A man's clay-caked shoes came up a few moments later.

Michael's face was ecstatic. "'Someday I will go to Aarhus,'" he quoted, "'To see his peat-brown head,/ The mild pods of his eye-lids,/ His pointed skin cap.' We are here in Mayo," he added, bowing. "We honor your sacrifice."

The only one listening to him was Morgan. The others seemed to think the past was simply over.

"We might be making history, folks." Michael was so turned on he could explode. "This guy might be another Tollund Man. You know, 'the bogman.' They're all over the country—and Europe."

"Who?" Morgan caught hold of him, sharing the electricity.

"Do you not know that poem about the guy sacrificed in the bog? Heaney's prize poem?" Michael looked a bit disappointed in Morgan, whom he considered "up to snuff on all smart Irish stuff."

"The Tollund man was an Iron Age guy found in a Danish bog. We're talkin' BC. Maybe this is an Iron Age guy, too."

"I don't know how old he is." Padraig was hanging in there, still on edge from all the "craft" talk—and now, ancient mythology! He gingerly moved grass away from the frightening head with his walking stick. "But the IRA do not have the humanity to weave their victims a shroud."

"Mister Moore is right on that." Michael seemed to be leading the investigation. "They're not going to take time out to sew a victim into a bag." He laughed. "And look at those stitches. That takes practice."

The inspector's little eyes tightened, and his gray lips pursed. "Yes. The IRA would be more into plastic."

"Celts required human sacrifice," Michael went on. "Or at least the Goddess did. After all, this is the Lady's Well. Hey, Miss Kenny—perfect timing!"

"Timing?" Morgan was puzzled.

"Yeah. This is the Beltane, old Celtic time. The Celts always took a sacrifice on the Beltane—now, May first. Kind of synchronistic, don't you think? Finding a human sacrifice on the old religion's Feast of the Beltane! Well, they do say the veil is thinner."

"Why was that, Michael? Why sacrifice on May first?"

"To make sure the crops would be successful. It's like insurance for the Lady—or the tribal god, the *Teutates*—to yield a good crop. Blood is really a spiritual fertilizer. *Teutates* always preferred his sacrifices in a watery grave, too."

"We know, we know, like a sacred well." Padraig showed his irritation by giving a singsong response.

"You can see the guy outside the well, on the tarp over there, was not a premeditated sacrifice," Michael said. "He was just murdered. Sacrifice had ritual requirements. That guy was just buried in the field. Not a ritual act *per se*. It might be Christian, but not very Celtic."

"Not to mention the hole in his head from a slug," Padraig said. "Now that's Christian!"

Michael joined the laughter. "In terms of the Goddess," he went on, "you had to enter the otherworld headfirst, the way you were born into this one."

"You know about sacrifice, do you?" F. X. moved back in. "Know anything else about that?"

"In terms of this case, well, the severed human head to the Celts was like the sign of the cross in the Christian times." Michael smiled.

"What's that mean? Murder?" The inspector did not catch his drift.

"No sir, mythology. That would make this person a sacrificial victim, not a murdered one."

"What kind of mythology would that be?" The inspector's mouth tightened.

"Irish mythology, sir." Michael returned the glare with a bit of glee.

Upstaged, the inspector quickly walked back toward his team.

A broad, red-haired man appeared on the scene. It was Grady, dressed in a long plastic raincoat. He bent down a few yards from the well and appeared to wash his face in the May morning dew. A few of the crew saw him and made the sign of the cross.

He went to the well and began taking flash pictures as the team inspected what was left of the bag. He took a small tool from his pocket, cut a piece of the turf from the area outside the tapes, and slipped it into a plastic envelope. The burly forensic doc shook hands with him and motioned for his photographer to take a few more pics of the other cadaver on the tarp.

As soon as Grady came on the scene, he seemed to elevate the importance of everything—especially this new corpse from the well. Some of the onlookers drew closer to the yellow crime scene tapes. The team knew him. Some smiled and waved. Subtly or not so subtly, he became a magnet that drew the crew, and they began to wait for his direction. Even as a mist began, the mood lightened.

"Hello, Grady, lad," called out the blond pathologist, who may have known him from his student days in Dublin.

"There's some kind of ornament falling out of the bag. Will someone please lay it carefully on the cotton mat?" Grady spoke with authority.

"Looks like a watch and fob," the blond doc said.

"I guess the 'Tollund Man in Castlebar' is out," Padraig said. "Unless he could sew and tell time." He punted to Michael, grinning ear to ear.

"Yeah, but the guy in the bag still went in headfirst, a ritual requirement. He still could have been a sacrifice." Either way, Michael was enjoying it.

"What do you think?" The pathologist looked at Grady.

"Well, the gent in the bag was not from the Iron Age. He's not very old at all. Maybe fifty years at the most in the well? I'm surprised he isn't older; this is one of the old wells … yeah, pretty old." Grady was on his hands and knees. "Time of Maeve. The Queen of Connaught, the holy Mare herself. Listen, lads, this gent may have been a lover gone astray." A few Mayo boys chuckled.

"When d'you say, Grady?" The doctor hadn't caught Grady's references.

"What I mean is, the well was built in virtually mythic time. A long, long time ago. But we're finding it now—and in the Beltane. That is not a coincidence, lads. Timing is everything, in life, death, and at the track." There was brief laughter.

"What I'm saying here is that although this guy is a recent addition to the well, he still could have been ritually executed."

All the parts were assembled and laid out. He was male, short—about five-foot-five—and the front of his skull was missing.

They hadn't found the missing piece in the mud. Undoubtedly, it had floated away before his body got stuck in the stone shelf area. Grady's specs matched up with the forensic doc's on the head taking a solid bash, and then the piece "sailing away" some years after. It was loose, and therefore lost. He'd worn tweed trousers, probably an animal-skin vest, knitted tie, wool-and-cotton shirt—most of which, though eaten by water, worm, and time, was still sufficiently identifiable to place him in the recently completed century.

The watch and fob proved to be gold plate, but blackened. "It's engraved, sir," a detective said. "Four numbers, '1 … 8 … something, something,' and a 'K,' sir."

"K" was the only letter discernible, but two other letters appeared after some cleaning. "A" for Anthony, and "P" for Patrick. The watch and fob belonged to Anthony Patrick Kenny—the father of Aran, Mary, and Lily Kenny, the great-grandfather of Morgan. But Anthony Kenny died in the 1930s, and it was doubtful such a poor man would have owned such a watch. And if he had, surely he'd not have been buried with it, but would have bequeathed it to one of his daughters.

"Yes, that's a telltale sign, is it not?" Francis X. remarked.

A perfect sign for Michael. A telltale that it was a sacrifice.

"Was this stolen? Or given to someone else in the family?" F. X. was going to play the inquisitor.

Morgan looked away from the second body, as though she did not want to find someone she knew. Even strewn in parts among a hundred objects, the vessel of a human soul still demanded respect. There were signs of the cross in the crowd, and not a few *Aves*, even among the police.

Morgan could hear the Naughtons talking in Irish. They were trying to come to agreement about the body. Finally, a few words in English; and soon after, young Liam came over.

"My great-grandmother wants to tell you that this is *not* the body of Mister Anthony Kenny. Mr. Kenny was a very tall man, says she. Also, my great-gran went to his funeral."

Francis X. added his sarcastic twinge. "But this man wore Mr. Kenny's watch, lad. Who might be a recipient of his fine timepiece? Was this a member of the family?"

No response was offered, although everyone could feel the holding back.

The old matriarch of the Naughtons signaled that it was time for her to go home. Grady caught up to her and her trailing family to ask a few questions. Francis X., looking down his thin aquiline nose, would not look up from his clipboard; he would suffer his questions until he could get Grady alone.

Padraig used Mrs. Naughton's departure to move in that direction himself. He motioned Morgan to get into his Jeep. She gave the whole excavation site a last look and then got in beside Padraig. *Maybe this is the last time*, she thought. They were still shoveling as she got in. She waved good-bye to Cyril. But then she saw the red hair and heard that full-bellied laugh, and she knew Grady had probably gotten a good nugget from the Naughtons.

"We have to talk, Morgan. About the land, I mean," Padraig pressed. "I've continued to work on your case. I've been in contact with another solicitor from Dublin about exceptions in confiscation."

Morgan was listening, but closely watching Grady across the field as he directed people around the well. He was in control.

"When I began looking into the descendants of Welch," Padraig continued, "of course, I found his primary living heir to be his daughter, Barbara. But today I'm convinced of her involvement with Cyril's insurance investigation.

The many burglaries we've heard rumored about her have materialized, right on her property. I suspect staking a claim to the land will not be her greatest priority. She's probably in South America by now, and my hunch is we shall not expect her presence in Ireland anytime soon. Anyway, there is still another living relative."

"Little Miss Goodchilde *Walsh*," Michael interjected from outside Morgan's window.

"Well, yes, that is a new piece," Padraig replied. Then to Morgan, he said, "She then would be the next in the Welch line for the property. But there is still another angle."

"I'm sorry?" Morgan's eyes held confusion. "I always heard Welch was a Brit who could be part of the IRA."

"Well, I think you're right about the IRA thing. I guess he ran that in the West of Ireland with a smooth hand. But he's not British. He's Irish. Only he's a Protestant. Under British occupation, Irish landowners had to become Protestant or lose their lands. They had to give allegiance to the English crown and separate themselves from any allegiance to the Church."

"So you're saying his side of the family made the switch from Catholic to Protestant in order to save their estate?" Morgan still wasn't getting this.

"Yes. Well, probably his great-great-grandfather made the change. A number of landed gentry did that under the British. Many others fled to France or, as in the case of my family, to Spain." He laughed out loud. "I'm sure you've heard of the saying 'To hell or to Connaught.' Well, a lot of people were already in hell *in* Connaught."

"The Walshes?" Morgan's voice dropped as she saw men take away the corpse from the well on a stretcher.

"Welch's side had the grace to use the Anglicized pronunciation—from 'Walsh' to 'Welch.' The rest of the family, Goodchilde's side, remained Catholic."

"Man, is this a hairball!" Morgan exclaimed.

"I love hairballs," smiled Michael.

"Another little tidbit from the records is that the Walshes were the lairds of a good portion of Castlebar, *fado fado*. Which included what would have been your great aunts'—the Kennys'—field."

"I thought you said if they became Protestant ..." Morgan was getting an overload.

Padraig was getting heated himself. "Right. Well, a deal is not a deal with the British. It's obvious from the records that the land agents at the time of the option—we should really say 'the steal'—only gave the Welch-Walsh family a fraction of their lands back."

"How could they have gotten away with that?"

"That's another long story, which probably needs something to wet one's whistle. Nevertheless, we have to find out why your family let go of their property fifty years ago. This is crucial. Motives, coercion … many things can change the outcome of this story." Padraig spoke gently, paternally.

"Maybe some of these finds today will yield an answer."

"I think Miss Goodchilde is your answer," Michael put in.

By now, Padraig had opened the passenger's door and helped Morgan out.

"I have to get back, Morgan," he said, having sensed Morgan's hesitancy when she watched Grady. Padraig was a smart man. "I hope Grady can shed more light on this." He waved. "See you later."

She walked over to what was left of the well. Grady was there, talking to the Chief Inspector, who looked a little more conciliatory. The police seemed to be closing down the scene, carefully removing the body now to a waiting van. It was interesting to Morgan that the Chief Inspector never addressed her, hardly looked at her even, though the land was Kenny land for more than a hundred years. She smirked. *Just another Yank,* she thought.

"Don't go yet," Grady said. "I want to make you a good fish dinner at my place. We can pick up some fresh salmon on the way. Here," he said handing her the keys to his wagon.

No question, Morgan thought, *this guy has great eyes.* But she said, "Are you almost done?"

"Yeah," he replied. "Just wait till I take one more look at this other guy, before they move him for good."

Grady crossed the yellow tapes again to prod the ground around the cadaver that lay outside the well complex.

"This guy has been here quite a while," he said to himself. "He's not some 'screw' checking up on the IRA some fifteen years ago. More like 150 years ago. He's on his face, and only a few feet under. Someone shot him, and that someone was in a hurry. He dug a bit and pulled the stone partly over him. Either the guy had no clothes on when they buried him, or he's been there a long, long while and he just disintegrated—or he'd been stripped so he couldn't be recognized. Or all three."

Grady bent almost parallel to the ground; he prodded something green. It was a clay-covered button. He paused to pull off some of the crust. It was copper or brass. A very old button, a blurry Union Jack encircled in laurel? Then he found another.

"I must have been standing on it," he mused. "This stiff must have been an English officer. Shot at point-blank range, with a uniform on. Maybe the rest of the buttons were stolen, as were the boots." He put the buttons in his pocket and picked a bit more around the body.

The horn of his wagon pulled him back into the present. Dinner. Morgan. A good bottle of chilled white wine. Even a couple of cadavers couldn't turn him off.

16

Dream After Excavation: Sacred Space

Morgan woke trying to catch a dream. It was a whopper, and it was still on the line. She was reeling in as much of it as possible. In order to retain its oracular effects, she reached for her notebook.

The moon on the water outside Grady's cottage illumined the room. Like Psyche, she awoke to find her Eros, a golden-haired hero or god, lying next to her, with a large naked foot protruding from the covers.

"It will surface if I am still enough," she whispered.

Julian sits cross-legged in her prayer space, she wrote, *in what feels like a cave. Her snow-white hair radiates from her head like an electrified Statue of Liberty. Silver stars spread out across the dark blue ceiling, a dome of stars that at first look like candles burning—or candles that seem to reach the stars are burning.*

I see an altar of colored icons in the wall. Wine-red rose petals are sprinkled among them. The icons are Madonnas, some regal, some warmly human. I recognize Our Lady of Guadalupe, her eyes cast down on Julian praying, and the

Green Madonna & Child painting my Aunt Mary left with the nurse, Winnie Shanahan. In the center, glowing, is Vermeer's Girl with a Pearl Earring, *reinterpreted. The wide-eyed girl is here depicted as Raphael's Madonna della Sedia, with a striped turban, sitting in a farm chair. Instead of the fat baby boy of the Renaissance, she is nursing a wraithlike infant, his skeleton-thin fingers and thin lips pressed against her adolescent breast, his haunted eyes looking straight at the viewer, at me, as if to say: "She was there, but it's all about Me."*

Vigil candles burn before family photos, just as in a church. One catches my eye—Aunt Mary as a young child, sitting on her mother's lap.

Some shifting happens. Julian morphs into Donna, the Western woman on the bus trip to Omey Island. She now is meditating under the stars. She opens her eyes, looks at me, and says: "It was a murder. Consider the obvious. The Mages found the good Christ Child, didn't they?"

She says nothing more. She closes her eyes and returns to meditating.

Morgan felt she had reeled it all in.

She lay still, peering out the sliding glass door at the moon on Grady's lake. Her heart experienced an outpouring of gratitude. *Someone must be praying for me,* she thought, *to be given so much and to be able to receive it now. My soul friend Julian and the nuns from the order are present for me. 'All shall be well,' Julian wrote, but this is the first time I've felt it would be.* Morgan thanked the Great Mother, who nourishes us with Her love.

Is she telling me all of this family mess is in our Lady's hands? Yes, I think so.

Still, why are there so many Madonnas? The image is repeated over and over again. Does the dream maker repeat so that I will not miss the message, to emphasize a change in focus? That it's not about my inheritance and the land?

The issue is the mother and the child. Not the land, but the baby. Whose baby is this, anyhow? This isn't baby Jesus, is it? This baby looks almost like a skeleton. Maybe this baby died? But the Girl with a Pearl Earring is still nursing it! Aunt Mary is the Girl ... so here, she is the Madonna of the Chair. This baby looking straight at me is Aunt Mary's baby!

Then another Madonna, and another aspect. The Madonna and Child are older. Their bodies seem shorter than adults' bodies, but their faces are developed. Aunt Mary sits in the lap of her mother, the psychic from Clare. (No doubt this is where she was instructed in the old ways, the old religion.) And the baby sits in Mary's lap. Something is coming down through these women, coming down through the family. From mother to daughter. The gift of sight?

The rose petals. What about them? They only tell me the reference of T. S. Eliot's poem … "The fire and the rose are one." The roses scream out Aphrodite, love, sex … that seems obvious. All of this comes out of passion? Was this a crime of passion?

The Madonna and Child, the mages, these are all images of Christmas. A babe is born, but then he is not safe from the wicked king. The infancy passages seem to say the wondrousness of Christmas still has shadow around the edges. The child is hidden amid the ordinary but then found by the wise men.

The atmosphere of Morgan's dream reminded her of early morning Mass when she was a girl. The nuns carrying tapers into the ink-dark chapel, chanting in Latin, bowing before the icons in their long black capes and veils. Morgan was there with them. They were the priestesses of her childhood. *It was mysterious and holy, and yet we did not understand a word they were saying.* The moon and stars still shone on the water, even as the rosy-fingered dawn appeared at the horizon.

She lay still in the bed, appreciating that Julian had given her another key to this Mayo mystery, still feeling that "All shall be well"—including making love with a beautiful Irish pagan. The pagan turned to take a nibble of her shoulder.

"Are you awake?" she whispered into the covers.

"Of course not. It's still dark out." Grady pulled her over closer to him.

"Julian told me what this was all about," Morgan said.

"Yah, so what?" Grady wasn't the least bit interested.

Then she said, a little more excitedly, "It's about Christmas." The priestess whispered in the dark.

He groused a bit and then smiled. "I like Christmas. It's the best part of Christianity."

"You were right last night about 'the stiff in the well' being Horsey Neary. Julian said the same thing … or at least, she said, 'Consider the obvious.' I took that to mean Horsey—he was the most obvious."

"Yah, well, Julian didn't figure that one. Mrs. Naughton did. She was the one who said Horsey left some fifty years ago. And he fit the corpse's description. To consider the obvious, you'd have to consider a few other obvious facts that at first aren't so obvious."

"Like?"

"Truth serum, truth serum," he mumbled, pulling the quilt over his head.

"What is truth serum?" Morgan had never played this game.

"Chocolate latte. It's what the torture victim needs at 5:00 a.m."

The torture victim was served a frothy coffee in bed in return for divulging all he knew.

"Well, consider this: Horsey really doesn't disappear until the year 1950 even though he has never been fully employed in his whole life. He could have gone astray at any time, but he goes in 1950. Such a coincidence!

"Then, the story is told that he goes to Dublin. Holy Mother of God, he's probably never been out of Mayo. Yet he leaves at this particular time, same year the church burns down and the priest dies in the fire—all 1950. Fishy enough for you?"

Morgan demurred.

"The tip-off is your great-grandfather's unique gold watch. Your aunts, I take it, were a shrewd bunch. Thus, no gold watch for Horsey, the layabout husband, who sucks up their savings in pints and ponies. But wait a minute— the bloke has the watch anyway. Why? Not because they gave it to him."

Morgan listened, seeking a loophole. "Why?"

"Simple as one, two, three. But you may not like the math." He sipped his latte.

"We have to eliminate immediately the IRA doin' him in—or bookies, because they'd never have left him with a gold watch. Or a high-class leather vest or a swell pair of leather high-tops. That's for starters. But he winds up with the watch.

"Number One: He stole it." Another sip.

"Number Two: His killers are too much in a hurry to think about carefully searching him for the loot he habitually nicks, because they're extra busy sewing him up a shroud. That's the Christian thing to do after you've just bashed him dead, right? The police are not called, because … Instead, the body is gotten rid of in the holy well, to cover up the crime of murder." Another sip of latte.

"Number Three: A problem. Someone is at the well watching when Horsey Neary is being initiated into the next life. Yes, here I do agree with Michael—I think this was a ritual murder. Because in addition to Horsey being forced in headfirst, they decide to put him in a holy well—of all places. They're sitting in the midst of acres and acres, in fact, a whole country and the entire ocean, but it is *the well of the Lady who is the initiator, She who is the womb into the otherworld*—that's what they push the body into. These perps have a pagan bent to them, yah? But—" Another sip.

"The 'voyeurs' scare the bejaysus out of our amateur killers. They blackmail the ladies, being witnesses to the crime or at least the disposal of the body. What's the price of their silence? Well, the aunties don't have any money, but that's not what Welches want. It's the thing all Irishmen never think they have enough of—*land.*"

By now, Grady's voice had gotten decibels higher.

"Land in exchange for silence. Of course, the watchers are at the scene because it is *their* usual hiding place for loot, nicked from the museums by Barbara and her IRA lot."

It was a lot to process at five o'clock in the morning, but it was crystal clear to Morgan.

"So you think my aunts killed Horsey?"

"I'm not sure of that. But I am sure they sewed him up and brought him to the well. Whoever did it in this manner had to believe they were giving him a chance at a new life. This is a pagan mind-set, but hey, these ladies weren't all Catholic." Grady took the last swallow of his latte.

"Chief Inspector Whatshisname and Cyril have already established that about half of the loot was thefts by the IRA. The Welches were in the well complex, burying their own stuff, when *ping!*—they witness your aunts dumping Horsey Neary. Who else gets your aunts to sign the land over to them? Right now, Welch knows something that nobody else knows."

"Wow. You have the answers for everything. Why'd he die?"

"Yah. You're right. That's the big lacuna. We don't know why. Maybe the three things that occur in 1950 have to be investigated, because maybe they're related."

"Which things?" Morgan asked weakly.

"Your inheritance! Your aunt's green box has the answer, I think. We don't know how to decode it yet, but it was left to you—so somehow, you'll be given the key to the code. It's the only thing we have to go on, the only thing that was actually hers."

"What are the three things from 1950?" Morgan intuited that Grady was so close to a solution that she wanted to draw back from all the facts, facts, facts.

"First, Horsey. Second, the priest. Third, the will."

"What about the other body? The guy in the meadow?"

"They took him to Dublin for tests. But they'll find he's not from the same century as Horsey. See what I found?" Grady leaned over the bed to take something from his jeans on the floor. He slowly uncurled his arm, showing her the corroded uniform button. She was looking at it, but she was also staring at the strength in his arm and upper torso, the reddish hair on his forearm and chest. Now she knew: she was so infatuated she could cry.

"You can just make out the Union Jack on this one," he said. "A common soldier wouldn't have this elaborate button. Good chance he was a British officer in the Mayo Rebellion. The timing's near perfect: the eighteenth century. It must have been the year of the French."

"There are just too many questions. I'm focusing on my aunt, and now another body—why?" Morgan was frustrated with Grady's professional approach to her personal pain.

"You of all people should know," he said. "That famous passage in Rilke: 'Be patient to all that is unsolved in your heart, and try to love the questions themselves … Do not seek answers, which cannot be given you because you would not be able to live them. And the point is—'"

Morgan lost a sock as Grady pulled her back into bed, kissing her ear and then her eye, nose, and mouth, many, many times.

"'And the point is,'" Grady mumbled into her neck, "'to live everything. Live the questions, now. Perhaps you will gradually, without even noticing it, live along some distant day into the answer.'"

What an odd man, she thought. *Him licking my tears and my ears …*

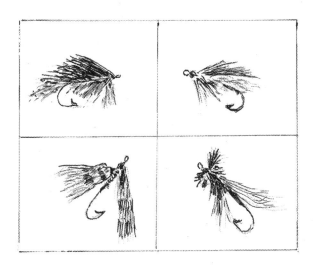

17
Fly-Fishing

Legend has it that the wise hero-king and poet, Finn MacCool, became so by eating a certain salmon—a mystic salmon found in a certain well. For so long was the fish free as a farkle, impossible to catch—he was almost invincible to time—a fish which had a great knowledge of all things ...

The note under Morgan's door read:

My Report—

Found Sean O' Toole (curate, Castlebar '44–'50) in the archdiocesan office files. Not much on him as a priest. The only thing for sure—he was the best fly-fisherman in all of Ireland back when! Fishing awards, pics with some bishop. Second thing: a note in the file with the name and address of a Father Finegas MacCahill, and a newspaper blurb on his appointment to St. A's, the Church of Ireland parish in Newport. On the very grounds of the Old Newport House

Inn (where you had your posh dinner with Grady)! I assume this friendship was significant, or why would the archdiocese record such a thing?

So, #1. Is Finegas still ticking? Could he fill in O'Toole's empty personnel file—like, how much of an *anam chara* was he to Aunt Mary? #2. Mrs. MacCahill is a Mayo writer, so I think the MacCahills are our next hit. # 3. This old record shows Fr. O'Toole had asked for a transfer. Why? To where? No answers here. I'm finished with my tests tomorrow.— Michael.

PS: The Dublin inspector was putting the screws to Mum this morning about *you*—and your aunt Aran's husband, Emmet Neary. (Mum doesn't have the info on your land, though. Being grabbed, that is.) *Also*, saw the garda waiting on the bell in front of Miss Goodchilde Walsh's. They took my tip!—M.

PPS: Thanks for the pay—I can use it at University. If I get in.

* * *

Reggie was walking up and down the alley in the rear of Timmons' Teatime, smoking a tiny cigar and looking worried. His face reddened when he glimpsed Morgan coming out the back door.

"Am I glad to catch you, Reggie!"

His eyes widened on the word "catch."

Morgan smiled as she thought of cornering him, since he had slithered away from the crime scene at the Lady's Well yesterday. Now her mind raced as to what Reggie might know. She had a hunch he flew the coop when he saw all that IRA loot. Padraig's tip about Reggie being an old IRA guy was probably right. *Could he have known about the well murders from his IRA contacts? Was he old enough to have heard about Horsey's disappearance?*

After all, he was a handicapper, too. He had to have heard about Horsey. Both of them had won, lost, and borrowed how many life savings on the ponies. At any rate, Reggie probably knows a lot more about the robberies—and the bodies at the Lady's Well. Just nobody's asked him.

"Reggie, I need a fast lift to Newport. I'm looking up old acquaintances of my aunt's—the MacCahills. Father MacCahill was pastor of St. A's, the old Church of Ireland in Newport." Morgan was back in "the mode."

"Mrs. MacCahill? Aye, she's a real corker." Reggie lifted his porkpie to smooth his bald pate.

"Do you know her?"

"Do I know her? The whole of Ireland knows her. Well, for sure, Mayo."

Morgan hadn't seen Reggie this animated since he drove them out from Shannon on the day of her arrival. He took one last drag on his cheroot and stamped it out slowly in the cinders, saying, "God willing, she'll be easy to find. That is—" he paused, giving her a wicked smile "—if she's still with us."

The two took off in the smoking blue cab with the gusto of kid racers. Morgan opened the *Castlebar Dispatch* to a headline: "MURDER IN MAYO: 2 Cadavers Found in Castlebar." A photo of Aunt Mary's dismantled well, a pile of the best antiquities, and both cadavers stretched out across the centerfold; it also featured the prominent profile of Dublin Inspector F. X. Mahoney, who appeared to have solved the case already.

She was torn. Should she sniff out what Reggie knew about the murders, or get some background on the MacCahills?

They drove together chatting like kin, father and daughter. Did she know that the family of Princess Grace of Monaco came from Newport? Morgan felt an odd closeness to this slippery old IRA guy. Maybe it was because both of them were resident outsiders.

For the next twenty minutes, the length of the ride, Reggie talked about "Minnie Mac," as Mrs. Minerva MacCahill was called. For many years, she'd been his favorite opinion-page writer, an indefatigable commentator on every aspect of Irish daily life—gardening tips for tidy towns, views into the ongoing Irish curse of "the drink," moral poems, fruit preserves without sugar, and last but not least, horses. She was a veteran handicapper, and surely, it was rumored, she spent as much time at the track as she did in the pew.

"Quite a 'capper, herself." Reggie shook his head in approval. "Very talented." He smiled. "Picked a number of Kildare winners. Sweeps, too. Think her son or grandson owns trotters out of Derry."

"Did she ever write about Shergar?"

"Did she? Mother of God! Shergar was her number one opinion piece for a while there. 'A horse like no other.' His destruction gave Miss Minnie a particular perspective on the IRA."

"What was that?"

"Well, she felt they turned the corner that time. Art thefts, okay. Ransoms without murder, okay. But to kill great horseflesh …" he slowed to find words lofty enough for Shergar … "to destroy great beauty … 'tis the act of savages, not activists!" Reggie was riled himself. "The IRA had tried to get justice from the Brits, and now they were no better than the likes o' them. Many got off the IRA then. A lot of Irish and American supporters left, Miss Kenny, a lot of monied people."

"Ruthless."

"Yes, ma'am, that's the word. 'Ruthless.'"

"She must be up in age now, Minnie Mac?" Morgan was figuring she was a contemporary of Aunt Mary.

"Must be in her late eighties. The mister was a Protestant cleric, but she's no 'holy moly,' not Minnie Mac. I guess Father Mac was a fine gent in his time, too. Great fly-fisherman, they say."

"I'm not going to phone her. Do you think I should? I don't want to take any chance at being rejected. Or put off for a week, since I'm leaving on Monday, back to Chicago. I have to get it right the first time." Morgan was feeling rushed.

"Well, if she's not visitin' *Tir na Og*, she'll be there." Reggie looked back in the overhead mirror at Morgan and smiled.

"I don't know if I'll ever get another chance for a visit, with all the buzz about the …" she was fumbling for a more neutral word … "the *recovered bodies*. I mean, they were both definitely done in." She couldn't say the dreaded "murder" word. *This is my chance to see what Reggie knows about the guy in the bag, the one with the watch fob.* "What do you think about it, Reggie? I mean, the whole thing at my aunt's well?"

"What happened to the gentleman with the watch is fairly certain, Miss Kenny."

"Oh, I mean who killed these guys? And why?" Morgan pressed a bit.

"Well, we know the one guy, the gentleman from the well, did not sew a shroud for himself and then dive into the well. Did he now?"

"That's right. I guess somebody would have to have put him in that bag." *Hundreds of stitches in that bag; and many years ago, I recall Aunt Mary sewing a little nightdress for me out of a flour sack in just a few minutes before bedtime.*

"What IRA man would take his sewing that seriously?" He chuckled softly. "One must consider the obvious, and that would be—a woman was involved. Whether she put him in the bag or bashed him in the head, no one knows." Reggie was being gentle.

"I wonder how old that body was."

"They've already got that sorted. 'Inspector the Chief Inspector' was 'round Timmons's place this morning. Late 1940s or '50s, said he. Quite a while back, anyway." He took a breath. "Around the time of that devastatin' church fire, wasn't it? 1950, right."

Musing on the fire, Reggie spoke slowly.

"Ireland has had her tragedies. Castlebar has had hers, too. It was May 13, 1950, the night of a vicious and powerful Beltane storm. Odd, though."

"How so?" Morgan hungered for more.

"Well, the winds whipped down the chimneys of cathedral and cottage alike, and many a house burned to the ground. Lightning started the fire, they say. But the odd part is, the church and rectory both had lightning rods. Yet they still burned down."

"That is odd."

"A mystery." Reggie was aching for a cheroot.

"Did many people die in the fire?" Morgan spoke softly now.

"I'm not certain. For sure, the two priests from the Transfiguration. It was a turning point in all our lives, you know. It was 'before' or 'after the fire' for many a year as I was growing up."

Morgan's mind rewound to the date on her old convent calendar. *"May 13: Julian of Norwich. Anchoress, mystic." When the fire and the rose are one. You're here again ... Don't worry, I am attending to this piece.*

Morgan was beginning to think everything important in her family's life happened around the fire—only no one had ever mentioned it to her.

"Maybe your Aunt Aran gave Mr. Neary her father's watch." Reggie began slowly; he seemed to want to convey something without being intrusive.

"That's what some folks are thinkin', anyway. It might make sense to some, as some kind of a wedding gift to her spouse.... But nah, I've heard your Auntie Aran was a strong woman, how she herded cattle, made fences, hired out to thatch folks' roofs. It makes no sense she'd give a 'capper like Horsey a golden watch, does it now?"

He's getting at something, Morgan thought, but she was too afraid to ask.

She sat silent as the cab passed farms, thinking of her Aunt Aran. *A strong, big-boned woman. I remember Papa saying Aran was the smartest of the Kennys. Reggie's right. It would have been more in her character to wear the watch herself, or at least pass it to one of her sisters, Mary or Lily. Was Grady right, too? Did Horsey pilfer the watch to pay a bookie debt, but the sisters were too busy—and scared—to search him before they sewed him up? Now, that makes sense.*

They drove on. It seemed a very long two minutes of silence.

"They're checking in Dublin whether Neary was an IRA man. Ask anybody around here, and they'd tell you he was more of a tippler than a tough." Reggie shot a look into his mirror to check if that was too impertinent, but he found her fairly distracted. "Well, whatever happened, it was a long, long time ago, Miss Kenny."

He's sly enough, Morgan thought. *Maybe he's come to the same conclusion, but he's trying to assuage my fears.*

Morgan pondered the family's story of Horsey. Grandma Lily always told it this way.

"That year, Aunt Mary came home to live, 1950. Aran's husband, Emmet Neary, left for Dublin—or maybe it was London—looking for work. We kept expecting to hear from him—where he was working or where he was lodging—but we heard nothing and he never returned. After a number of years, he was simply declared dead. Aran's work and the farm supported them, God help 'em. Mary kept a little kitchen garden, pigs, and caffeen. And after Aran died, Mary worked both farms, but it was subsistence. Until Mr. Welch rented some acreage."

"It was your aunt's well that seemed to be the center of everything yesterday. All those flags brought that point home, did it not, Miss? The goods and the bodies. I mean, that was a complicated scene there." Reggie stared in the overhead mirror again, smiling.

"It seems ironic," Morgan said, "in the light of all this … crime, but my aunt always said it was the most blessed place on our land. The Lady's Well. When I was a child, she would bless me in its water whenever I arrived … and then again, when I went back to the States." Morgan fell back into silence. She didn't add one of her aunt's favorite lines: *"Sacrifice makes holy what we cannot."*

* * *

Newport was a town of about 450 souls. At the head of Main Street, every shop and business could be seen in one visual sweep. Although Westport, a few miles south, was an aesthetic heritage town, designed a century ago by the occupying English, Newport had her own fame—at least in Grandmother Lily's memory—for its courageous rebels, who stood until their deaths against the Redcoats in the Year of the French. Including the parish priest, who was hanged in front of his own church.

Everyone at Newport News, the magazine and tobacco shop, knew Minnie Mac. As Reggie testified, Minnie was a person in her own right. She was ahead of women's liberation—even the Protestant part, so they said.

Reggie opted to stay in Newport News, perusing the *Times* and the *Castlebar Dispatch*'s sensational issue on "THE MAYO MURDERS." What's more, he could have a fag here without compunction. Morgan would walk the block to Minnie's, and they'd meet up in an hour if all went well.

Minnie's place was an ordinary, tired, turn-of-the-century brick row house a minute from her husband's old church—at the back of the Old Newport House, just as Michael had said. Morgan had imagined Minnie Mac's garden would be an elegant, lavish, old English traditional one, like the house-and-garden magazines—but it was a mere postage stamp, with a few weedy hanging pots and a bedraggled climbing rose against the entrance. She had a feeling that age played a part in the scene's sad quality.

Maybe Minnies's place felt the neglect of her family, just like Mary's. It appeared Minnie Mac was mostly on her own. Maybe she was always the "outsider," being an opinionated Scot, a Protestant, and a widow. Aunt Mary was the consummate outsider, too—but maybe she made herself one, because she had too many secrets.

"Yes?" the thin voice responded to the bell. The door cracked an inch.

"I am Morgan Kenny of Castlebar, come to see Mrs. MacCahill."

The formal presentation flowed from an old convent reflex. But it was just the right tone for Minnie to open the door wide.

"Kenny? Oh, yes. You've come for the flies."

"Sorry?" Morgan spoke back. "Mrs. MacCahill?"

"Yes, Mary Kenny?"

Morgan's heart sank.

"It's Morgan Kenny, Mary's great-niece. I'm sorry to bring you some bad news about Mary Kenny."

"Not bad news."

"Miss Kenny died a few days back."

"Oh? I thought she died long ago." She sounded puzzled. She opened the door and herself to Morgan—fresh visitors were at a premium.

Minnie Mac was a real talker. She'd slowed down over the years, but was still a contender the like of which an American like Morgan had never seen.

After rambling through Scottish nobility bloodlines, Scottish Celtic place names in Ireland, and the fate of the Church of Ireland, Minnie Mac let Morgan steer her back to her deceased husband Finegas and his Catholic friend Father Sean O'Toole.

"Such a tragic thing about Father Jack," Minnie mused on a long-gone life.

I knew it. "Sean" turned into the English, "Jack" … the last words of Mary.

"My husband and he were the best of friends, in spite of the Catholic church's pressure. How Finn missed him. He was so young." A pause. Minnie stared at a picture of Finegas, vested in long white garments, standing before his church at Old Newport House, a miniature stone medieval church. "We were all young."

She walked into the den, motioning Morgan to follow. A corner of the brown study was a sanctuary devoted to "Finn's delights." His favorite fishing rod was mounted over a shadowbox of ornate, rainbow-colored flies sewn to burlap. Hot pink, fuchsia, lime green, bright yellow feathers beautifully crafted of wire and thread. Each was an intricate work of art, comparable to fine jewelry.

"Yes, they are beautiful. If you could have known Finn, you'd say he was an artist. An artist with a great sense of humor. Everything he did was art. Fishing was his art. 'Soul making,' he called it. 'You don't have to go to church to make soul,' he'd say. Making art, making love, making soul is the same thing, isn't it?" The older woman looked with longing on the colorful wall, gazing as if upon an icon of her heart's worship.

Morgan caught Finn's humor displayed next to the flies, a poster reading: "Some go to church and think about fishing—Others go fishing and think about God."

"Here's a picture of Finn and Jack fishing at Delphi Estate in 1945." The framed photo showed a shadowy silhouette of two fishermen standing in a boat at sunset. Neither face was discernible. Behind them, the massive fireball of the sun melted into the silvery river. The breathtaking scope of nature rendered the two men mere objects, victims of a much larger plan. It was the only photo of Finn and a friend on the wall.

"Finn made each fly himself," Minnie purred. "Miss Kenny, what an opportunity you have afforded me." She took the hanging masterpiece from the wall. She stretched out her offering to Morgan.

"Here, please. Please take the ones you like. Ecclesiastes does say, 'There is a time for everything under heaven, a time to gather and a time to give away.' My time now is to 'give away.'"

Morgan chose two flies. One for herself and one for Michael, her partner in the quest.

"You know, that is exactly the kind of gesture Finn would have made. He simply was a 'giver.' Father Jack used to come on Saturday nights to make communion bread with me and Finn."

"He made his own altar bread?" Morgan felt she would have liked Finn.

"I suppose we could have purchased those little wafers, but Finn felt those things were soulless. 'They're cardboard,' he'd say. 'We have to put our consciousness—man's soul—into this.' Jack often took part in our Saturday-night altar-bread baking. I think that big Catholic rectory was very lonely on Saturday nights."

Morgan tried to steer her back to Mary.

"You said you knew my Aunt Mary?"

"Yes. Well, no, I didn't really *know* her. Father Jack spoke of her often. I think she might have come with him to some Saturday-night baking. He definitely cared for Mary."

Minnie put her hand on Morgan's.

"We spoke to him thoroughly. He took much counsel from Finn about all this. Mary was, after all, his housekeeper, and not schooled. She could not disguise her class," Minnie sighed. "There were difficulties all the way around. Jack was thinking of coming into the Church of Ireland, to save his priesthood, that is. Finegas told him that was the only option. 'The Catholic church does not have a corner on priesthood!' he'd often said.

"But Jack's bishop was not going to let him go. There was going to be a fight over this, Jack said. They were furious, slanderous! On the other hand, we were not so sure of our own bishop, either. I mean, politically, His Grace didn't want to anger the Catholic Archbishop of Mayo over a love-struck priest. Obviously, no church on *our side* could be gotten for Father Jack in this part of Ireland. Archbishop McCaskill was a powerful figure. Powerful and stubborn."

"Could they have survived? Financially, I mean, without a parish?" Morgan was all the way in now.

"They could have if they'd have gotten the O'Tooles' support. But there was none there. Nor anywhere. Those times were ..." She stared out the window musing. "If only it had been later."

She spoke so well, Morgan thought. *No doubt Minnie and Finn had hashed and rehashed Jack and Mary's options.*

"Father Jack was a very popular priest. He would have lost most all his friends. It would have been the end for him here. The O'Tooles of Clifden have money, but can you imagine the sting of it?"

"You said Finn was a 'giver.' Was Father Jack a 'giver,' too?" Morgan had to be careful that she did not offend.

With a sigh, Minnie lowered herself slowly into a soft, flower-covered chair.

"Finn always said the reason Jack O'Toole made such a great fly-fisherman was because he understood its essence."

"Its essence?" Morgan could feel a slight flutter of her heart.

"Yes."

"What is that?"

"Deception," Minnie Mac said flatly. Morgan was taken aback.

"Fly-fishing, after all, is a lie. You have to fool the fish into thinking he's going after a real fly."

"And Father O'Toole?"

"Well, that's where the beautiful fly comes in. The fly has to imitate an insect or a minnow to attract the fish—and Father Jack was a beautiful fly. He attracted a lot of people to his church." She winked. "He also had a lot of young girls fooled into thinking he was the salmon of knowledge! He let them take a nibble."

"My aunt, too?" Morgan asked, worried. Even though everyone was dead, they were feeling very much alive in this moment.

"The odds say, 'aye.'" Minnie Mac minced no words. You knew exactly what she thought of this whole affair.

Morgan felt she was tiring Minnie out, but she knew Minnie had more. She had to press a bit, a last chance to find out the "more."

"My great-aunt had a funeral card of Father O'Toole in her belongings. She kept it all these years."

"You know, every culture, in its myths, finds its own way of expressing deep wisdom. For much of the world, it's in the image of the dragon. Something dangerous, eh? But for us Celts, wisdom must be caught ... as in the sacred fish. With Father Jack, I'm afraid, some were wiser after tasting that fish—but some got burned."

"I'm sorry I'm pressing you to remember things of so long ago, but you are the only person who knew the two of them ... you are the last one living."

Minnie Mac was looking back. Wistful eyes told their own story. "It's all right. I've been working on my memoirs rather piecemeal, and I'd almost forgotten this chapter with Father Jack. I remember that special occasion quite clearly. The marriage! The utter shock of it." She closed her eyes and winced.

"The marriage?" Morgan was fearful.

"Yes. Suddenly, Finn said, 'Things have changed. There'll be no more discussions with Father Jack.' We would have the ceremony at St. A's. He wanted me to be their witness. Finegas had the documents, too. I remember this in particular, because I laid out his new white vestments right next to them. But at the appointed hour, Father Jack and Mary did not show up.

"We waited and waited. I think the bishops—the Catholic Archbishop and Jack's pastor—told him they were going to throw him out. Well, that's the sad part, isn't it? The marriage was aborted."

They were both silent for a moment, the word "aborted" hanging in the air.

"That whole day we thought maybe Jack had changed his mind. The pressure was so great ..."

"Our family didn't know," Morgan breathed. "My great-aunt's secret went to the grave with her, Mrs. Minnie."

Morgan felt Minnie's conflict about this, even after all these years. She felt her own conflict regarding her aunt's long silence as well.

The old woman seemed to have it all at her fingertips now. Memory's lens was washed clean in the telling.

"But we will never really know, my dear."

"Why? Did Father Jack never reveal the reason for their not coming?" Morgan sat at the end of her chair.

"That was not the only shock. We never saw him again." She shook her head. "Such a tragedy, and in the prime of life."

"What do you mean, 'tragedy'?"

"Why, the fire." Minnie looked oddly at Morgan, wondering why she didn't know something so seminal to Mayo's history. "The cathedral … Father Jack and Father McGinty died in the fire."

"You mean the fire was on the same day when the wedding was supposed to be?"

"Well, yes. It began in the middle of the night; the fire raged all the night. There was a storm. Many houses were hit by lightning."

Morgan shook her head in disbelief. *Why have I never heard of this from anyone before today?*

"I don't remember hearing what happened to Mary after the fire. I hoped all would be well. Finn … Finn was devastated by the loss of Jack, devastated. I canna' tell you how often I looked in that study and found him with his head in his hands …"

Minnie Mac was obviously strained by the visit. Morgan could feel her heaviness.

"He always said, 'If Jacko hadn't died in the fire, they'd have transferred him north, anyway.' Of course, the church—and the O'Tooles—probably preferred him dead to wed!" Minnie almost snarled.

"That may have been true back then," Morgan whispered.

"Come now," Minnie spoke with bitter alacrity, "the bishops are still that way! Even though the church turns faithful priests into drunkards and keeps lecherous ones among lambs, Rome flies above it all! Or rather, lies about it all!"

Minnie's face softened for a moment. "They're gone now. My Finn never had another friend like Jack again." She sounded sad and protective, like the mother of a young son.

Morgan put her two flies in her purse and quickly assessed that, even though she had almost touched the third rail, it was all right to give Minnie a small hug. She did.

Reggie was standing next to the cab. He ran around and opened the door.

"Well, how did it all go? Isn't she an interesting lady?"

"Oh, yes," Morgan said vaguely.

He looked closer at Morgan's strained face. "Are you all right, Miss Kenny?"

"Yes, yes, I'm all right. A bit confused is all."

Morgan needed time to grasp this last piece of the puzzle, this enormous piece in Mary's life.

Mary was about to marry the local parish priest, a handsome, popular guy with community status—and she an ordinary housekeeper. It seems discordant, or at least that's what Minnie Mac was trying to tell me. That was what Finn was trying to tell O'Toole, too.

Something pressed them to attempt marriage anyway. What?

But then, why didn't they show up? Somebody besides Father Finn must have gotten to O'Toole. Then the fire.

Morgan wished she could share this new piece about the essence of fly-fishing with Grady. He would have loved Minnie Mac's fish stories. For the moment, though, she'd have to settle for a chat and a snack with Michael. She was beginning to feel some of the pain they'd caused—Mary and Jack.

18

Saying Good-Bye

"Rosie New Girl," the Timmons's new housemaid for the B&B, had neither uniform nor manners. She shuffled to the front door with scone dough still stuck to her fingers, lifted the special delivery letter with her "good" hand, and stuck it in her apron pocket. Leaving a faint flour trail on the polished hallway floor, she sauntered back to the kitchen to pull her pastry out of the oven and then hung up the apron.

In another part of the house, an insistent knock at her door brought Morgan back to this world.

"Hey, Morgan! Miss!"

It was Michael, telling her Mrs. Timmons was having a proper "fry-up" to send her back to the States. He'd be back for her luggage in fifteen minutes, at eight o'clock.

Morgan sat upright in bed.

"Any messages? Any tea?" No answer. Michael was already whistling down the back stairwell.

She was hoping for a "valentine" from Grady, but he was so busy—

probably on a dig. Or, as Reggie said yesterday, "Still workin' on the stiff from outside the well."

She searched her purple-flowered wallpaper for better answers. She was sad to say she'd have to put Grady in the category of "summer romance." Did she believe in miracles? Yes. In fact, she had come to rely on them. "All would be well," and she'd dreamed it true.

In the shower, sadness flooded her—what her father would have called "an Irish melancholy" at having to leave Ireland, Mayo, Timmons', even her Purple Bower. She began to let down. Tears welled up. At this sentimental moment, Timmons was as much home as her old convent—or her parents' house—ever was. Whoever said things don't have soul? This ordinary B&B room had taken on the semblance of the heritage home she felt she'd never had. It seemed these ordinary people had more interest in her than her own parents had. She had lots of roots in her life, but few connections.

She looked out the back window to Miss Goodchilde Walsh's garden deck. Miss Walsh, her long white hair flowing down her back, was on her veranda in a pink kimono, watering pots and pots of primroses—yellow, orange, purple. The parasol of colors relieved some of Morgan's blue mood. *Thank God, spring doesn't have to be solved.* Seeing Goodchilde Walsh stirred the dream she'd had the other night at Grady's. *Julian said, "The Mages found the good Christ Child, didn't they?"* How Goodchilde Walsh fit in, Morgan didn't know.

What she did know was that she was going home, with everything still up in the air.

She would have to let go of the investigation about Mary. Mayo, the County, would have to follow up with the Grailside people on the body and burial stuff. F. X. Mahoney and Grady would figure out the fifty-year-old homicide, Horsey. *Actually, Grady's got it put together already. And the soldier outside the well, well, they'll all have to deal with the Brits, if that follows Grady's theory of the Mayo Rebellion. And I'll have to let Padraig deal with any new land developments; he's a hands-on guy anyway.*

I'm good at letting go, she anguished. *Maybe that's my cover for not having to achieve much in life. Not being possessive was rewarded in the convent. Taking hold, that's hard.* The first example was letting good men and good jobs slip through her fingers, while others made the catch. *Making decisions is hard, too. If I'd had the chance, Grady could have been an exception. But I have to admit, I can't run after him from the other side of the Atlantic.*

She'd have to let go of him, too. Or maybe he'd done that already. No word.

Minnie Mac's revelations were even more confusing than the green box. *Why didn't Mary and Jack show up for the wedding? I have another hunch about that, but I'll have to get that piece of the puzzle from Winnie.*

She took one last look around the Purple Bower to make sure she had everything. Opened the flaking green box to take one more wistful glance at Aunt Mary as the Girl with a Pearl Earring.

You had a lot more to you than I thought, she told the presence in the photo. Then she wrapped the whole flaking box in a Timmons' Teatime towel and set it in the bottom of her suitcase.

Breakfast was served in the Timmons's private blue dining room, in honor of Morgan's departure. The usual suspects were seated 'round a massive oak table laden with old Waterford and filled with Mrs. Timmons's specialties—extra portions of Morgan's favorites, black pudding, buttered brown bread, and hot berry scones.

Even Mr. Timmons, often thought to be a fiction, showed up smiling and frail, looking kindly on a plate of rashers.

"God save all here," he said, standing heroically at the threshold.

Mrs. Timmons cheerfully bossed the new servant girl, Rosie, who was about fourteen and was ladling spoons-full of porridge from a black kettle, her bobby socks rolled down to her ankles. Michael, Reggie, Padraig, and—to Morgan's surprise—Miss Goodchilde Walsh. And Liam Naughton, sitting in for Old Mrs. Naughton. A full circle of friends awaited her, just like a real family farewell. Only Grady was lacking, but he was in Dublin that day. Wasn't he?

Mr. Timmons said a mythic grace over the food:

"O Jesu, King of the poor, Thou who wert sorely subdued under the ban of the wicked, hast become victorious in the blood of the Lamb. This house gives Thee thanks. Amen."

He seemed an eloquent actor in the final act of the American girl's play. As the hot tea went around, a pile of small gifts was assembled next to Morgan's plate, with Mrs. Timmons handing her a neatly typed recipe for her "Do It by Memory" Brown Bread.

2 cups buttermilk
2 cups stone-ground whole wheat meal

2 cups rough flour (1 cup oats, ½ cup wheat germ, ½ cup white flour) and more on the board
2 tsp. brown sugar
2 tsp. salt
2 tsp. cream of tartar mixed with soda
2x2 tbs. butter

Knead lightly, form into round loaf, bake for 1 hour or more in a hot oven of 400° F. Cool. Lather with butter.

A farewell card from Padraig held a silver Claddagh necklace, the card's inscription telling her he'd be coming into New York the following year, signed, "Affectionately, P. M." He clasped the necklace onto Morgan, his hands trembling. Morgan gave him a hug.

Liam, the dear, shabby country boy, stood and handed Morgan a faded brownish tintype of two laughing teenage girls coming up from the surf on a beach at Achill Island. "Mary Kenny and me, 1938," it read in Mam Naughton's shaky script. "God speed ye, Naughtons."

"Thank your grandma, Liam." Morgan was glad to have one playful picture of Mary.

"I am glad that Mary Kenny and Mrs. Naughton had their good times," put in Mrs. Timmons.

Michael's gift, in a little white box, brought Morgan to tears. It contained a dime-store family crest key ring, imprinted: "KENNY," with three hoops and a fleur-de-lis on a blue-and-yellow divided field. The motto: "TENEAT LUCEAT FLOREAT"—"May it hold, shine, and flourish"—"VI VIRTURE ET VALORE"—"by virtue and valor."

Morgan looked at Michael. He received her affection, gratitude, and sisterly pride. He held back his own tears, too.

"Everyone knows Michael has been the best friend a Yank could have," Morgan announced. "We've had a genuine adventure together. I promise to be back for your college vacation." Raising her orange juice, she toasted him: "To Michael and Julian, my two guardian angels. And to Prudence Timmons and all of you—my Irish family."

"Who's Julian?" Mrs. Timmons whispered to Michael.

He was about to give the whole truth, about how Julian was an English mystic who was a soul-compass directing Morgan to just the right places and conclusions about her aunt's life—but then he thought better of it.

"Her patron saint," he whispered back.

Miss Goodchilde Walsh just sat there, looking like it was her cake and her birthday. She seemed to be giving a regent's approval to the whole thing, smiling vaguely, enjoying the breakfast and not requiring formal exchange.

A few inquired as to Morgan's aunt—careful to leave out the problem at the well—and what Morgan would be doing when she got home. She said her hospital employment in the States was on hold, due to a nursing strike. But this was a question she worried about: What *would* she be doing?

As the breakfast wound down, Morgan leaned over to Padraig. "Will you please sit a moment with me and Miss Goodchilde Walsh? I have to ask her about the land, and I need a legal witness to the conversation."

Padraig nodded, and the two moved Miss Goodchilde seamlessly into the parlor. Her maid observed her leave, but did not absent her post in the dining room. Flanked by the two younger people, Miss Goodchilde Walsh felt important.

To Padraig's chagrin, Michael followed them and sat down next to Miss Goodchilde Walsh.

Morgan looks particularly attractive this morning, Padraig thought, *in her high black riding boots*. And his Claddagh necklace stood out on her exquisitely simple gray linen shift, which quietly matched her gray-blonde hair done in a soft braid.

Today, Michael thought, *she looks a little famous*, and he felt she was something more than a friend—at least a mentor.

"Miss Goodchilde, do you remember me, Morgan Kenny? My land is next to your cousin, Angus Welch. Do you remember when I made a visit to your home last week? We talked about the great fire."

"Oh yes. I was there. I saw it. My father planted the rose garden there in 1905. They always had roses on the altar."

"Do you remember you told me that you saw them bury my Aunt Mary? Do you remember that?"

Smiling, Goodchilde Walsh nodded her head. "Of course, I remember Mary Kenny." Sitting next to Michael, she seemed small, like a colorful little bird.

Michael took her by the hand and said to her, "It's okay. Tell them where they buried her. Angus is dead now. And Barbara's moved to the States. No one will know." He seemed to have won Miss Goodchilde's confidence long before.

She covered their hands with her right hand and spoke directly to him as though the other two weren't there.

"I saw them. They buried her in the Lady's Well at the Kennys' place. Angus told me to wait in the truck, but I couldn't."

"Why couldn't you wait?" Michael asked gently.

"It was dark out. Angus was supposed to take me right home. He said he had to pick up something over by the well. So he left me out on the road. He knew it was a place of the *siogi*. And he knew I was afraid out there. One time he told me old Mrs. Kenny was a *cailleach* and she'd put the 'curse of the crows' on me if ever I played with her daughter Mary. When I saw Mary and Aran pushing the cart, I had to follow. They weren't afraid of *siogi*. It was Angus's fault, because he didn't come back."

"What was in the cart, Miss Goodchilde?" Michael coaxed.

She delayed. Padraig was about to ask her a question, but Morgan touched his hand to stop him. She thought Michael was doing just fine, and she didn't want to scare Goodchilde, not now.

"A big bag." The small voice was that of a young girl, fifty years past.

"Tell them what was in the bag, Miss Goodchilde," Michael pressed.

"They threw the bag in the well. Aran prayed in Irish on it, though. 'Get back in the truck, you bad girl!' Angus told me—but he and Seamus stayed and pulled the big bag out again. I was there. I saw him cut open the bag."

"You knew who was in the bag, didn't you?" Michael coddled her. Morgan felt he genuinely liked the old lady.

"Oh, you know who it was, Michael." Miss Walsh liked the attention.

"I know, but tell Morgan."

"Aran's husband, Mishter Horsey."

"Who was Horsey?" Padraig had to be sure.

"Mishter Emmet Neary, sir."

Padraig pressed her: "And Mary? Where was Mary Kenny?"

"Mary was in the fire with Father O'Toole."

"Oh, my God," Morgan gasped, startled by the horrific image.

"Then what happened?" Michael patted Goodchilde's hand to continue.

"We went home, and Angus told me never, never to tell anyone or my friends would hang."

Michael smiled at Miss Goodchilde Walsh and led her back to the dining room.

Reggie broke into the parlor to announce that the time of departure was pressing closure to the familial scene.

"I'm so sorry, Padraig," Morgan began. "I thought we were going to get her to speak about the land. I didn't think she knew anything about the murder of Horsey Neary. I don't know, perhaps this was better, really." She paused for a moment to swallow, maybe even to swallow the story. "Goodchilde seems to have been a real witness to the disposal of Emmet Neary's body. She saw my aunts in the cover-up, even if she didn't see the murder."

Padraig took out his pipe and began fidgeting with it as though he were going to fill it, but then saw the sign about no smoking; he seemed almost hampered in speaking without it. "Obviously, Miss Goodchilde has some things mixed up. I don't think she even knew about the bodies being dredged up yesterday, either."

"She still puts the action at the Lady's Well," said Michael, rejoining them.

"Oh my God, fifty years ago—she was there." Morgan put her hand to her mouth. "She was sitting in the truck, and she saw them all pass her. That's what she meant by 'I saw them bury Mary.' She saw them bury Emmet Neary." Morgan gulped air. "He was in the bag, not Mary."

"Yeah, Goodchilde's mix-up could be existential ... like all of them were jumbled, but all of them went together, existentially." Michael was throwing in notes from his latest psych class.

Padraig cut in. "Yes, maybe the priest's preferences went beyond Goodchilde's moral sensibilities. Thus, the offending priest must pay for his sins, so he dies in the fire, obviously her idea of God's justice, and she throws in Mary Kenny for good measure. For Miss Walsh, maybe that's tantamount to hell. Who knows? That mix-up makes perfect sense." He lifted his unlit pipe. "*And* I'll bet my last quid that this was the time and the place Angus Welch cut the deal on the land with your aunts—at the well, with Miss Walsh crying to go home. And all of this Walsh-Welch material is blarney. Morgan, they were damned well at it with the IRA!"

"The thing about it is," Michael put in, "if you erase the Walsh-Welch Brit history thing, you've wrecked Welch's motive for doin' all this blackmail to the Kennys, yeah? We know about a fifty-year-old homicide, but we still don't know where your aunt is."

Reggie was on the car horn, wanting to get going to the airport. Morgan was torn.

Padraig felt good about the conclusion, but he hadn't noticed how Morgan was taking it. Morgan's mind felt like a cartoon. All the words seem to jiggle into a brain slot, swirl, gurgle a bit, and then came out ... bingo.

"For the love of God," she managed, "what she's sayin' is that Aran and Mary killed him and sewed him up in the bag. They were the ones pushing him in the cart to dump him in the well when Angus caught them in the woods, because he and Seamus were in the process of hiding some IRA contraband. Or dumping someone else, for all we know."

"She sees Angus pull the bag out of the well," Padraig took up the tale. "Yes, the rest of the story falls into place. Welch blackmails the two sisters. And he can still use the land as a 'burial ground' for his IRA loot. Isn't that what Miss Goodchilde is saying, in her own odd way?" Padraig was a bit winded, but felt he'd got it right.

Morgan was shaking. She felt as though she had crawled out of a big, dark hole.

Padraig was nodding.

"Maybe Aran and Mary had to agree to the land sale to shut up Welch," Michael offered.

"Blackmail sounds right to me," Padraig said. "We've gone through this before, I know, but this is the first time I find a compelling reason for them making such a deal at all with Welch."

Morgan said, "But he really didn't need their land."

"Of course he did. You have to consider the obvious, Morgan. He was hiding his stolen stuff all over Aran and Mary's property. Maybe the police had been keeping an eye on *his* land and *his* house all the time."

"I don't think the land was ever the point," Morgan countered. "Keeping silence about the IRA's activities at the well, that was the point."

Padraig was firm. "The IRA had been disposing of their own loot, apparently for a goodly time, among the *cailleacha* gifts. We agree on this. The blackmail was the serendipitous opportunity, when they saw Mary and Aran with the bag."

"Yeah, that's probably one of the reasons," Michael said, "but maybe there is a deeper 'soul reason.' That's what psychologists would say. We have reasons we do things that we can't explain even to ourselves. Anyway, maybe some of it has to do with the other guy who was murdered. I mean, it is synchronistic, isn't it? That there's another dead guy next to the well?"

Reggie came in, cap in hand, saying Morgan was sacrificing her "duty-free time" at Shannon.

"Morgan, Michael, I'll have to let the inspector know about some of this conjecturing." Padraig sounded a little desperate.

"Padraig, wait. Wait a few hours, until I'm on my plane. He'd keep me here for days with questions."

Reggie was in front of his cab, fidgeting and smoking a butt. Morgan jumped in and motioned Michael to come to the window.

"Michael, this is for you, buddy." She pressed a Marlboro box into his hands. It contained one of Finn's salmon-and-lime-colored flies and a wad of rolled-up twenty-dollar bills.

He responded, "Listen, I'm takin' you to Shannon, Morgan. We've got too much to process for trans-Atlantic phone calls. The Green Dino's full of petrol—come on, now."

Morgan made an "I'm sorry" face to Reggie and climbed out of the cab.

Reggie looked disappointed. He hadn't planned on liking a Yank or caring whether rich people worked out their losses, but this time with Morgan and the adventure all about her, something caught him. Soul-wise, it might have been Morgan's likeness to his daughter. Something ... Of course, he couldn't admit the obvious.

"Let's roll," Morgan smiled at Michael.

As Mrs. Timmons and Rosie New Girl cleaned up the morning dishes, they found Grady's letter to Morgan on the floor beneath the apron.

"From the University College, Dublin, no less. It's probably a farewell note from Grady. Maybe we should open it 'just in case.'"

"In case what?" Rosie was still innocent.

Prudence Timmons, being prudent, ripped open the letter and read. She smiled and put it in her pocket.

"That Kenny girl must have the luck of the Irish, landin' a lad like Grady and havin' him send her off at Aer Lingus. I'll bet he'll be bringin' roses, too. Well, all's well that ends well."

from the Gundestrup Cauldron

19
Conversations Before Closing

Michael and Morgan waved good-bye to Castlebar and Timmons' Teatime. The Green Dinosaur roared, and they were off to Shannon Airport on the Newport Road, by way of the Atlantic Coast.

"I know this is going to take longer," Morgan admitted, "but it's such a beautiful drive on a good day. I'd like to see Winnie Shanahan in Connemara, to ask her a few questions about the green box."

Morgan hadn't quite left the spirit of the Timmons's sitting room.

"Michael, I'm not sure I know what you mean when you talk about 'the Walsh-Welch Brit history thing' being the 'unseen motive' for Angus Welch blackmailing my aunts. That's a mouthful."

"Okay, okay. What I mean is that Angus Welch jumps at the opportunity to blackmail your aunts, doesn't he? Because, lucky for him, he can cover his robbery activities in the woods with Seamus when he sees the sisters trying to get rid of something. Which we now know is Horsey. So, Welch can accuse the aunties and distract them from what *he's* doing with all these stolen things. Okay, that's what's on the surface. Welch's MO is to put the squeeze on whomever.

"But the subliminal thing, the hidden motive—I mean, hidden even from himself—is synchronously keyed to the other dead guy, on the outside of the well. The bloke who's been in the sod for over a hundred years! Do you get it? Welch may not even know about the dude!"

Michael was only going forty miles an hour, but on these coastal roads, it felt like he was doing eighty.

"Probably the guy was buried when it still was the Walsh Estate, back in the seventeenth or eighteenth century, I'll bet. I'll bet twenty punt! Welch's mind-set has to go all the way back then. The Brits gave Irish lands as gifts to their military, for serving in their wars—even your American Revolution. The point is, the Brits had stolen that land from the Walshes, even though they became Protestants—Welches—to save it. I think Angus Welch always felt it was still his land. To Goodchilde, too, this was all Walsh land. They were lairds of the Lady's Well and a whole lot more, not those raggedy tenant farmers, the Kennys! The dead guy is merely the symbol of the larger split."

"Now you've lost me. What split?"

"Yeah, England and Ireland, Catholic and Protestant, the landed and the tenants. The punch line is: We were all tenants in our own country! I'll bet Grady is finding out right now in Dublin that this guy, the one outside the well, was somebody in the English Army who took away the Walsh's lands. That's my hunch.

"Maybe, just maybe, one of the Walshes-turned-Welches did him in. Maybe he was some kind of a crown bailiff during famine times, and they didn't appreciate the gesture. That would have been Angus's great-great-grandfather. Do you feel the reflex?"

"Michael, I think you've got something there. Tell me more about your theory of synchronicity." Morgan was beginning to think Michael should go on in psychology.

"Miss Kenny, this is a no-brainer. It's *chronos*. It's the timing. Two bodies are being dug up at the same time, one in the well and one outside the well. On the surface, they don't seem to be related. They may be hundreds of years apart, but somewhere—in heaven?—they are linked." Michael is ready for another long-winded explanation, but they have arrived.

"Newport. Let me take you past the church where the Brits hung Father Manus Sweeney, who sided with the Irish rebels in 1798."

Michael slowed the Green Dinosaur and turned the corner of a prim, fenced churchyard with a man-size cross standing in it.

"Tell me more about this rebellion, what you call the Year of the French."

For the next ten minutes, Michael gave her a history lesson on the Year of the French, the annexation of Irish lands, and Mayo's two-century-old inferiority complex.

"Michael, I did find Minnie Mac. Reggie called her a 'corker,' and indeed she is. Actually, she lives across the street, right down there." Morgan pointed out the window. "Oak Park Street, near her old parish—St. A's, in back of Old Newport House. Her husband, Father Finn, is no longer 'ticking,' as you say, but I did get you one of his hand-tied flies. What was troubling is that to hear her tell it, O'Toole may have been a rake."

"A what?" Michael was too young for the term "rake." By the time Morgan finished telling him Minnie's take on the whole Mary-Jack thing, he was fairly well silenced.

"Well, what do you think?" Morgan asked gingerly. His silence scared her a bit.

"I think it changes everything," Michael said stoically.

"Clew Bay," he pointed out the window at a sixteenth-century castle, with its keep in ruins in the water. "Now we're passing the great pirate queen Gracie O'Malley's castle. Yes, yes, she kept Queen Elizabeth's pirates at bay for a few years. Newport-Westport Road is full of history, too."

The two sped down the newly constructed road that tilted slightly to the sea. Morgan could taste the salt of it today. *Does that portend a storm?*

* * *

Morgan lifted the knocker and looked through the window in the front door.

Winnie had added a candle before the Madonna painting hanging in her hallway. It was lit. *So the painting has become a prayer icon for her.* Morgan supposed, now that she knew more about the painting's origins, that she could see a resemblance to other Leonardos—especially the face of the Madonna. *Seems unfinished. It's supposed to be* The Madonna of the Yarnwinder, *but the Holy Child just looks like he's holding a cross. Guess I'm not much of a knitter.*

Well, Winnie should be set for life and beyond with this piece. Morgan felt a deep satisfaction that she could do a favor for a woman who had been so kind to her aunt.

Winnie appeared.

Morgan put the green metal box on the kitchen table. Michael took up a position near the fireplace, somewhat like the recorder of note.

"I've been studying this box since you gave it to me, Winnie, and it has led me to a very different Aunt Mary than the one I knew as a child coming to Ireland." Morgan spoke stiffly.

Winnie's reaction was one of worry.

"It's as though each object in the box is a clue to a secret life, a double life, as it were. As I decode each one, it seems to open up another mysterious facet of her life story."

"Does it, now?" Mrs. Shanahan wiped her hands on a towel. "I don't know what you mean exactly."

"For instance, these certificates of birth." Morgan held up the two blue cards. "They revealed that both Aran and Mary had different names. Aran's name on them was Arianhood, and Mary's was Meredith."

"Odd. But they are lovely," mused Winnie. "I wonder why she didn't use it?"

"That was my question. Maybe these names were considered too 'old religion' by the local priest—or by their own father."

"They're not Irish names. Maybe Welsh?" Winnie was listening.

"For sure. They're names from Arthurian lore, a friend tells me. Well, the old stuff, the really old Welsh stuff, is Celtic myth anyway. But the point is, the choice seems deliberate."

"Do you mean English?" Winnie looked like she didn't know where this was going.

"Arthur of the Pendragon sounds like the Welsh to me," Morgan said, "but the English wrote big Christian stories about those Arthur tales."

"So these are pagan names, from pagan versions of the grail stories?" Winnie caught it.

"You're a fast study, Winnie. It has taken me some time to figure out where they came from and why."

Winnie sensed that Morgan was different today. Something seemed to be pressing her.

"These records tell me there was purpose in their names. In Arthur's tales, these pagan names belonged to 'maidens at the well.' Like priestesses. Camelot and the land had miraculous powers—*if* the maidens kept up their duties of guarding the well."

"Oh yes," Winnie sighed. "That is interesting. Mary always talked about 'the duty of the well' in her family, how she and Aran were its guardians."

"Guardians. Exactly. I think their mother gave them those names so they would guard the well, the center of her old religion."

"But from whom, I wonder." Winnie seemed to be scanning her mind for hints.

"I don't know if they guarded it from anyone in particular. This may all sound kooky now, but they must have believed that the well was the source of their mother's healing power—and that of the other *cailleacha*. Maybe even Mary's?" Morgan left this hypothesis up in the air. Winnie looked stumped.

"I never heard Mary talkin' about any power." Winnie sat down at the table, a bit overwhelmed.

"They were supposed to use the well for inspiration and a place of transport to the Other Side, my friend Grady tells me."

"Who do you mean by *they?*" Winnie asked.

"Oh, sorry. The wise women, of course." Morgan was so excited about her own theory of the well, she had almost lost Winnie. "The *cailleacha*. Do you see what I mean? The pagans also used the well. It was the precursor to the baptismal font."

"So you are talkin' about the really old times, before the coming of Patrick himself." Winnie was tracking slowly.

"Yes, yes. Back then, you had to go through some kind of a ceremony or a ritual to get to the Other World. The well was the initiation chamber for admittance into the Other World."

"Wait a second. I've got a picture of this in an Irish myth book."

Winnie found her old book and opened to a picture of the famous Gundestrup cauldron found in a Danish bog, said to be a Celtic relic from the Iron Age.

This isn't like the bog sacrifice Michael was talking about when the Lady's Well was being excavated. Morgan was thinking ahead.

In the depiction on the cauldron, a man, probably a soldier, was being immersed headfirst into a deep cauldron or *graal* by a priestess or a goddess. The gesture was clear: death would ensue. But the meaning was ambiguous. Why was this being done?

Morgan was a little stunned that this centuries-old *graal* pictured what might have happened to Emmet Neary.

"Was the man being drowned? Killed as a human sacrifice? Or was he being initiated into eternal life, in the hopes that he would be renewed or resurrected?" she asked.

Winnie looked like a fourth-grader who didn't have the answer.

"Well, Winnie," Morgan continued, "which do you think it was?"

"You really want me to answer that? Okay, I think both are right. I think the guy is being baptized the way the pagans did it. They thought he was going to come out alive on the Other Side. Isn't that what we say about baptism—it's the ticket that gets us into heaven? Just one thing, though; in this picture, they're *killin'* him on this side."

"Thank you, Winnie. I value that. I think the same. I think the guy went into the cauldron so that he could have a new life on the Other Side."

The intensity between them subsided. Morgan was so tightly wound that she had made Winnie uncomfortable. Both took a breath and a draft of tea.

"From some of the things Mary said, I always wondered if she had been a *cailleach* herself." Morgan spoke softly. "Did she ever give you that impression?"

"Oh, there were some signs. She cursed a swarm of black flies one time and turned them into honeybees. She had the respect of the residents, because she had no fear of the banshee or the pooka, nor anything else for that matter. Sure, she had the gift of blessings and curses. You know, she still could do all that in Irish, and it seemed the right thing in Irish, you know." Winnie's eyes mellowed, thinking on times past. "On the other hand, she had total devotion to our Lady. She always said her beads—and prayed them on her knees, mind you."

Winnie slowed to consider her next words.

"If that be true, that she would be priestess of the well, then God knows she would be hiding her old-time name and the works of her mother from the wrath of the priests."

"The priests don't have the same sway anymore, Winnie."

It quickly crossed Morgan's mind whether to show her the funeral card of Father Sean O'Toole, the "Jack" to whom Mary called out in her last hour in Winnie's presence at Grailside. She saw how stirred Winnie became about the *cailleach* matter. Perhaps Morgan had opened too much. Despite Winnie's traditional view of religion, there seemed to be room for a wise woman or two. Nevertheless, Morgan decided not to question a cherished memory of Mary by bringing in O'Toole and a heap of questions.

With some vigor to her voice, Winnie said, "To end it for you, Morgan, I don't think your auntie was any healer at all, at all. I think Mary Kenny inherited a lot of the old ways of her mother, just like she knew the songs and the curses in the old Irish. She was gifted, yes, but she was not a wise woman in the sense they're speakin' about it nowadays."

Morgan got up and gave Winnie a brief embrace. There was no doubt, Winnie had felt uncomfortable in the exchange—not unlike a priest divulging scraps of a confession.

Morgan opened the green box, gently dislodged a dirty envelope from the black tea, and gave it to Winnie. On the back of the envelope was number code.

"I wish I knew what this was about." Morgan pointed to the faded numbers.

Winnie stared at them for a few seconds. "No. No, dear … that is a mystery." Winnie pressed the envelope open and withdrew the dried flower. She perked up. "That looks like a common iris." She seemed happy to offer something.

"But what are all these little black things?" Morgan asked. "Tea?"

Winnie wet a finger and put it in the box. She touched it to her lips.

"Nay, this isn't tea, dear. Though many people used to drink it like a tea during the hard times. It's bladderwrack. Seaweed. Kelp, some call it. Many mornings I would see the tenants from Grailside Estate raking it up on the strand below, by Omey Island. There are kelp forests in the waters off Omey, not far offshore. Sure, the cooks wash the salt and sea creatures out of it in good fresh water. Chop it. It's good in soup, healthy for ye. But this stuff must be very old. That's why it's in such shreds."

"Is there any particular power associated with kelp?"

Winnie's nose scrunched up at the question.

"It's important," Morgan said.

"Yes, yes. Times past, every herb had a special purpose or meaning in

Irish; you could even call them sacred meanings from the old times. 'Are you lookin' for money, are ye? I recommend Irish moss.' 'Do you need to remove a curse, do ye? Add angelica to your bathwater.' 'If you don't want rain, lassie, then don't light your fire with heather.'" Winnie was having fun, but even hearing it reminded Morgan of her Grandmother Lily, who had a saying for everything.

"Kelp brought 'coin and consciousness.' In other words, what gives you power equals money and knowledge. Isn't that right, now?" She smiled at Morgan. "It all may sound superstitious to you, dear, but everyone used to live on two planes at once. There was the thing itself, and then you also had its hidden self, its magic meaning. The priests couldn't beat it all out of us. The one level we paid our bills with. That's when you use the kelp for soup. But the other level was always hidden inside—the lucky meaning. That's when you keep the kelp for greater 'mind.' Or you even eat it to recall the dead."

"Are you kidding?" Morgan was almost laughing. *Was Mary trying to call someone back?*

"Of course, when those you love are beyond the ninth wave, maybe you need their consciousness from the sea, you see?" Her eyes held steady as she looked at Morgan. "Mi mather told me about those out there, 'Be about the sea, eat the fish of it and its plants, and listen to their voices in the wind.'" Winnie spoke in a rhythmic fashion.

Morgan was not quite there, but she knew Winnie had once lived the "old times." She would have to learn more of the ninth wave, but there was no time now. Morgan got enough of the idea.

Winnie pushed her finger around in the box. "I believe this other odd plant is nettle. These dried berries were a common aversion herb. Stinging nettle, they call it, to keep out nosy people—to sting them, in other words—but also to avert danger."

"You mean like the protection of Michael the Archangel?"

"Exactly. But you can't put Michael in your tea." Winnie smiled; she enjoyed Morgan so. She dug out more from the box.

"Everyone knew that if you threw it in a fire, it would ward off ghosts." She could see Michael's eyes enlarge. "I'm not joking. Sure, those people who lived on the Blaskets threw a handful of nettles into the fire every night before they slept. With those kinds of winds, I would, too.

"And in case none of those meanings work for you, throw it together with potato and cabbage for dinner. It's great in stew!" Winnie was pleased with herself.

Morgan began, "But why—?"

"No doubt your auntie wanted to keep the wrong people from lookin' in this box."

"Well, I hope this kelp is the real McCoy, and it helps me find out where Mary—or Meredith—is buried."

"Oh, it will, dear," Winnie replied without missing a beat, "but you'll have to drink it. None o' this lookin' at a few kernels in a box and wishin'."

"Put the kettle on, sister," Morgan laughed. Winnie took a few pinches of the kelp and threw it into the teapot.

Moments later, they tossed back a quick cup as though it were a whiskey. Then Morgan put on her sweater to leave. Michael, silent for once, was still standing next to the stove, finishing the last magic draft.

"Thank you, thank you very much, Winnie," Morgan said as she descended the front steps. "I have found another aunt in you. 'I shall arise and go now.'" She smiled. "I think I know where I must go."

"But the painting! Don't you have room to take the painting on the plane?" Winnie ran back in to get it.

"No. I want you to hold onto it, Winnie, until I get back."

Morgan was hesitant. *I don't have time to unwind Angus Welch's convoluted IRA robbery story. How he probably stashed the masterpiece with Mary at the nursing home, because who would ever think of checking up on his aged tenants? How wonderfully ironic that Aunt Mary gave it away to her sweet old nurse! He must have thought he'd be back to claim the Madonna when Mary died. But God had the last laugh—Welch died first.*

Morgan hadn't prayed in a long while, but she would thank God for the Madonna and the last laugh.

"For now, Winnie, it's too clunky for me to be carrying around. It's safer—and actually prettier—in your front hallway."

So, Winnie's "testimony" is the confirmation. Everything in the green box has a double meaning. In the old times, everything had double meanings. Maybe everything had a double meaning in Aunt Mary's life, too. A double life doesn't seem so incongruous; it makes sense in this way of thinking. The apparent world and the magic world. In Ireland, it works.

20
Steadfast Love

The Sea Road, from Cleggan to Claddaghduff

"Is that a fishing fly on your jacket?" Michael exhibited interest.

"Yes. It's like the one I gave you, a gift from Minnie Mac the day I went to Newport. Father Finn was a great fisherman, as you know from your research at the archdiocese." Morgan's voice trailed off.

Finn's fly feels like a talisman to me, something like a saint's relic. Maybe Finn's wisdom in landing the big ones will work for me in finding Mary's body today. And if that doesn't work, I hope the bladderwrack I drank with Winnie does! She laughed at the whole malarkey-thinking of it. *But wouldn't it be a pretty perfect ending before I go home?*

This was the first moment Morgan and Michael had been silent since leaving Mayo that morning. And the first time Morgan noticed how exposed and windy the sea road in Cleggan was.

The Green Dinosaur was making good time. Even in "the tank," they wobbled against the wind on the gravel road. Morgan was concentrated, collecting her thoughts for the next move: Omey Island. Michael felt tense about having enough wiggle room to make Shannon comfortably. It was only the second time he'd ever driven there.

Morgan pulled the green box out of her suitcase yet again. She lifted out the tattered envelope with the cryptic writing and studied it for the umpteenth time. "41 s … R 13." Then she put the envelope in her breast pocket. Pieces of black kelp fell on her skirt. *Coin and consciousness*, she thought. *I need both now, Julian.* She smiled, humming the music from *Fiddler on the Roof—A little bit of this, a little bit of that … a wish, a prayer … and some bladderwrack!*

After Cleggan, they arrived in Claddaghduff.

"Is that Inishbofin?" Morgan asked.

"I don't rightly know. I've heard it's hard to sight—too misty. One of the reasons Granuile, the lady sea pirate from Mayo, used it for her ships' hideout. Maybe that's Crow Island; that one's supposed to be only a few miles off the coast."

Morgan wanted to pass Grailside Nursing Home one more time. It was true: for her, there still was energy there. *Maybe it was Aunt Mary's energy, radiating from the once-great Victorian mansion.* She peered over the cliff edge at Grailside Estate. She got a telescopic view of the wild Atlantic, with misty Omey Island below, grazed by low clouds. She hadn't quite appreciated, on the day of the tour, how high above the sea the elder home was situated.

The clouds parted a piece, and she could make out a fuzzy procession of people, probably paying their last respects in the old-fashioned way, carrying a coffin overhead to its burial place on the island. No car could have maneuvered among the gerrymandered graves on the hillside. Omey, with its walled fields full of rushes, boulders, and bogs, had been for sometime a graveyard, a place of memory. No longer the summer retreat for the wild O'Flahertys and their right hands, the O'Tooles.

She felt a twinge of loneliness, not for Aunt Mary but for Grady, who gave her her first tour of "the sacred isle." Maybe Julian found the one guy who would understand this island for her. Was that synchronicity? Or malarkey?

* * *

Grady was also speeding toward Shannon, hoping to see Morgan off. But the thought of her leaving permanently made him feel a little apprehensive. He had the nature of an angler, as fisherman and wagerer. He had to almost blind himself to the extent of his affection for her—somehow, he felt, he was not in charge of this. In his belief system, he had to just allow it to unfold. If it did, it did. If it didn't, it didn't. He supposed his was as cavalier a philosophy as hers was supernatural.

He wanted to give her a real memento, though, of her time in Ireland. An old friend from Dublin had found him the perfect vintage leather box for his newly published *Ireland's Islands*, a going-away gift for her. What to do about herself was another problem. He liked her too much to write her off as just a visiting American. And yet that's what she was. He needed more time with her—or more something, maybe a couple of more trundles in bed. He recalled her hopping around his kitchen in his winter nightshirt and wool socks, making chocolate latte and singing "You Are My Sunshine."

She was an awkward bed partner. Well, that made sense, considering she'd spent most of her life in Catholic schools and the convent. Something he could teach her. But she did have a great sense of the ridiculous. He smiled. And she was well-read (for a woman). So why was he letting brains *and* beauty go? He didn't want to. ("Just yet," his inner corrector added.) It had to be clearer to him—clearer for the next step.

She was too independent to want a commitment. So what was he worrying about? She had a kind of flaky, free quality. Cathy, his old reliable, on the other hand, was from Connemara—hardy, sexy, but she would never be a peer. *Probably never read a book or wanted to*, he thought. Over the long haul, Morgan could be a better mate—if ever she wanted a mate. But she definitely was a maverick ... though he supposed women would just consider it "having her own mind."

Then he wondered if this wasn't just a silly obsession, or even competitiveness on his part because of Padraig's apparent interest. He had plenty of time to make Aer Lingus before her flight.

* * *

No clouds could possibly obscure the sign on Sweeney's Bar—it was the biggest sign in the West of Ireland. Michael could wait there for Morgan. She had decided to go to the island alone. And go quickly.

As they pulled up to Sweeney's, she stretched over the front seat, pressing a few punt into Michael's hand.

"Have a pot of tea, Bucko Mike," Morgan mimicked Mrs. Timmons's brogue. "When it's time to go, come to the edge of the strand and whistle for me." She winked at him.

Michael had no trouble having a second pot of tea and scones, extra butter, extra jam.

Directly across from Sweeney's, halfway between the bar and the strand, was a large stone church. A gravel path ran alongside it and down to the strand, where it was about a mile across to Omey Island.

Morgan hurried toward the strand, pulling a plastic poncho over her head. As she drew parallel to the church, a shingle clanged on its post:

ST. MARY'S
STAR OF THE SEA

The words from her dream echoed in her head: *"The wise men found the good Christ Child, didn't they?"* *The Mages followed the star. O my God*—the church is the star, *the star of the sea. This is my clue! I'll find something here. The wise men followed the star—how about the wise women? How about the* bean feasas? *The wise women?*

Morgan laughed at the utter congruity in it. *Hah ... me, too. I'm following the star of the sea. I'm on the right trail.* "I'm going to find something here!" she yelled into the gale. *How did the dream maker know about the church, the sign ... all?*

Already Morgan was breathless, and she was only on the winding beach road that ran to the strand. She turned to look for Sweeney's, but it was totally out of view. She'd forgotten that the strand was more than a block or two from the bar on the downcurve.

Wet sand flew up her skirt and fell into her boots. "Why don't I ever learn my lesson about this country?"

The tide had run out, but a spring storm seemed to be turning the tidewater back onto the cream-colored sand. The wind raked the grasses and threw Morgan's hair across her face.

"All shall be well. All manner of thing shall be well." This is going to turn out. *"All shall be well."* Even Grady? Yes, even Grady. *"All manner of thing shall be well."* She whispered Julian's revelation over and over as she stepped onto the strand. The salt air filled her nostrils and began to cake her tongue. *This is a baptism of sorts for me.*

"This was the place where prayer was made valid," drifted into her ear from the wine-dark sea.

The black hearse and the gray mourners she had seen from the sea road earlier were on their way back to the mainland and a hot whiskey at Sweeney's. They honked and waved at Morgan, thinking she was an islander. She waved back with Mrs. Timmons's bent umbrella. The truth was, only one old gentleman, who herded cows, still lived on the island. One of the entourage pointed to sea, where a school of bottle-nosed dolphins was cavorting in the waves. Her heart was pumping extra.

At Star of the Sea vicarage, the pastor was staring absentmindedly out his study windows as he worked on Sunday's homily. He blinked awake at the hearse's horn. Attuning to the strand, he vaguely watched Morgan walk away from the group and head toward the island. "Who the hell is that?" he groused, but so absorbed was he in the bishop's tirade against abortion that he registered no alarm. Father Moroney had managed to stay afloat in this stringy parish by the sea in spite of the drift away from the church. He was a good man, just the last vestige of the old ways.

Morgan was nearing the edge of the island. Salt spray on her lips led her to think again of Baptism … *"Receive the salt of truth."* "I hope this will reveal the truth," she prayed under her breath. *"Be preserved in the faith,"* the rite said. "Preserve me, O Lord, from madness," she chuckled to herself. "And all my crazy relatives."

With the roar of the sea and the hope of a good find, she was almost high, excited, giddy. She was wading through black slimy stuff. "Kelp!" she yelled. The storm was stirring the ocean floor, throwing up long ropes of kelp and other seaweeds from Omey to the mainland of Claddaghduff.

Morgan reached the island's shoreline and the first terraced graveyard. *They must have had a big blow last night. The waves have eaten the hem of the shoreline.* She wondered why the people continued to bury on Omey, when the sea would eventually claim the graves. *The sea will consume it all, maybe the way death consumes us all.* Over time, graves floated out to sea. Bones of small animals and even skeletons were scattered on this first tier of graves. Morgan had noticed this the last time, with the tour. But now she grimaced; it all seemed more menacing alone.

Soft terrain. She didn't want to sink in. Deftly, she hop-stepped up the hill. She knew this first graveyard was not the one she was looking for.

She was trying to recall something Grady said in his "Omey lecture" about the O'Tooles' connection to the island, but thinking was impossible in the howling wind.

"Keep steppin', girl," she knew Michael would say. As she climbed the hill, she positioned the umbrella against the wind with her left hand, and with her right she kept fingering the envelope in her pocket.

When she got to the top, she stood up to survey what was beyond the plateau and was stunned by the glow from the glen. Masses of purple and yellow iris trumpeted *Glory!* in this sunken gully, deeply carved by a century or two of wind and shifting sands. *Why didn't I see this glow ten days ago, on the tour?* she thought, surrounded by the purple and gold. *Simple: too early. They hadn't bloomed yet.*

There's no cross or ornamental gate, but this is a church! She had no doubt this place was holy. *This must be the "baby graveyard" Grady talks about. The garden is a little church for the unbaptized, a* killeen. *So many flowers. Were there so many little ones who were thought unclean, unfit for the proper rites? Were these dead babies stillborns? Abortions, too? Miscarriages? A miscarriage of pity, one might say. Doesn't the church sense the sacrality of this place? All our preoccupation with virginity, our pinched vows of chastity. How could we understand the blood, milk, and tears of women who have lost a child?*

It hit her in the middle of her chest. Morgan touched the dried flower in the envelope in her pocket. *It's an iris from this little graveyard.* She knew it. *This is the May flower Aunt Mary could never forget. The Beltane bud—her child! Only a mother or a lover would keep a pressed flower for fifty years!*

"Mary, O Mary," she whispered into the wind, "I am humbled by your secret."

Beyond the glorious iris glade were the remains of St. Fechin's Temple, a seventh-century ruin once the core of the ancient village. "Covered by storm sands for centuries, unearthed in 1981," said a historic site marker. Morgan stared at the bell tower of the once-submerged church.

Maybe the tower was the only thing sticking out of the ground some time ago? In Mary's time, anyway. It looks like the triangle on the envelope. A triangular marker ... three-sided, for the third graveyard.

"A triangle!" she said out loud, pulling the envelope from her pocket. *The inverted caret could be the tip of the tower, St. Fechin's. If the tower is the triangle on the envelope, maybe the numbers are gravestones? Or steps?*

She turned around slowly, taking in the whole space. Her mind seemed to plummet to a deeper place. She realized that the whole island had become a graveyard, indeed a series of graveyards. And Ireland?

Maybe Ireland, the Island, is a graveyard that for centuries held fast to a harsh and obsessed way of life on the edge of the world. A life filled with so much hardship it was accepted as a holy penance. And the paradox of it all is that it was seen as a sign of God's affection. Maybe such an obsession makes for great fairy tales. Ireland may have saved Western civilization from spiritual eclipse in the Dark Ages, but she paid the price. Alongside her thousand saints were her Crazy Janes and Aunt Marys.

Morgan's foot hit a stone. This was the graveyard nearest the temple, so maybe it was oldest. She looked down at the gravestones at her feet. She couldn't read many of them. They were in what must have been old Irish and had few dates. *They look more like rounded boulders than grave markers. All are individuals, primarily men, if I'm reading it right. Could that be possible, a men's cemetery? Or maybe a monastic one!* She took more steps, calling out the men's names.

When she squinted, she could see pieces of a wavy, wrought iron fence defining this cemetery. Just beyond it was another, perhaps an older one, with gravestones, Celtic crosses, and a high cross. She couldn't make out the shingle, a black plaque with gold letters. *How can I get to that private graveyard except by tromping through these magnificent spring blooms? Time is of the essence now. The "blow" feels imminent. I wish I knew Grady's secret shortcuts.*

As she stepped into the flowery glen, everything rolled in a downhill slant toward the sea. It was an unsettling feeling, everything being "off" by some inches. *But then, everything's a little off in the whole country.*

She made it through the irises to the fence. "TOOLE," the sign said. Time had almost erased the "O." *Yes, the O'Tooles are here, just as Grady predicted, hundreds of 'em.*

The O'Tooles, she thought, remembering Grady's tour speech. An ancient Gaelic-Irish family, among the list of clan chiefs before they became slaves—of British kings, law, and language. *"Tuathal,"* Toole, meant "ruler of the people," although in Connemara, they may have found the O'Flahertys their rulers and their liege lords.

She could hear Grady: "What's known of their connection with Omey is mostly tragic. Their clan chief was executed there, along with members of the O'Flaherty clan and Owen, the 'fair-haired' son of Grace O'Malley, the pirate queen." But the family had recovered enough to keep a guesthouse on Omey for pilgrims.

"From the early middle ages,' Grady had said, "Omey Island has been a place of hospitality, a way-station island for pilgrims on their way to retreat on High Island. In these modern times, Omey is the final destination."

The varied gravestones, carved of marble taken from the Connemara hills, numbered in the hundreds—a bumpy medley, haphazard, unlike the ordered graveyard at the Dominican monastery in Newport. Omey's probably dated back five centuries further, to the 800s.

These O'Tooles have had a corner on heaven for more than a thousand years. And they could probably never get a hearse up here.

Before Morgan had finished counting her steps, she saw it: a path freshly trod. A very recent addition had been made to the O'Toole section of the cemetery. A two-wheeled cart, no wider than a wheelbarrow, had ridged a new path through the sandy surface and long grasses. She stood in reverential stillness before an old stone: "Father Sean Fintan O'Toole, 1913–1950." Beside was the new grave: "Meredith Kenny O'Toole & Infant Son, 1909–1999."

There was no time to savor the moment. The wind and soft rain had turned into a gale and downpour. As Morgan bent to touch the new gravestone, the head of her umbrella was turned inside out and then pulled off the handle by the twisting wind. Then it blew away. She watched it lift over St. Fechin's steeple and disappear.

It was all dawning on Morgan at once. With her umbrella gone, she felt naked, and her whole family was exposed.

That's why she didn't tell anyone ... the baby. But would not they have been happy about a baby? What would Aran and Horsey have done? The baby died. My God, marrying a priest in 1950! The iris Killeen, the baby graveyard, the priest.... Oh, my God, my God.

But Minnie Mac said they never came for the ceremony; they never showed up for the wedding. What happened?

What is the worst-case scenario?

Did she kill the baby, set the fire, and kill the priests to cover the whole mess up? Did he refuse to marry her—after everyone's advice—and did he file for a transfer to avoid the consequences?

But then how is she an O'Toole? That cannot be; she was the mildest old lady. She said her beads.

Morgan was winding up again. Added to the impact of finding the graves, losing the umbrella was tipping her toward hysteria.

Sean O'Toole was buried as a priest. What about the O'Toole family? Did they know about the marriage plan? Did they just bury him as a priest to cover up the woman?

For a few minutes, Morgan struggled with the shame of this—the reflex reaction to hide the sin, to blame the sinner—blame morality—at the bottom of every choice. That was the Catholic guilt method, and it usually worked. She struggled against the old nuns' voices on the inside as hard as she pushed against the wind on the outside.

She was transfixed to the spot, holding the umbrella shaft up as though it were whole, like a sword. A sharp thunder crack—flashes of lightning lit the sky. Morgan fell to her knees. The Kenny keychain memento Michael had given her, with the key to her aunts' cottage door, fell into the mud of the fresh grave. She stared at it.

"Steadfast love." This is my Irish inheritance. This is the thing my mother told me would bring me through the hard times. A key without a house … a will without the land.

I am here at your shrine, steadfast love. You held fast for fifty years to your secret husband and baby.

Finally, I've found you, Meredith. You had a bigger life than any of us knew. You heard the music of the universe. Someone of the underwave loved you in its song. Would it have been so bad to have trusted us, Mary? Would you not know how lonely we all were for a chance to have known an aunt with such heart, with such loyalty to love?

Morgan made no sound in the beginning, just tears flowing down her face; then came a soft whine. No longer a mental conversation, her words moved to her lips. She was speaking to the aunt who was buried there.

"I don't have … I don't have … I have nothing. I am almost forty, and I have nothing to show … no husband, no child, no home. They didn't even leave the barn. The inheritance, the land. Nothing. I do have a beloved memory to cherish. You and me at the well.

"My life is nothing. Do you understand? Who will ever love me the way Jack loved you? I spent fourteen years in a convent, and I didn't learn to love anyone, not even Jesus Christ. You held onto your lost loves your whole life! Your flower."

She could not stop. The wind picked up her uncontrollable wailing like the umbrella and carried it over the water, beyond the ninth wave, where prayer is received. The rain and wind had almost beaten her plastic poncho to pieces. She was still on her knees.

When she was all but exhausted from crying, she looked up to see a line of cows alongside the fence, lowing and moaning as they moved past her. The big blow was here, and even the cows knew it. At the end of the line, a black-and-white collie was barking. She was herding them somewhere. Was she bringing them home to the old man who lived in the caravan on the other side of the island? The dog gave Morgan a bit of hope that someone was "in charge." The wild winds had frightened her and brought her to stillness. So she followed the cows. The shepherd knew her task.

* * *

Michael had finished his pot of tea and was enjoying the conviviality of the burial crowd's stories. This bunch was from Mayo and a few from Dublin, but they had continued an old family practice of burying on the "holy isle." The round-faced narrator took up the traditional place next to the fireside. With a foot on a chair, waving what was left of his pint, he led them in "I'll Take You Home Again, Kathleen," which indeed they had. The bar lived off of the funeral trade, and without an order, set out trays of ham-and-butter sandwiches on the bar.

Remembering Michael had said he was waiting for someone, Mrs. Sweeney told him the priest from Star of the Sea had just called inquiring about a girl crossing to Omey alone in the storm. Michael jumped from the stool on the word "storm," since he obviously was not aware of it.

Mrs. Sweeney had a protocol for such emergencies and immediately rang a bell inside the bar, halting the singing and bringing a sudden churchlike atmosphere. She told the assembled Michael's story of an American lass by the name of Kenny, who came to bury her aunt, who wanted to pay her respects to an auntie on Omey before she flew back to the States.

Mrs. Sweeney didn't have to explain that Morgan was in real danger now and that any rescue was to be done in pairs. She gave them a handbell to shake when they had found her. A few recalled her on the strand before the heavy gales. The hearse driver, a few slightly buzzed mourners, and Michael volunteered to cross the strand and search Omey's graveyards for Morgan.

21
Cattle Shed

Once in royal David's city
Stood a lowly cattle shed,
Where a mother laid her Baby
In a manger for His bed:
Mary was that mother mild,
Jesus Christ her little Child.
Who is God and Lord of all,
And His shelter was a stable,
And His cradle was a stall;
With the poor, and mean, and lowly,
Lived on earth our Savior holy.
And through all His wondrous childhood
He would honor and obey,
Love and watch the lowly maiden,
In whose gentle arms He lay.
*   – Traditional hymn*

The collie was working the cows to the far end of the island. They seemed accustomed to the wild sheets of rain and the peals of thunder echoing over the ocean. Morgan, emotionally exhausted, followed the animals as one of them. The path was well-worn. There were no graves here. An attempt at a garden some time ago left remainders of wild dill and clumps of chives. Morgan must have been approved of by the dog—she looked back several times at her as if to say, "Come along, lassie, I know where I'm going."

She brought them out of the storm into a cave-like shelter. Four cows, two calfeen, the collie, and Morgan crammed into a cattle shed honed out of the hillside rock probably sometime in the Middle Ages; the only additions since were an extended metal roof and a rusting bicycle leaning against the inside wall. The interior was snug as snug. No sound, and the warm cattle breath insulated Morgan from the wind. The deeper she entered, the dimmer and more womb-like it felt. Somehow it fit those monastic manuscripts on religious life, where the dreariest places seemed to be the best ones for meditation.

Grateful for a dry place to rest, Morgan saw that the dog was sitting on a raised stone stair in the wall—*a place for hay*, she thought, *added sometime in the Middle Ages.* She found a place for herself next to her, with a view over the cattle's heads to the sea.

When the fog lifted, the vast horizon made Morgan feel that life—and her own life—were beyond her ken. Angry and violent Poseidon, or Manannan mac Lir, drove his chariot over the wild, white waves. *"You may not be in charge, Morgan Kenny, but you're still to blame!"* She sat quietly, listening to old rage tapes of her mother, dead for years but still harping. Rose was barely audible in this storm; nevertheless, the negative mother kept up the fight.

Morgan didn't know what time it was, but she knew she had missed her plane. It didn't matter that much now—actually, she felt relief. Somehow, during this time in Ireland, she was nearing some kind of a breakthrough, if only it would come. But she was stuck in a cattle shed on a peninsula on the Atlantic Coast of Ireland, and she couldn't withdraw her mental wheels from the rut they were spinning in.

Why did Aunt Mary and Aunt Aran do in Horsey Neary? Did he find out about the priest? And the baby? Could Mary and Aran really have killed him? Was it an accident they tried to cover up?

And how did the baby die? How old was he? Was this baby baptized?

And however can we resolve the huge coincidence of the priests' death in the fire on the same day as the wedding? Did somebody try to kill Jack for fooling around with a laywoman? Did they set the church on fire? Was it the lightning?

Or did Mary start the fire at the rectory because her Jack wouldn't marry her? Did she just fake the headstone, about being an O'Toole? Or did they truly marry? And then what about Minnie Mac, her piercing analysis of O'Toole? Deception. Deception. The O'Toole family appeared to prefer him as a priest, labeling the gravestone "Father" ... or was that an archdiocesan cover-up for a priest gone AWOL? Why was there so little in this guy's formal file? Was Michael right—did somebody empty the file when they knew O'Toole was leaving the priesthood in disgrace? Did they know they would never be found out, because of the fire?

She couldn't get off the wheel. She was too scared to think of the alternative.

What would a jilted, pregnant woman do in small-town Ireland in the 1950s? The silence in the shed, and the liminality of the moment, magnified her questions.

Perhaps the guiding emotion of the Kenny family could be defined as taking account of the appearances of things. Not the *quidditas*, the whatness of the thing, but rather the value of it, how good is it, does the thing, person, gift, and so forth, measure up to a hidden Kenny standard? Does it look better than all the rest?

A well-developed judgmental reflex accompanied everything. Every Irish scenario was capable of hiding sin, especially the carnal kind. So when Morgan began to take pity on her great-aunt, her mother's disapproving voice tamped down that move toward forgiveness with the same fierceness that she used to denounce Morgan's weak will for failing to "stick it out" in the convent.

Morgan wondered in the cattle shed if anyone had taken pity on Mary, offered her consolation. *At least you escaped the Magdalen Laundries, dear aunt.* Then she heard her mother: *"How can we count Aunt Mary? She's just an odd duck."* Reconciliation could not come from the negative mother. Surely it must come from another quarter.

And it did.

A cow laid down with her calf. Morgan stared at the two. They looked just like the wooden carvings in her childhood Nativity set. The rest of the pieces from the crèche gradually inserted themselves into the scene from her memory. To the Greeks, anyway, memory was sacred, a goddess, *Mnemosyne*—and it was from her, a pagan, that Morgan received forgiving ablutions for Mary—and herself.

Memory took her back to a heavily draped Victorian living room in Grandmother Lily's rooming house in St. Michael's Parish in Chicago, where a single candle wreathed in holly was set alight in each window on Christmas Eve, in hopes of directing the Holy Family to take shelter there. After midnight Mass, the house flooded with guests, and a party was held for His coming. The elegant and the odd, blended together by Old Bushmills in the bottles and in the cakes.

Usually, the odd were old-country types, tenants of Grandma Lily's, mainly older gentlemen stiffly outfitted for her annual party. Morgan recognized their faces now, but recalled few names after so many years ... except for the Lincolnesque Englishman, Mr. Radcliff, sous chef at the luxurious Germania Club, who (the coroner relayed) died of virulent tuberculosis. And tiny "Mr. Fitz," who always left Morgan a stick of Juicy Fruit along with his rent, tucked under the dresser scarf. There were many more FBIs (foreign-born Irish) who were honored to celebrate the feast of the Nativity with the Kennys and to remember and remember again old rhymes of the country they could never leave behind.

The elegant appeared primarily in the high formality of Grandma Lily herself, who "received" people after the Mass, to recall once a year the poverty she came from in Mayo and to sing in their once-forbidden tongue. Every Christmas, she wore the same floor-length blue velvet gown, weighted down by brooches, gold crosses, and diamond clips, with golden braid epaulettes at her shoulders and little red velvet opera shoes—"just like the pope wears."

Morgan remembered everything golden. Everything wrapped in gold. Gold was the spirit that invited *Memory* and Mayo into every Christmas feast of Morgan's childhood.

The elegant also appeared on the piano in gilt frames—those from beyond, made eternal in the Mayo of long ago, "God help them." Lily introduced them to guests by raising a picture and saying, "Mr. Fitz, I would like you to meet my sister Mary Kenny. *Slainte.*"

So Aunt Mary was always there with us at Christmas, as Grandma Lily had last seen her: in front of the Lady's Well, a summer child in her cotton shift and bare feet. The rituals, the sacrifices at the altar of *Memory,* had ended when Grandma Lily died. No one sang in Irish again nor paid for a harper nor wept at the stories of their Great Hunger nor invited in the neighborhood with lavishness. No one recited poems in front of the fireplace anymore either, for the bard was no longer prized. Morgan had even lost her grandmother's recipe for whiskey cake.

In ten years' time, the Kennys were like everyone else in America—with a Christmas tree and mountains of gifts tied with paper bows one didn't have to iron. The community of the foreign-born Irish—or the community of anything else—slipped away from the feast like the old language. Aunt Mary and the rest of *"those beautiful lofty people never to be seen again,"* who had been held by *Memory,* were forgotten.

But in this moment, She gave them over to Morgan's imagination to edit—and to pay the price for neglect: copious tears and *mea culpas* for stingy love. And Morgan deserved the penance.

The little match girl in Morgan warmed her hands at the Christmas fire of times past and smelled Grandma Lily's turkey roasting, Grandma's favorite expression of America's "plenty" over her childhood want. Morgan's soul composed the crèche from these familiar figures of childhood for her meditation on the incarnation. *Because if it isn't incarnated, flesh and blood with us, it just won't last.*

All these faces, especially those from holy Memory, is how God comes into the world, she thought. *We cannot separate them out from God, even if they sinned. It is through* them *that the Child of Christmas became incarnate in us! Because Julian said so,* she sniveled.

She thought it a little odd how seldom preachers reflected on the fact that our Lady was in similar straits to Aunt Mary's—unmarried, but with child. *Wasn't Jesus born to an unwed mother? Wasn't Joseph going to silently "put her away"?* She supposed there were some people who would not have forgiven either Mary, whether she'd been "overshadowed" by a god or a man. *What our Lady had going for her was a love that gave her hope about life. I pray that Mary, or Meredith, had that hope of God's love for her—no matter what she did. Love is it.*

That was Julian's main message: *"Know it well, love was His meaning."*

"That's why I love you, Julian," Morgan said out loud to the faces of the cows. "You are so-o-o-o-o-o-o big! Love *is* stronger than death. Love wipes out sin."

Even murder?

"Yes, Morgan, even murder." Well, Julian was never into punishment for sin. Mary had enough torment—having the love of her life die, her only child die.

Impropriety with a priest could not compete with that. Morgan could almost feel her eccentric aunt's aloneness, her purgatorial withdrawal from the world, her self-punishment.

She did not trust her secret with even one person. What a burden! The good Christians?

"No, no," Julian says. 'No blame.'"

Mary was an odd duck, a wild woman who was better equipped than most to live out a harsh life and think it a grace.

Outside of her Church's and family's notions—which meant, aside from her heritage—Morgan believed that a child was always a gift, a grace, and that legitimacy made not a difference in that at all. She believed Aunt Mary knew some of the consolation of God's love because of one thing: *She was always humming, singing ... somehow it was courting company to hear the music, a sign of God's 'courtesee' to her.*

At last, Morgan could understand why Mary chose Grailside, overlooking Omey, the isle of Killeen. It was her secret future with *them*, her lover and her child, who had preceded her.

Winnie had drawn her story about Mary calling out to Jack in death to come to her over the waters. Morgan grasped it. *Mary's secret internment had to be realized right here—she had to lie where her life's loves had lain.* She smiled, thinking of Mary and Jack's graves in the O'Toole graveyard and their meeting on the Ninth Wave, forgiven and transfigured ... *where the fire and the rose are one.*

It was late afternoon. The sun had almost fallen below the horizon line of High Island, five miles out. Morgan would remember her meditation in the cattle shed on Omey Island for the rest of her life as "the Mayo mystery of the incarnation." It was a mystery she could not explain to Michael, and maybe not completely to herself. She did not learn it in church or in school, nor in the convent of the Benedictines—but from love, Julian, and maybe from the islanders (*Lucht an Oileain*).

Still, the event was marked by a nature phenomenon. There was an ancient monastic belief that climbing high on the hills on Easter, at sunrise, could give you a glimpse of the sun dancing. If you saw it dance, it was a sign that a miracle was happening to the viewer, a resurrection.

From her perch in the back of the cattle shed, Morgan witnessed a hazy sun nearing sunset. It began slowly to swirl counterclockwise, its pink, jagged rays like the points of a Bridget's cross streaming out beyond the lesser islands, until finally it encompassed the entire horizon. *The Atlantic on fire with love.* It lasted a minute or two, permeating the island and the strand, making even the cows and Morgan golden. She closed her eyes. *"Thank you,"* she whispered.

Was the vision of the sun dancing a moment when outer illumination and inner awareness flowed together? The inner "dancing" was some kind of bridging between two very disparate forces in Morgan's soul—of love and of shame, of sin and of forgiveness. The reconciliation that Morgan longed for, but could never have accomplished without having come to know and love her "odd aunt."

"If you forgive her, then God must forgive her." That's the voice of Julian. It must be her. Yes, I forgive. That is miracle enough.

All the digging and sleuthing of the green box, all the meditating upon Meredith's vocation to protect the Lady's Well, had moved Morgan to cherish and embrace her aunt. The sun danced, and Morgan's heart danced, back and forth, back and forth, between the opposite poles, between the extremes in Mary's life, until Morgan found the core of her aunt's humanity.

She was not really sure how this happened, but she had accepted whatever her aunt did and forgiven it. It was a miracle.

"But it did not happen on Easter," her mother put in.

"Yes, yes, you are right, Rose. It is Christmas," Julian countered. *"It didn't happen on Easter, it didn't happen on the hills—she was in a cattle shed and it wasn't sunrise, but it is still a miracle!"* Julian was beginning to sound a little like the Baal Shem Tov, but Morgan was always glad to get any support.

Did Morgan really experience some kind of spiritual vision, like Julian, where everything seemed to come together on account of love? Or was it simply a daydream, compensating for what Morgan had hoped for all along? Then an answer came in the words of David Quin, Dublin poet and mystic, *Pity the Islanders, Lucht an Oileain*:

> *Praise the islanders* Lucht an Oileain
>
> *... for they feared vain glory
> and the evil eye, chewed bits of seaweed and prayed to the
> mother of God;*

... for they lived

before Descartes, Newton, Freud ...

... for they lived before the age of trivia
and never made it to the age of anxiety, and did not suffer
ennui because
there was turf to be cut ...

Spiritual vision? There is turf to be cut!
The dog jumped down off her perch and stood alert at the shed's entrance. She cocked her head, listening. A bell's gonging carried over the water and was quite clear across the island.

"Morgan! Morgan Kenny!" A voice rose above the gong. It was Michael, shouting as the rescue hearse drove slowly over the strand.

The first person she saw as she edged to the mouth of the shelter was Michael, jumping off the hearse's running board. He sloshed through the waters of the incoming tide in his bare feet, smiling through his tears, holding open a blanket for her. A few curious mourners from Sweeney's and the priest from Star of the Sea accompanied him. All were smiling.

When Morgan stepped out of the shed, a woman began clapping. Having listened to the deadening sounds of the "blow," the rescue crew was fully aware of the outcome it might have wrought. They appeared truly grateful to find her unharmed.

The priest held out a tiny silver cup, offering Morgan a draft from his flask. It was strong Irish whiskey, warming her all the way to her boots.

"I was hoping Juno would take care of you," he said. The priest's eyes were holding her up, if eyes could do that, perhaps the way her own father's might have.

"Juno," Morgan said, a bit dazed, petting the dog who had saved her.

"The tide's coming back," the hearse's driver announced, and everyone piled back in.

Morgan was not eager to leave. In a kind of salute, she faced the graveyard, then turned back to the cattle shed, and finally faced the sea, lingering a moment in the changing light, mauve and silver white.

On the way back to Sweeney's, a soft conversation ensued about old Malachy's dog Juno, the spring storms this year, and more. One of the women, wishing to break the chatter, touched Morgan's shoulder: "Your auntie, was it? Surely you'll get a blessing for your perseverance. You're a lucky lassie, out in that storm."

The survivors reappeared at Sweeneys, and pints went all round. Storm stories and tales of Yanks in general, until the talk began to slow. At last, Michael and Morgan waved away the rescue crew and were back on the road again.

The Blasket Islands

22
A Necessary Step

Shannon Airport

It was Grady's fourth phone call to Mrs. Timmons', maybe his fifth, and his third Bloody Mary. (He thought that might be a synchronous cocktail, now that they knew Aunt Mary probably did in Horsey.) The effect of the calls had been to bring Prudence Timmons to hysteria. But he thought one more would be all right—a phone call, that is.

Whispering at the top of her lungs, Mrs. Timmons told him Michael had at last called from Sweeney's in Connemara. He and Morgan had stopped at Omey Island on their way to the airport; Morgan had crossed the strand alone, to search for a grave, and got caught in the storm. A priest had seen her crossing before the blow. And a bunch from Sweeney's had gone to try to find her—but the storm was too big right now and the tide too high. As soon as possible, they would try again.

"Can she find shelter on Omey now, Grady?" Mrs. Timmons asked nervously.

Grady winced but presented a good front. "She's been on Omey before.

I'm sure she knew of the caravan up on the hill." He wondered himself if she could even make it to the old man's house in such a blow, if she even knew which side of the island he was on.

Walking back into the bar, he realized he'd left his drink in the phone booth. A woman from Dublin, with whom he'd shared an hour of *craic* and light flirting, pointed over his head to the TV: "Look at that Yankee cow! They always think they know it all."

Her friend, at least as drunk as the Dubliner, copied her sarcasm. "Looking for your roots, are you?"

Grady turned on the stool, half thinking he might see Morgan. Then he stood up and said to the bartender, "Who do they think they're talking to?" The bartender looked at the two, but did not register either interest or concern.

"They're just Friday regulars." He leaned over the bar to give Grady a private message. "Watch out, Gov. They're out for wallets and ... well, you know."

Grady turned and gave the two a final gray glance. The Dubliner in the polka-dot dress with extra cleavage leaned forward and demanded, "What the fuck are you lookin' at?"

Suddenly, he had such a revulsion he felt like vomiting.

"Can you give me a black coffee, takeaway?" he asked the bartender. "Make that two."

The barman left and returned with two cartons. "Do you need change, sir?"

Grady gaped with such incredulity that the man explained, "Three punt, sir?" Obviously, Grady had mistaken his words. He'd thought the man said, "Do you need *to change,* sir?"

* * *

Grady sat in the car park, slugging black coffee, repeating the synchronous question a number of times.

Do I need to change? Probably. From the amount of punt I blew in an hour—about six punt apiece times three ... There's no mistake, I need to change. Maybe I still have a small flame of a conscience left in the bottom of all that dross.

"Let the good times roll," they say in New Orleans—and as the Celtic

Tiger began its roar, the Irish could feel the roll of "the money" comin'. Grady could feel the inflation of it, even before the euro became official. *In some way, the expansive spirit is Irish. The soaring movement fits us too well,* he thought. A little later, he added, *But could it drive us higher and higher?*

Are we going beyond the pale with this little draft of hope in our future? Do we have to act like thieves and grab at life and overdo it? God knows Ireland deserves a time without hardship. Still, something is pulling me apart, something I know in my gut I must pull back from.

"Holding back? That's not very Irish—not the Irish we know!" Morgan's father would have told him.

What made me so sick at Shannon? What made those girls so disrespectful of the American on TV? They weren't being oppressed. "The old chip on the shoulder" … drunks and pugilists, they say … maybe it's true. Those two pretty girls were cursing and swearing like a couple of stevedores. It made them look ugly, revolting.

What the hell has happened to us? Can no one speak in this country without saying "fuck"? Are we so bloody ignorant that we cannot speak without fouling ourselves? We were a welcoming people, a lyric people. Whatever happened to our gift of language? Did we only lend it to the playwrights? Our deep faith, is that gone, too? What's happened to me? Like a stone skimmin' the top waters.

The revulsion clung to him like a damp Aran sweater all the way to Omey Island and Sweeney's Bar.

He began to think of the Atlantic blow. He began to recall Morgan the morning she'd awakened in his one-room house wearing his flannel nightshirt. She filled his senses now with a tinge of guilt. Aphrodite, the golden goddess who laughs and has the scent of roses, dancing around his kitchen, striking an invisible tambourine, making chocolate latte, singing her version of that song from Fiddler on the Roof … *If I met a rich man, dooba dooba doo, All day long we'd deedle deedle dum, if I had inherited some! Oy!* He smiled, thinking of the quirky paradoxical mix: a nunny American girl in an Irishman's room singing a Jewish song. He loved it. She was different. It was okay.

He could see Sweeney's from the road, and he finally realized: *She was probably following my lead on the motive, the linkup between the three things that happened in the Year of the Fire—Horsey's disappearance, her aunt's will, and the funeral card of the young priest in the green box.*

When he said "funeral card," it all became frighteningly clear.

Mother of God—she went to Omey to see if the priest, the O'Toole, was buried in the clan graveyard. She's a sleuth all right.

Well, Julian, wherever you are, I'm back in your corner, Sister—and I hope to hell you shield her on that island. Not because of me, but because of her great loyalty to you. I don't know if that's a prayer, but I send it up into the universe. In the name of the Father ...

Grady hadn't "sent up a prayer" in many a year, and that's probably why he was rather impressed, awed, by his dialogue with a fourteenth-century English mystic.

* * *

As they set out on the road that would have taken them to Shannon Airport, Michael and Morgan began to normalize.

Morgan had missed her flight hours back, and the Green Dino needed a petrol fix.

"Now what?" Michael asked. "We don't have to go to Shannon. There's no flight to Chicago until tomorrow. I called my mother and told her you were out on Omey Island, in a big blow. Holy fright! She told us to come home. She said Grady called from Shannon, quite a while ago now. Well, we scared the hell out of her!" He smiled broadly. He was in a high devilish mode.

Within a few minutes, Morgan called out, "Stop!." They were rolling into Clifden, a picturesque town in Connemara, a few miles from Omey. Michael pulled into the town parking lot so they could figure out their next move. Morgan just sat there, still stunned from the violent blow, from finally finding her aunt on Omey, and maybe from finding what life was all about. Slowly, coming out of deep silence, her voice sounded rather flat.

"I found her there, Michael. Just as we had suspected. She was buried in the O'Toole graveyard .... next to the killeen."

Michael turned slowly to give her his full attention. She wanted to tell him everything that had happened in the graveyard and in the cattle shed. But Morgan could not possibly communicate now—or perhaps ever— the forgiveness that she now knew was in Christmas, or wherever love is incarnated. The incarnation of love in each one of us who loves, regardless of how high or how crazy the love may be. The spectacular vision of the sun dancing, confirming for her that *"All shall be well, all manner of thing shall be well, by the purification of the motive."*

She did tell him, "There was an infant buried with them. Mary and Jack and a baby."

She spoke as though they all had been mutual acquaintances, friends even. In some odd way, they had.

"Yeah, yeah, I wondered about that," Michael said softly. "A baby would have been the ultimate pressure permittin' him to leave."

Consider the obvious, she thought.

"Yes, Michael, that sounds right. I just didn't fit that piece into the puzzle until you said it right now."

She bowed her head and, seeing the blue-lime fly on her lapel, said, "I think Father Mac's—*Finn's*—flies brought me some luck out there."

"I'll say."

She smiled at him, only now noticing how streaked his face had become from tears.

"I'm not going back to the States, Michael. Not yet. I'm not done with Ireland."

"You bet. I don't think Ireland is done with you, either."

"I don't have long to spend this punt!" Morgan was holding an Irish one-pound note, with the mythic Queen Maeve on one side and the three classes of woman on the other—one of them a deer-robed wild woman, an archetypal relative of Aunt Mary. "That's an identity, you know. We were ourselves, then. Here comes the euro!"

Then, more seriously, she said, "Ireland is changing so fast. I can't stop that. Still, I want to take into myself, to incarnate in my bones, who *she* was before it's gone. I'm going to squeeze the last of mythic Ireland out of the wild woman on this one-pound note."

At that moment, Michael's theory of synchronicity began working again. The Michael Nee Independent Bus Company pulled into the parking lot. A passenger got off. The driver got out and began turning the front window stile for the bus's next destination.

The sign was illumined from within: "Galway, Dingle, Blasket Islands."

This must be where I should be going now. Morgan began perking up. Her heart beat faster. She reached into the backseat for her luggage and pulled out the green box.

"Hold on to it for me, Michael. I think we know all we need to know—for now."

She stepped from the Dino, waving to the driver of the bus.

"How long will you be here?"

Looking at his watch, he said, "Just time enough for me to get a tea takeaway. Five minutes."

Morgan gave him her luggage. "Just beep when you're ready to take off."

By now, Michael was standing beside Morgan and the bus driver.

"Excuse me, sir," Michael said in a badgering voice. "Where are you overnighting?"

"We overnight in Dingle Town, and we'll make the ferry crossing to the Blaskets after breakfast." The driver was now crossing the parking lot, headed to the tearoom.

Michael's face was puffing up. He looked like he was going to jump out of his skin, he was so irritated. All this spontaneous stuff was just too much for him, after a day trying to bring Morgan to safety. He called across the lot, "What's the name of the ferry?"

"Julie's Joy!" the guy yelled.

Morgan threw back her head with a good hoot. "You see, you see! I don't even have to tell you. My spirit compass is working!"

"Morgan, you don't understand. Nobody lives on that island. It was abandoned in the fifties."

"Don't worry, Michael. I know someone who lives there and works on the ferry—all summer."

"There's no electric. Progress never reached the Blaskets."

"Thank God. Then they haven't put a hotel there. Well, she's a weaver, and she doesn't need electric. There are still the moon and the stars." Now Morgan was almost giddy. "'Let's praise the islanders, *lucht an Oileain* … for they lived off the pick of the strand and the fish of the sea … they do not fret about tumbler driers or grouse about the menu.'"

The driver returned. Morgan put her arms around Michael. She gave him a hug and a kiss on the cheek, and he stood limp with his arms hanging by his sides. She stepped on the first stair of the bus.

"Michael, don't be sad. Listen, I have to catch the end of this era. Story or lie, it's passing. If I'm not back in three weeks, call Padraig. Tell him about the

Madonna painting, the Leonardo that's in Nurse Shanahan's front hallway. Tell him about the reward from Mr. Matthews's insurance firm."

The bus doors closed, and the bus began to move slowly. Morgan moved quickly to a window seat, yanking up the window. Michael was next to her, walking and looking up at her in a bright moon.

"Tell him, Michael. Tell him I want some good to come out of Welch's theft. Something for Miss Shanahan and you. Tuition money." In the midst of her craziness, Morgan tried to be prudent. Her father would have approved. Michael felt empowered with this last request.

"Tell Padraig you need to get your tuition paid. Tell him I told you it's okay. And listen, Michael, if Grady ever calls, tell him I've taken his advice. I'm trying to 'love the questions ... to live the questions.' And don't look so sad—*All shall be well*. You've got to believe that."

It was going too fast; the bus pulled away. Michael had to let it go. He watched the bus lights streaming away from him like the tail of a comet.

"Yes, I think *All shall be well*, too."

Appendices

Julian of Norwich
1342–? (still living in 1428)
Medieval mystic

In 1373, as Julian of Norwich approached midlife, she did not pilgrimage to Canterbury for the cure of her soul. Rather, she stepped back into her anchorhold of two rooms and a garden attached to a church, and took a journey to the center of her self. When she arrived, she had a series of mind-blowing experiences, exhausting visions she titled *Showings of Divine Love.* In them, she found that God was all love, and basically we are, too, because "God is the very ground of our being"—regardless of what the church was teaching about sinful man.

Julian maintained this straight through her book. She wrote out these *Showings,* and they became her sacred text—a living record of her own experience, which she claimed was more powerful to her than the Bible. She opened each and every word, spoke with Christ in it, analyzed it, and prayed with it for the rest of her life. Some say she lived another half-century. Julian, of course, was reborn through her visions. She never gave up on them. She believed in them right up to her death.

Julian was never canonized "saint."

Madonna of the Yarnwinder
(1501) Leonardo da Vinci and his Florence workshop

Madonna of the Yarnwinder is one of several paintings produced by the Florentine student workshop of Leonardo da Vinci during 1501 to 1507. Produced between two of his world-renowned paintings, *The Last Supper* and the *Mona Lisa*, the *Yarnwinder* is considered by critics to be a flawed masterpiece, in which the face of the Mother may have been the prelude to the enigmatic Mona. There is no doubt that the original *Yarnwinder* has been lost. But as part of his studio's work, several copies were made; these practice pieces were dismissed as student efforts, and not seen as authentic Leonardo. However, contemporary technology has revealed in each an underpainting in Leonardo's own hand, giving outline and tone, though the pieces were most likely finished by students. Each copy had a different background and—typical of a study—a predominant color. This new information brought the *Yarnwinder* to a value of $50 million when assessed in 2003.

 The *Madonna of the Yarnwinder* has a checkered history in terms of its being stolen and recovered a number of times. The last time occurred in the span of this novel's writing. Burgled for the third time in Scotland in 2003, it was recovered in 2009.

Born and raised in post-Depression Chicago, Lillian Lohr Lewis was tutored in "the malarkey" by her eccentric but lovable Irish grandmother, learning the stories and dreams of her ancestors. She holds an M.A. in theology and a Ph.D. in psychology. She raised four daughters. A lover of poetry, and Celtic lore, Lil walks easily on both inner and outer paths. This is her first book.